KU-456-556

Mystery
at the
Old Mill

BOOKS BY CLARE CHASE

EVE MALLOW MYSTERY SERIES
Mystery on Hidden Lane
Mystery at Apple Tree Cottage
Mystery at Seagrave Hall
Mystery at the Old Mill
Mystery at the Abbey Hotel
Mystery at the Church
Mystery at Magpie Lodge
Mystery at Lovelace Manor
Mystery at Southwood School
Mystery at Farfield Castle

TARA THORPE MYSTERY SERIES
Murder on the Marshes
Death on the River
Death Comes to Call
Murder in the Fens

Mystery
at the
Old Mill

CLARE CHASE

bookouture

BOOKOUTURE

First published in 2020 by Bookouture, an imprint of Storyfire Ltd.
This paperback edition published in 2023 by Bookouture.

1 3 5 7 9 10 8 6 4 2

Copyright © Clare Chase 2020

The moral right of the author has been asserted. All characters and events in this
publication, other than those clearly in the public domain, are fictitious and any
resemblance to real persons, living or dead, is purely coincidental.

All rights reserved.
No part of this publication may be reproduced, stored in a retrieval system, or
transmitted, in any form or by any means, without the prior permission in writing of the publisher, nor be otherwise circulated in any form of binding or cover
other than that in which it is published and without a similar condition including this condition being imposed on the subsequent purchaser.

A CIP catalogue record for this book is available from the British Library.

ISBN: 978-0-34913-267-9
eBook ISBN: 978-1-80019-002-3

Printed and bound in Great Britain by
Clays Ltd, Elcograf S.p.A.

Papers used by Bookouture are from well-managed forests
and other responsible sources.

MIX
Paper from
responsible sources
FSC® C104740

Bookouture
An imprint of
Storyfire Ltd
Carmelite House
50 Victoria Embankment
London EC4Y 0DZ

An Hachette UK Company

www.hachette.co.uk
www.bookouture.co.uk

For Hilary

PROLOGUE

Thursday 2 January

The Old Mill stood on the raised bank that bordered the River Sax, on the opposite side to the village of Saxford St Peter. The large building looked threatening against the night sky. It had been converted into an upmarket residence years earlier, but its huge sails remained.

It was 2.30 a.m., and there was no visible moon. Thick, dark cloud cloaked the sky and snow was forecast. It was the perfect night for murder. Any footprints would soon be hidden by a white blanket.

The mill was overlooked by just one building: a large house which stood on the opposite side of the ink-black water. Most of it was hidden behind dense leylandii, but part of the driveway was just visible. The car that normally sat outside the garage was missing. Upstairs, the windows were blank, their curtains half-drawn, as though to fool burglars. A light had snapped off fifteen minutes earlier, but it had done the same the night before, at exactly the same time. Everyone knew the owners were away for a few days; news travelled fast in Saxford St Peter.

There was no outward sign that the mill was under attack. Not yet. But inside, the start of a catastrophic event was already unfolding.

There were hints that Harry Tennant, asleep on an upper floor, would never wake to realise his last night had come. Under a corrugated iron shelter sat a boxful of wine bottles waiting to be recycled. He liked a drink in the evenings.

And it was doubtful anyone else would raise the alarm before daylight. Saxford St Peter was a sleepy Suffolk village, not known for its nightlife. With the New Year celebrations recently over, the locals would be tucked up in bed, thankful the strain of enjoying themselves was done with for another year.

At last, the first slender red and gold flames licked the window to the left of the solid oak front door. As the minutes wore on, the glass cracked, breaking the silence, and the taste of smoke drifted in the air. The stealthy fire was already consuming the stairs.

It did its work with frightening speed and awful inevitability.

CHAPTER ONE

Eleven days earlier

It was midwinter, and Eve Mallow's home, Elizabeth's Cottage, was full of villagers. The wooden-beamed living room where she stood smelled of heady mulled-wine spices, woodsmoke from the roaring fire and someone's expensive scent. Eve packed in the hordes twice a year, when she opened her home to the residents of Saxford St Peter and its outlying hamlets.

The biannual gathering stemmed from her cottage's turbulent history. Back in the 1720s, its owner, Elizabeth, had hidden a servant boy to save him from the gallows. His crime was to steal a loaf of bread from his wealthy employers to feed his starving siblings. He'd shrunk, shivering and terrified, in a space under the house, while a hue and cry thundered after him: wolves scenting blood. Elizabeth's Cottage stood on Haunted Lane, named for the thudding feet you were meant to hear late at night, echoes of the men who'd chased him. The villagers said the sound signified danger.

But the story had a happy ending. In the dead of night, Elizabeth managed to smuggle the boy, Isaac, down a lonely track to the River Sax, where she'd rowed him to safety. He'd travelled north to Norfolk, found work and sent money home to his family. Elizabeth's heroism had been celebrated ever since, and her grandson, who'd inherited her cottage, renamed it after her. Eve was proud to live in her old home, but it came with responsibilities. Each new owner was known as the 'keeper' of the cottage and was expected (by tradition) to open it at midsummer and midwinter to raise money for children's charities.

For Eve, there were personal benefits to the arrangement. As an obituary writer, she interviewed the living to understand the dead and was fascinated by what made people tick. Although she liked her private space, the gatherings were a chance to pursue her passion: people-watching.

She'd spent weeks preparing. The menu had been in place for two months, the helpers booked since the summer. After some thought, she'd invited villagers with small children to come first, followed by those who weren't ruled by early bedtimes, allowing some overlap between the two so they could mingle. Eve hadn't had to tidy up beforehand; she was tidy already.

'It was a good move of yours to stagger things,' said her friend Viv, scooting past with a tray of tiny mince pies, dusted delicately with icing sugar. She'd warmed them and they smelled divine. 'I can't think why my parents never did that.'

Viv's mom and dad had owned Elizabeth's Cottage before Eve, and Viv and her brother were helping host the event, just as they had in times past.

Eve couldn't suppress a tiny glow of pleasure and pride at her words. 'They were probably more relaxed than I am.' She wished she'd known them. They were dead now, but if Viv was anything to go by they'd probably been so laid back they were horizontal.

Living in Elizabeth's Cottage wasn't Eve's only connection with Viv; she worked at her teashop, Monty's, too. The part-time job meant security, with her freelance journalist's income always a little uncertain. Eve had been taken on to bring order to the place, which was a challenge. Viv's baking was creative and sumptuous, but her organisational skills were non-existent.

'They were more like me than Simon,' Viv said with a grin, as she squeezed between the vicar and Moira the storekeeper at speed, managing not to lose a single mince pie. They were her handiwork, and with Monty's providing the food, a packed house was guaranteed.

Simon seemed to have bucked the family trend, keeping his hand firmly on the administrative tiller of the riding stables and other businesses he ran.

Even he might not go as far as Eve, though. She'd filled a notebook with to-do lists before the open house, causing Viv to shake her head when they'd met for a planning session. (Eve knew Viv thought having a meeting at all was over the top.)

But now, the results were showing.

Viv gave her a look as she came to a halt after delivering the mince pies to a side table. The intense blue of her eyes contrasted her latest hair colour: holly-berry red in honour of the season. 'You've got "I told you so" written all over your face. And all right, I admit it: everything's running like clockwork. Maybe I should finally accept there's something in your weird passion for planning.'

Eve allowed herself a small smile.

They'd laid out batches of cakes before the guests arrived. The oven was set low for the mince pies, and Eve had limited the types of drinks on offer to keep things simple. The mulled wine sat in a pair of slow cookers, with ladles on hand, so people could help themselves. Other than that, it was just spiced apple juice (hottish to start with but gradually cooling – it tasted good whatever its temperature), chilled Prosecco or sparkling water. Side tables housed rows of hired glasses that sparkled in the firelight, white china plates were stacked high, and so long as she, Viv and Simon replenished the cakes occasionally, little intervention was required.

Alongside Monty's mince pies, there were chocolate clementine cakes topped with miniature orange truffles, perfectly iced fruit and peel cakes and layered red velvet sponge, decorated with vanilla frosting and angelica.

Viv had been training her up. Eve had cooked the fruit and peel cakes herself and was secretly proud of the results.

'Even the Christmas decorations work well,' Viv said.

They'd balanced red-berried holly and white-berried mistletoe over the paintings on Eve's walls, and hung sprigs from the cottage's beams too.

The meticulous planning meant Eve had time to do the guided tours that had become an expected part of the open-house formula. Villagers were already loitering around the bottom of her cottage stairs, next to the latched wooden door at their base. She'd take them up in small groups to see Elizabeth's old room (which was also her room) and show off the moonlit views of the lane and the marshes through which woman and boy had fled. After that they'd come back down to view the trapdoor in the understairs cupboard and the area below, where Isaac had hidden.

'You carry on and do your thing,' Viv said. 'I'll keep an eye on everyone. Make sure no one pinches all the bakes!' She grinned and swooped in for a chocolate clementine cake herself.

'Hmm.' Eve folded her arms. 'Maybe I should ask one of the kids to come and keep an eye on *you*.' With Viv's laughter in her ears, Eve switched her focus to the people in line for the tour.

Harry Tennant was closest to the door to the staircase, just to the left of the inglenook fireplace. She hadn't seen much of him to date. He was even newer to the village than she was, having arrived just nine months earlier.

A striking woman with beautiful olive skin and silvery grey hair had just knocked into him on her way through from the dining room.

She put one hand on his arm for a moment, apologising profusely. 'What a way to meet a neighbour.' Her voice was carrying and melodious. Yet another visitor Eve hadn't managed to identify; there'd been no time to greet everyone personally. She, Viv and Simon had been taking it in turns to open the cottage door to guests.

Harry had frowned with irritation as the woman made impact, but the look morphed into an easy smile in an instant as he waved away her concern. A moment later, he turned back to the person he'd been talking to: another taker for the house tour, presumably.

Eve considered Harry as she crossed the room. The converted windmill he owned was outside the main village, along the River Sax, away from the sea. The remote location added to his air of mystery. Eve had been told he was hazy about his occupation, and she wondered why. Perhaps he did something that halted conversations. She could relate to that; some people dried up when she announced she was an obituary writer. They seemed to think the job was morbid, which mystified her. It was people's lives she wrote about, not what happened afterwards. The stories were often uplifting and always fascinating. Maybe Harry Tennant was a taxidermist. Or a sewage expert.

She hoped she was about to find out.

CHAPTER TWO

As Eve neared Harry Tennant, she continued to review what she knew of him so far. He must be well paid or have family money. The windmill he'd bought had been on the market for well over a million pounds.

He looked relaxed, standing just to one side of the inglenook fireplace, his weight on one hip, one hand on the door frame, the other holding a glass of mulled wine. He was around her age, Eve guessed – late forties or early fifties – and quite handsome, she had to admit, with laughing brown eyes and brown hair. There was just a touch of grey near his temples.

Moira, the storekeeper, appeared to like his style. Eve had seen her glance repeatedly in his direction, while patting her dyed auburn hair. She was talking to the vicar and it was clear Jim Thackeray knew he'd lost his audience and was amused by the fact. The almost permanent twinkle in his eyes was especially noticeable.

Of course, Moira was married, but to Paul, who'd be a strong contender for the world's grumpiest man competition. You couldn't blame her for looking longingly at someone who smiled on a regular basis.

Next in line after Harry, leaning against Eve's mantelpiece, was a woman who might be in her early sixties. They were chatting, their body language relaxed, and Eve guessed it wasn't the first time they'd met. The woman was all polished smiles and small talk, neat in pristine blue jeans, dark-blue pumps and a pinstripe shirt, though only its collar was visible outside her navy crewneck sweater. Eve bet it was cashmere, along with all the other knits in her wardrobe. She and Harry were laughing now.

She was saying something about retirement, and looking forward to 'a few weeks in the sun, just when "we" fancy it', so Eve guessed she was talking about herself and a partner.

Harry looked over the woman's shoulder as Eve waited for a pause in their conversation. 'Hector's committed to retiring then?' He smiled and leaned forward, his eyes bright in the firelight.

The woman pursed her lips and raised her eyes to heaven. 'So he tells me, though he's said it before…' She glanced at the man behind her, laughed and patted him on the shoulder.

He was Hector, then. It figured. His outfit mirrored hers, except his sweater was a V-neck and he had leather boat shoes on his feet. He was a little older than the woman.

Eve double-took. The tumbler next to Hector on the mantelpiece contained something which looked suspiciously like brandy. Had he discovered her meagre spirit collection, hidden away in the kitchen cupboard? She'd bought it to flavour the fruit and peel cakes she'd practised at home and had planned to drink the remainder as a treat.

Hector was studiously ignoring his wife's teasing words, focusing instead on the partygoer he was conversing with: a dark, bearded man with intense, brooding eyes.

The bearded guy had a glass of mulled wine in his hand, but Eve hadn't seen him sip it. Was he too intent on what Hector had to say? Eve happened to glance at Harry at that moment and noticed he was watching the intense man too. He frowned and Eve wondered if he'd overheard part of their conversation. Before she could consider it further, there was a general lull in chat, and she stepped forward. Harry noticed her immediately.

'Tour time?' He gave her a twinkly smile. 'I've been looking forward to it. I missed your midsummer do, so it'll be my first. It must be amazing to live in a place with so much history.' He lowered his voice conspiratorially. 'And I take my hat off to you, welcoming us lot in!'

She laughed. 'But you've invited most of the village to your mill in January too. That's just as brave.'

He raised an eyebrow. 'Only as a one-off. Special occasion... A very different kettle of fish.'

'I bet everyone's looking forward to seeing inside though. They'll probably be clamouring for tours too.'

He shook his head. 'There, you see! That's where I have a bone to pick with you; you've got them used to it. It's what they expect now. But my party will be strictly ground floor only. I think I can promise a few surprises, but nothing resulting from a tour of my bedroom.'

Surprises? Eve wondered what he had in mind. She sensed several of the gathered villagers had picked up on his words too. There'd been something theatrical about the way he'd spoken.

She suddenly realised she'd fallen silent, just like the people nearby, and focused again. 'I love that the mill still has its sails.'

He gave a wry smile. 'You can hear them creak in the wind. I sometimes worry I might take off.'

The mill would have been a hive of activity at one point. Hearing the wind in the sails must bring the past to mind as Harry lay in bed at night. Eve loved that feeling of history. When she looked up at the beams over her own bed, and thought of the generations who'd occupied Elizabeth's Cottage before her, it filled her head with stories.

'I guess I'd better start the tour. I don't want to build it up too much. It's a tiny place, as you can see, but Elizabeth's story is special, so it's good to keep it going.'

Harry stepped forward, ready to follow her.

'Who's joining us?' Eve turned to the woman Harry had been talking to, Hector and the man with the beard and brooding eyes.

The couple stepped forward (she agile, her other half lumbering), leaving their drinks on the mantelpiece.

'I'm Tori,' the woman said, holding out a golden-ringed hand. 'Tori Abbott. And this is my husband, Hector.'

The intense bearded guy edged back. It looked like he hadn't been lining up for the tour after all. A moment later he began a conversation with another villager.

Eve was curious. There was no obligation to take part, but most people would, out of politeness. There were only three bedrooms; it wasn't a time-consuming commitment. 'I have to warn you all, the stairs are perilously steep.' She went ahead, then turned to check on them. Hector was last of the three, gripping the banister, his ruddy face bathed in the landing light.

Eve always showed parties each room upstairs; the tour wouldn't be worthy of the name otherwise. They found Gus, her beloved dachshund, in the second bedroom they entered, which faced up Haunted Lane towards the village green. He'd lapped up the attention on offer when the first handful of guests arrived, but had run out of patience a short while later. A small boy had become fascinated with his tail and after pouncing on it a third time, Gus had had enough. She'd taken him to the quiet spot where she'd moved his bed for the evening. He looked at her over his shoulder now, more in sorrow than in anger.

Eve pointed out of the window to where the hue and cry had come from, and told her visitors about the legend of the footfalls. After that she let them have a closer look at the room.

Hector and Tori were the first to walk through to Elizabeth's old bedroom – her room – next door. Harry was busy saying hello to Gus, who'd accepted his attentions rather austerely at first, but had been won over. The dachshund was on his back now, accepting a rub on the tummy.

'So, I gather you're relatively new to Saxford too?' Harry said, looking up from where he'd crouched by Gus's basket. 'Of course, I can tell from your voice you're not local!' He grinned.

'You got me! I was born and raised in Seattle. My mom's American and my dad's English. I've been in the UK since I was eighteen.'

'Your family moved over here at that point?' He was facing Gus again, but glanced at her momentarily as he spoke.

'Actually, I came alone. To study in London.'

'Got to admire you for that. And you stayed on.'

She hesitated. Passing on the details to someone she barely knew felt weird, but it would seem odd if she didn't explain. 'I met my husband at university and stayed on in the city while we raised our family. Then I moved here.'

'I see.'

His tone was sympathetic, and it made her want to elaborate again. 'The move wasn't triggered by a change in my circumstances.' She didn't want him to think the actions of her ex, Ian, controlled her life. 'My husband and I split, but that's unrelated. I came here on a work trip and loved Saxford so much I decided to stay. I thought I'd miss London – the crowds, you know – but I love village life. Really getting to know a fixed group of people.' It was practically professional development.

'I love that too,' Harry said.

It was interesting; she'd always had the impression he kept himself to himself.

'What's your work?' he asked.

'I'm an obituary writer.'

'That must be fascinating.'

She breathed a sigh of relief. 'It is. I guess we'd better catch up with the Abbotts.'

'Of course.'

As they crossed the landing, she asked about his job.

'I'm a consultant. I tackle all kinds of problems, and I get to know a wide range of people. I find it endlessly interesting too.'

She wanted to hear more, but as they entered Elizabeth's old bedroom, Tori asked about the age of the cottage, and the upkeep involved with a thatched roof, and the moment passed. The group admired the house's thick old walls, beamed ceiling and leaded casement windows. Ahead of them lay moonlit fields, the marshes and the estuary. Somewhere, an owl hooted.

A moment later, Eve escorted them back downstairs, to reveal the trapdoor and space under the house where Isaac had hidden.

Tori Abbott shivered. 'How horrible to know his life would be over if the hue and cry discovered him. To have no other options. No chance of a future. And all for one small, forgivable misdemeanour.'

Harry was behind her, peering in too, and nodded. 'Thank goodness we live in modern times, where punishments fit crimes.'

'His employers at the local manor house weren't well liked,' Eve said. 'Anyone with an ounce of conscience would have felt it their duty to help Isaac and his family.' The people at the manor had been ancestors of Viv's mother-in-law, and Viv always maintained you could tell. Viv's husband had died young, and as Monty's had once been his business, Mrs Montague liked to check in on a regular basis.

Harry and the Abbotts thanked her for taking them round, and she went to escort another group upstairs; longstanding locals this time, who'd all been before, but looked again for tradition's sake. Moira the storekeeper was amongst the party.

'I think it's only fitting to visit Elizabeth's bedroom each time I come, Eve,' she said. 'As a tribute to her.'

She'd said the same at the midsummer do and was clearly making sure Eve hadn't forgotten her excuse for snooping. If ever she saw anything untoward in Eve's room – any sign of a male visitor, for instance – it would be round the village in half an hour. But she wouldn't. Eve had been gloriously single since the end of a very brief series of dates with Viv's brother, Simon. And before that, nothing since Ian. He'd been the one to walk out, but Eve had acclimatised to life without him a lot quicker than she'd thought. Her current feelings could be summed up as blissful relief. As for their twins, they were adults now. Although they'd been sad at the breakup (and concerned for Eve when Ian instantly moved in with a woman called Sonia), they'd adapted well.

Once Moira and her group had had their eyeful, Eve returned downstairs to see the intense, bearded guy she'd noticed earlier was now talking to Simon.

Eve went to the kitchen to fetch a fresh tray of chocolate clementine cakes and caught Viv's brother on her way back. Mr Intense had moved on to speak with someone else.

'He's Judd Bentley,' Simon said, when she asked. 'He came to work at the stables in October.'

'I thought he must be new.' She frowned. 'I don't remember seeing him around the village much.'

'He's one of those very self-contained sorts. I've tried to chat – I like to get to know my workers – but he's not one for small talk.'

That was interesting, considering Eve had seen him work his way round the guests that evening.

'In any case,' Simon added, 'he lives outside the village, with a sister – according to one of the other grooms – so he's not knocking round as much as the rest of us. They're in that pale blue cottage with the white gates on the Blythburgh Road. And I only know *that* because of his employment records.' He laughed. 'Hell. I probably shouldn't have said. Goes against data protection.'

'Your secret's safe with me.' She felt relaxed around him, despite their brief relationship.

As Eve put the tray of cakes down, she saw Judd was talking to Harry Tennant. It looked as though Harry was finding the conversation hard going. He was smiling just as easily as before, but his jaw was taut. Was he trying to draw the man out and finding it challenging?

It was a mini mystery. If Judd didn't like chatting, why approach each new group who arrived at her house? In fact, why attend the party at all?

CHAPTER THREE

It was another hour before the guests began to thin out, by which time Eve had started to feel like Gus: you could have too much of a good thing. Her feet were aching.

She was about to leave the kitchen when Viv grabbed her arm so forcefully that the cakes she was carrying slid forward on their platter as she braked.

'What?'

'Stop!' The look in Viv's eyes was severe. 'There's enough out there to be going on with and if you keep delivering more, the stragglers will never go home.'

She had a point.

'You've gone into management overdrive. It's time to release the reins now.' Viv took the platter from her, put it down and shoved a glass of Prosecco into her hand.

'All right. Thanks.'

'What's up, anyway? You seemed fine until you looked at your phone half an hour ago. Worrying message?'

The thought made Eve's insides pull tight. 'Ian.' Her ex had wished her a happy Christmas, then ensured she wouldn't have one by announcing his intention to visit her in January.

She passed the news on to Viv, whose face contorted in agonised sympathy. 'Hell.'

Eve could hardly say she'd be away. He knew she was anchored to Saxford by her job at Monty's. Other than that, she'd be prepared to leave for New Zealand to avoid him. She could go by boat. It would be more environmentally friendly and ensure she was absent for longer. Ian had no idea where to get off. It might be he who'd left her, but he still tried to run her life. It was like he thought she couldn't cope on her own, and owed it to her to wade in. A noble favour to his abandoned wife. It sent Eve's blood pressure through the roof.

'You'll just have to come clean and say you don't want to see him,' Viv said, topping up Eve's drink, and pouring herself one while she was at it.

Viv was right, but it was difficult. Eve didn't want a complete breakdown in communications. She was determined to remain civil for the sake of the twins. She was just about to explain when she heard a familiar-sounding throat being cleared behind her. Turning round, she came eye to eye with Moira.

'I do apologise, Eve. I didn't mean to interrupt a private chat.' She was leaning forward eagerly, her lipstick gleaming in the overhead light. She must have reapplied it, probably in honour of Harry Tennant. 'I only came to see if you needed a hand with the dishes.'

Really?

'But having accidentally overheard your conversation, maybe I can help.' Moira saw herself as village counsellor as much as storekeeper. 'Are you aware of Pippa Longford?'

'No.'

'She's the agony aunt on the *Real Story*.'

A national magazine, but not one Eve read.

'She's really *very* good,' Moira said, before adding hastily, 'or so I've heard. Everyone seems to be talking about her at the moment. I'm sure she'd have suggestions to help with, erm, your little problem.'

Hearing Ian referred to that way made Eve feel slightly better, but the boost to her mood was short-lived. Glancing up, she saw various partygoers had gathered in the doorway just behind Moira, probably waiting to thank her and go home. How much had they heard?

Harry Tennant was at the back of the group. His eyes met hers, eyebrows slightly raised. 'I think we're all just about off,' he said, over the heads of the other guests. 'It's been wonderful. You must be exhausted. I'm looking forward to returning the favour and chatting some more.'

'Lovely.' Eve pasted on her best smile. 'It'll be nice to have something to look forward to after Christmas.' At that moment, people-watching opportunity or no, only the thought of peace and quiet appealed.

Harry's twinkly eyes met hers. 'It will be a chance to see if everyone's keeping their New Year's resolutions. There's nothing like sharing news over a glass of mulled wine.'

He laughed and Eve thought back to his promise of surprises at the mill party. What was he planning? For a moment, her tiredness fell away, and she was impatient for January.

The crowd shuffled towards the front door of Elizabeth's Cottage and Eve followed them. Judd from the stables was amongst the last to leave; he'd stayed the course, then. She still hadn't spoken with him, though she had the impression he'd intended to introduce himself earlier. In the end, a cry from a stray child, stuck under one of the beds, had robbed her of the chance to talk.

The Abbotts had done the full stint too. Eve hoped they'd join the rest of the leavers. Unlike the others, Hector was still standing where he'd been earlier, close to the fireplace. He was leaning, rather heavily perhaps, on the stone mantelpiece. Tori, all cashmere and pearls, slumped against him suddenly and giggled. 'Come along, Hector; I've definitely overdone it.' She turned to Eve. 'Thank you for having us.'

Hector pushed himself up straight, put an arm around his wife and together they moved rather stiffly towards the door.

At last it was just Eve, Viv and the washing-up. They'd told Simon to go on home; his fiancée was back from a business trip that evening.

Viv made sure they consumed the rest of the Prosecco as they worked. When she'd left too, Eve sank into one of the two couches in the living room. The fire had burned low and now that everything was cleared away, the space was calm and cosy rather than stifling. She'd opened the door at the bottom of the staircase before sitting down, and after a minute or two Gus appeared, looking anxiously left and right.

'You're quite safe. They've all gone.' He turned towards her and picked up speed, putting his head against her knee as soon as he was close enough. She stroked his ears. 'The things I put you through. Can you forgive me?' He had his head on one side. 'Still deciding, huh?'

But the evening had been a success, despite the tantalising number of neighbours she'd never managed to identify. Maybe some had come from small settlements outside Saxford, like Judd.

She got up to reach her laptop from the cupboard, then put her feet up. It was late, but although the evening had left her bone-tired, she was too stimulated to sleep straight away. Besides, she wanted to tackle Ian before she went to bed, so he didn't prey on her mind. Thoughts of Moira's advice drifted through her head. She booted up the computer and googled 'Pippa Longford'. Not that she'd consider writing to the agony aunt for advice. The idea of relying on someone you'd never met to tell you what to do made her stomach clench. She'd make her own decisions, thanks very much. But she was curious. She wondered if Moira had written to the woman, and if so, what about?

Eve clicked on a link to Pippa Longford's column and scanned the pull-out quotes from her readers' letters. There were questions about talking to teenagers and ways to patch things up with an aging mother who'd joined a hippy commune. Before Eve knew it, she'd read the lot and clicked through to a different selection. The next batch included pleas for help from a married woman who was regretting an affair with a next-door neighbour, and a guy whose boyfriend was losing interest.

The answers were beguiling. Pippa's confident, unequivocal advice instilled a feeling of trust, but Eve questioned her instinctive response. She herself went to great lengths when researching her obituary subjects. She dug deep to ensure she'd read them right and would do them justice in her articles. And several times she'd found, shortly before submitting her copy, that she'd misunderstood something fundamental. How could Pippa feel happy, proffering such life-changing advice without even speaking with her correspondents? All those words of wisdom, based on the contents of one short letter…

Was the woman's approach standard? Eve cross-checked. Other columnists came across as assured too, but they used words like 'suggest' in their answers unless the matter was clear-cut, and signposted their correspondents towards experts as required. That seemed more appropriate, but maybe Pippa's readers found her strident approach compelling.

Eve was almost tempted to write in about Ian after all, just to see what she decreed, but she wouldn't want to be a time-waster. Besides, her private life was private.

After a moment's thought, she composed a reply to Ian's text.

Thanks for getting in touch, but I feel you coming to Saxford for an extended visit isn't appropriate.

It was a horrible thought.

I'm happy to meet you for coffee if you're in the area though.

Preferably well away from the village, where none of her new friends could judge her taste in men.

His reply came back in seconds.

Oh don't worry – I wasn't thinking of an extended visit – only a day or two. I'll be in touch to let you know when I'll arrive.

CHAPTER FOUR

Eve pulled back her bedroom curtains on Christmas morning to reveal a crystal-clear blue sky, bright winter sunshine and hoar frost on the privet hedge below. It was beautiful, but wistfulness coiled its way up inside her chest. This time last year the twins had been with her to join in the festivities. They might be in their early twenties, but they'd bounded into her room as soon as they heard her moving, just as they had when they were six. They'd all sat on her double bed, under the encircling beams that reached overhead, and exchanged gifts, laughing and chatting.

This year the presents they'd sent were under the tree she'd installed in the dining room. The Norway spruce had enhanced the décor for the midwinter gathering, but it seemed pointless now. Gus had been giving it disapproving looks ever since he'd sneaked underneath its branches to explore and ended up with a bauble caught in his fur. She was secretly looking forward to taking it down again.

As for her presents for the twins, they'd be opening them at Ian and Sonia's place. Ian had told her they were having smoked salmon, scrambled eggs and champagne for breakfast. She and the twins had had toast and marmalade last year.

At that moment she heard Gus lolloping up the stairs and felt slightly better. Once she'd fed him, they were due at Hope Cottage across the road for this year's breakfast. Eve's neighbours, Sylvia, a photographer, and Daphne, a potter, had invited her. Afterwards they would head to St Peter's for the Christmas Day service, then join a larger gang, including Viv, Simon and his fiancée, Polly, for lunch at the village pub, the Cross Keys.

Wearing a plum-coloured woollen dress, long chocolate-brown boots and a matching overcoat, Eve crossed the road with Gus. Inside Hope Cottage, all was warmth and good cheer. The house was thatched and seventeenth-century, like Elizabeth's Cottage, and looked entirely traditional at the front, but to facilitate their artistic careers, Sylvia and Daphne had opened it out at the rear to form a large studio. Their six-foot Christmas tree was right at the back, between wooden shelves housing Daphne's latest ceramics and albums showcasing Sylvia's photography.

Sylvia greeted her first, leaning in for a hug, her iron-and-smoke-grey plait falling forward. It had a strand of dark red tinsel woven into it today, which Eve admired.

'Daphne looked askance at me when I put on jeans. She said I should make an effort, as we're lunching out, so I have.' She gave an innocent smile; the jeans were still present.

Daphne's exasperated sigh broke into a resigned laugh halfway through. She put the steaming coffee pot she'd been carrying on the living room table and came over to hug Eve too. 'Come and sit down. There's nothing to do; it's all ready. We've got some of Monty's cinnamon, cranberry and clementine muffins.'

In a moment, Eve had pulled up a chair at the table and Gus, who'd been having a tense stand-off with her neighbours' cat, Orlando, now walked with dignity to a spot by her feet. The cat stalked off, tail twitching, head held high.

'So,' Sylvia poured Eve a strong black coffee and handed her a tiny red cup, which was Daphne's handiwork, 'you survived the midwinter do!' She laughed. 'We tried to lead the way by leaving at a reasonable time but I could see some selfish so-and-sos weren't going to shift until they'd eaten their own bodyweight in cake.' Her wry eyes met Eve's. 'Either that or drunk enough mulled wine to pickle themselves until Easter.'

'Sylvia!' Daphne said. 'It was a party. People were meant to enjoy themselves.'

Her partner laughed again. 'Yes, yes. All well and good, but you can overdo these things.' She turned to Eve. 'You must have been awfully glad to get shot of everyone once they finally went home.'

'Don't put words into the poor woman's mouth,' Daphne said, shaking her head, but joining in the laughter too. 'It was a great success,' she added, turning to Eve. 'And what a crowd! There were people there I'd never met before.'

Sylvia passed round the muffins. 'Did anyone actually check who the visitors were when they arrived?'

'Not in a very formal way,' Eve admitted. 'But Viv, Simon or I made sure they all donated on their way in.' She'd hoped potential house burglars would be put off when charged an entry fee. Other than that, she'd made sure her valuables and spare keys were out of sight, just in case a stranger slipped through the net.

'That's the spirit! Did you make much?'

'Two hundred and fifty. Viv donated all the cake ingredients, and Moira and the pub the drinks, so we had no costs.'

'Well done. And you enjoyed the people-watching aspect of the evening, I imagine?'

'Don't let Sylvia make you feel awkward,' Daphne said hastily. 'As a photographer she's just the same. She sees each little cameo as a potential shot.'

'So frustrating, damn it!' said Sylvia. 'Not being able to act on my instincts, I mean, and actually capture the images.'

'I can imagine,' Eve said. 'I should have asked you to record the event. It would have given you a free hand, and people would have bought the photos too.'

Daphne half closed her eyes and inhaled the steam from her coffee. 'It's best not to encourage her.'

The spark of amusement was there again in Sylvia's eyes. 'Who was the striking young man with the brooding eyes and the dark beard, do you know? He introduced himself but I've already forgotten his name and he didn't mention his connection with the village.'

Suddenly Eve felt like Moira. She had the answer, her finger on the pulse of village gossip. 'Judd Bentley. A new groom of Simon's, apparently. He's only been with him since October.'

Sylvia grinned. 'You must have wondered about him, Eve? I know I did. So intense.'

'Simon says he's a loner who doesn't interact much with his colleagues; I was surprised he came. Yet he worked his way round the room, talking to people.'

'I noticed.' Sylvia sipped her coffee. 'You didn't speak to him yourself?'

She shook her head. 'I had the impression he was on his way over, and I was curious to meet him, but a stuck-child incident meant I had to leap upstairs.'

'Vexing.'

'Quite. So, you spoke to him? What did he say? Was it just small talk?'

'Initially.'

Eve raised an eyebrow.

'After that, he asked if we knew anything about the agony aunt Pippa Longford.'

'How strange.' Eve took a sustaining bite of her clementine and cranberry muffin. The tartness of the cranberries offset the sweet dough and orange flavours perfectly. She explained about Moira's recommendation.

Daphne put down her coffee cup. 'He said everyone was talking about her and that made him curious. I must admit, I'd never heard of her, but a little later I caught him asking another neighbour the same question.'

Had Judd Bentley braved the do specifically to ask the villagers about Pippa Longford? If everyone was talking about her, perhaps she was local, though it seemed like a long shot.

And why on earth would he want to know?

An hour later, Eve was sitting between Viv and Daphne in a pew at St Peter's. Jim Thackeray, the vicar, was standing at the front of the church, close to the altar, talking to one of the church wardens. He'd gone one step further than Sylvia, she noted, and was currently wearing a fetching pair of felt antlers.

'He did a children's service at nine,' Viv hissed. 'Do you think he's forgotten to take them off?'

Eve watched as Jim reached up and stroked the right-hand one absently. 'Hard to say, but I suspect he's probably left them on deliberately.' He was coming along to the pub for lunch too, and Eve was glad. He was one of her favourite villagers.

She watched neighbours from Saxford and surrounding hamlets file in. Several of her midwinter party guests were amongst the throng. Harry Tennant took a place in a pew a couple of rows in front, on the opposite side of the nave. He was looking smart in a knee-length black woollen coat. Somehow, he fitted the time of year: he looked plush, shiny and extravagant.

He'd settled himself next to Moira Squires, who was all of a flutter. Moira's husband Paul sat on her other side, hunched into his grey overcoat. He looked like an animal that had been forced out of hibernation.

Judd Bentley was there too. He arrived with Simon, Polly and a couple of others from the stables. He was ahead of the rest of his party and slid into the pew behind Moira and Paul, even though there was space next to Harry Tennant. For a second Eve remembered the look Harry had shot in Judd's direction while Judd was speaking with Hector at her party. That frown... Was there something amiss between them? They'd spoken later on that evening, but it had looked stilted. She shook her head. She was probably reading too much into it. Maybe Judd just figured there wasn't enough room for them all in Harry's pew.

It was only a moment before the space next to the mill owner filled up. Jim always drew large crowds, and at Christmas St Peter's was crammed. He welcomed attendees of all religions and none, and was persuasive as well as fun: a winning combination. Animals were gathered into the fold too. Gus sat at Eve's feet, waiting patiently for the first carol. He seemed to enjoy the music and occasionally joined in. Eve was still trying to perfect feigning nonchalance when this happened.

Looking round the church again, she realised the woman on Harry's left had also been at her midwinter do. It was the striking lady with the shining dark eyes, olive skin and silvery-grey hair. She and Harry greeted each other formally, but with a quick laugh, as though they were remembering their previous (literal) run-in. A family had followed her in, with four red-headed children exhibiting an extreme case of the fidgets.

Jim Thackeray's move to the lectern and microphone caused everyone to quieten, though his brief rendition of Mariah Carey's 'All I Want for Christmas is You' reversed the effect. At last he switched to 'The Holly and the Ivy', and the congregation rose to their feet and joined in.

At the end of the service, as Eve stood to make her way towards the nave, she happened to glance in Harry Tennant's direction. He'd turned to reach for his overcoat, having removed it during the service, and noticed Judd Bentley behind him.

It was slight, but Eve spotted a momentary flicker of nervousness in Harry's eyes.

CHAPTER FIVE

When Eve looked out from her bedroom window, early on Thursday 2 January, the scene took her breath away. Her eyes were met by the first snowfall there'd been since she'd arrived in Saxford St Peter. In the bright morning sunlight, the beauty of the glimmering crystal-covered fields and marshes made her throat catch. She was conscious of the feeling of clear, hard cold from the casement window, contrasting with the heat from the radiator, which almost burned her legs through her pyjama bottoms. And then the cool draught round her ankles (standard, in a seventeenth-century cottage), offset by the warmth of Gus. He was jiggling against her, his head raised towards the window as though he could sense he was missing out.

Suddenly, to her right, something startled the wintering wildfowl out on the marshes, and a huge flock of widgeon rose to the sky, changing its shape like a dense collection of iron filings pulled by a magnet. That sight would have had Gus attempting to leap out of the window.

Eve was still getting used to nature up close, though she'd lived in Saxford for over a year now. It filled her with awe, and made her wish she'd paid more attention when she'd visited parks in London. Her gaze was still to her right. She could see the snow-covered gorse which marked the start of Elizabeth's Walk, the ancient path that led from Haunted Lane, down to the marshes and the estuary. It was the route Elizabeth had taken with Isaac, the night she'd rowed him to safety.

If you turned right at its end you could follow a narrow path to the mouth of the River Sax and the sea. It wasn't far. The gorse bushes were glittering amorphous forms now. Everything looked strange: touched by magic.

In those brief moments, Eve felt like a child again, and forgot, briefly, the dream she'd had the night before.

She'd imagined she'd heard the hue and cry which had chased Isaac, back in the 1720s. In her dreams she'd conjured up the cruel determined faces of the men who'd hunted the small, starving boy. As always with these night terrors, she'd woken in a cold sweat, her heart thudding. And as always, she'd found Gus was awake too, whining. She'd peeked into the lane then. It normally helped to dispel the dream. Looking up at the sky she'd seen the odd flake of snow, but she hadn't imagined it would lie. The lane down below had been empty, of course. She didn't believe in omens, whatever the villagers said, but as time went on, it got harder and harder to explain the dreams away. On every occasion, trouble for the village had followed.

Gus was leaping up.

'We'll go downstairs in a minute. In a minute.' He knew that phrase, if she said it a few times.

He'd want to dash about on the lawn and she might join him. Back in Seattle they'd only ever had an inch or two of snow at most, and lately the falls in the southern UK hadn't been much deeper. Today was special, but she'd delay the trip downstairs. Just at that moment she was spellbound by the view from the window.

She took pity on Gus and lifted him carefully.

'My goodness.' He always felt more solid than he looked. 'If you carry on wriggling like that I'll drop you.'

As he settled, she turned left towards the village. There was Sylvia and Daphne's cottage, subsiding gently on one side, shrouded in a heavy, twinkling blanket. There were no signs of life yet; the pair weren't early risers. And beyond was the old oak tree and village green. In the distance she could just see Monty's teashop. It made her think of Viv, and her mind flipped back to Christmas Day, when her friend had landed a piece of pudding in Simon's fiancée's lap. To her shame, the thought made her laugh. In an instant the cold glass, so close to her face, misted.

And then suddenly, in the distance, beyond the green, the houses and the teashop, Eve saw a strange effect. The sky was clear in general, the day crisp and sunlit. But somewhere beyond the River Sax was a grey haze.

Just in that one patch of sky.

And now the dream of thudding feet from the night before came back to her. Her eyes met Gus's. She bent to set him down, and her mobile rang.

Robin.

She felt the hairs on the back of her neck lift as she took the call. Robin Yardley had been a mystery when she'd arrived in Saxford – a loner who kept himself separate. He beat Judd from the stables on that score. After a couple of chance meetings and some lucky guesses, she'd uncovered his secret. Though he now worked as gardener to most of Saxford St Peter, he'd once been a police detective, down in London. A fact he kept from almost everyone.

He only rang her about two things: gardening – and it was a bit early for that – or murder.

'Is everything all right?'

'*I'm afraid not. Greg's just been in touch.*'

Greg Boles – a detective sergeant on the local force, and the one member of the team who knew Robin's history.

'*The emergency services were called to a fire at the Old Mill at four thirty this morning. Some guy travelling home from a party spotted flames across the marshes, but it wasn't in time to save Harry, I'm afraid. I'm sorry. I saw you chatting outside the village store just after*'

Christmas. I wasn't sure how well you knew each other, but I wanted to let you know before you heard it on the grapevine.'

Eve's mouth had gone dry. Harry's friendly face filled her mind, so vivid, lively and full of charm. And then the thought of her dream brought her up short. The grey haze she'd seen outside must have been smoke. What time had the fire started? If she'd been looking in the right direction the night before when she'd drawn back her curtains to check the lane, would she have seen the flames? Had she missed the chance to save Harry's life?

'That's terrible.' She paused for a moment, assimilating the news, tears pricking her eyes. She'd hardly known him, really. He'd only paused at the store to ask after her Christmas, but she'd been touched at his interest.

He couldn't have been much older than her, if at all. He ought to have had years ahead of him.

'Are you okay?'

She swallowed. 'Yes. It's just hard to take in.'

'I know. It's a horrific business, I'm afraid.'

'Business?' The dream. 'It wasn't an accident?'

'The police think it was arson.'

She had to work to adjust to the extra news. 'It's so hateful!' She thought for a moment. 'He didn't have a smoke alarm?'

'I assume not, unless he was drugged, and failed to wake at the sound of it. Maybe he never got round to installing any after he moved in,' Robin said. *'Or what he had wasn't working. The CSIs will find out, if the evidence is there. But in that heat…'*

'Who would have done something so appalling?'

'Who indeed? Look, Eve, I assume you won't work on Harry officially.'

She'd written the obituaries of murder victims in the past, but the manner of their deaths hadn't been the reason. They'd all been high-profile figures; she'd have covered them anyway. On those occasions, Robin had secretly passed on information he'd been given by DS Boles to help keep her safe. There was always a chance she'd end up quizzing a murderer. And she'd played her part too, reporting any hard facts she found to the police. She'd ended up interviewing the same people they did. The friends, relations and contacts of the victims were essential when it came to researching her obituaries. She and Robin had worked on clues, and Robin had covered her back.

'That's right.' She had no excuse to write about Harry. A consultant. The job description was so vague. It might be fascinating, but it wouldn't allow her to pitch his obituary to the media. Suddenly, the thought of not having a ringside seat made her feel trapped. Harry's murder had been so chilling and callous; she wanted to find out who'd robbed him of his future. She'd done well in her previous investigations, secretly aided and abetted by Robin: come up with information that had led to arrests and saved the police time.

The local detective inspector, Nigel Palmer, was blinkered and snobbish. Nudging him in the right direction had been particularly satisfying.

And this time she'd dreamed of danger; sensed the death would be unnatural before Robin even told her. Was she really going to sit back and leave the police to it?

'*Although you won't be writing Harry's obituary, Greg says he'd be keen to hear your impressions of him. Anything interesting you saw or heard in the run-up to his death. He knows you're at the heart of the village. And didn't Harry visit your house on the solstice?*'

'That's right.' Her mind flitted back to the occasion. Elizabeth's Cottage had been packed. Robin hadn't come himself, of course. He avoided situations where he might have to make small talk; that meant questions about his background. He'd walked out of his old life after uncovering high-level corruption on his team. He still did some covert work for the police, but powerful enemies meant it was best his past stayed secret.

She turned her mind back to Greg Boles's request. 'And yes, of course, I can sum up what I know.'

'*Sounds good.*' Robin paused a moment. '*If you send the information via me I'll see Greg gets it without Palmer finding out.*'

That made sense. The detective inspector would be furious if he discovered Eve had contributed to the investigation, even in a minor way. 'Will do. You can take a look too; see what you think.'

He nodded. '*Thanks. Greg's keen to get the inside track and no one's got much faith in Palmer. I gather he's been cutting a lot of corners lately.*'

Lately? If past experience was anything to go by, he'd seize on the nearest, weakest contact of Harry Tennant's and try to make the murder charge stick so he could take the rest of the day off.

By the time she ended the call, Gus was leaping distractedly round her ankles.

'I know. I'm sorry.' The words were automatic. Her mind was still on Robin's news as she padded down the steep cottage stairs. She walked through to the kitchen, where she let Gus out to sniff round the garden, watching him navigate the new-fallen snow. He bounded about giddily, his stomach barely clearing the soft white blanket under him. She was still in her pyjamas, but pulled on a jacket she'd left on a hook by the back door and stood outside for a moment in her wellingtons, breathing in the cold air. Gus looked joyous, leaping about as though the snow spectacle had been laid on especially for him. It contrasted with the weight Eve felt in her chest. She kept seeing Harry Tennant's laughing face in her mind's eye, full of life and humour. But beneath the heavy sadness, a nervous agitation built: the need to act.

She would fix some coffee, shower, dress, and walk Gus on the village green. Then, as soon as she'd fed them both, she'd start on the task Robin had given her. She knew she wouldn't rest until she was on it. Memories of the midwinter gathering filled her mind. She needed to get them down before more time clouded the details.

Maybe her information could help catch a killer.

CHAPTER SIX

After breakfast, Eve sat down in the dining room at Elizabeth's Cottage, where she did most of her work, ready to start her notes for Robin and Greg. The room overlooked Haunted Lane on one side and Eve's garden on the other. It had been one of her favourite places when she'd first explored the house: full of nooks and crannies – narrow cupboards next to the fireplace, and an old sideboard and highly polished wooden table she'd bought with the house; they fitted the room so well.

She always faced the garden as she wrote. The scene was picturesque. At the bottom of a long, wide lawn, a beech tree stood, crisp against the sky, white-coated and glittering in the light. Nearer to the house, snow perched on the branches of a gnarled old apple tree and a magnolia. The beauty jarred with the news she'd had.

Inside, the dining room was cosy. It wasn't enough to alter her mood, but it had a cocooning effect, buffering her from events outside.

She'd gone through her usual winter ritual before sitting down: lighting lamps at either end of the sideboard, and switching on the classic floor-standing Anglepoise to illuminate her work. She'd plugged in the pin-prick fairy lights on the Christmas tree too. She was fond of them, despite this year's love–hate relationship with the tree itself.

To Eve's left was the fireplace. She'd banked it up with fuel the night before, after checking the weather forecast. The kindling crackled under the logs. Gus, who'd settled himself at her feet, lifted his head for a moment to glance in the direction of the flames. A second later he resumed his relaxed posture, nestled against her slipper socks. They both benefited from the arrangement.

She looked to her right, to the cupboard that led to the boy, Isaac's, hiding place, and let her mind drift back to the gathering on midwinter's evening. She began to write.

Time went by without her noticing, her fingers touch-typing at speed as she recounted events that day. As she focused, more details of Harry's interactions came back to her. He'd spent some time talking to a small, squat woman who'd reminded Eve forcefully of Beatrix Potter's hedgehog character, Mrs Tiggy-Winkle. Eve had seen her about the village before, but they'd never been introduced. She hadn't been able to see Harry's expression, but Mrs T had looked flushed and she'd wondered what was going on. Though of course, the room had been crowded and hot; it might just have been that.

Harry had circulated all evening, in fact, appearing to draw out each and every villager. She'd experienced personally how good he was at that.

His odd promises of surprises at his party took on a new significance too. He'd been killed the day before the event. Was he planning to reveal something about one of his neighbours? Information he'd unearthed at the open house, perhaps? Maybe someone had acted to stop him in his tracks.

The details all needed including, but they were so sketchy, and she hated submitting a report that referred to a Mrs Tiggy-Winkle lookalike. She shook her head, but then shelved her worries. It would have to do. It was time to move on to record her memories of Christmas Day and her meet-up with Harry outside the village store.

After she'd finished, she reread what she'd written. She'd treated it like one of her obituaries, and included her personal thoughts, so long as she could back them up with evidence. Judd Bentley's odd behaviour, the way Harry Tennant had been able to get people talking, and even Hector Abbott pinching her brandy (she was venting) were all included.

After fetching herself a coffee and some lunch (a slice of mushroom and Stilton Wellington she had left in the fridge), Eve caught her dachshund's eye.

'Robin and Greg will think I spend my whole time listening in to other people's conversations.'

Gus gave her a deadpan look.

She did, of course. Anyone would think her dachshund had picked up on the fact. 'Thanks for your support.'

She'd have to sacrifice her reputation on the altar of truth. It was no good holding back when it could be crucial. She pressed send and considered Robin's involvement with the case as she ate.

It was clear he missed police work. He kept his inside knowledge of local investigations very quiet but he always knew the latest within hours. And it was a risk: if DI Palmer found out, Robin's cover would be blown and his local contact, DS Boles, would be in trouble. Greg Boles was married to Robin's cousin, and had helped him relocate to Saxford, enlisting the support of the vicar, who'd officiated at Greg's wedding. Robin's recluse-like behaviour and unknown history made the villagers wonder, but they'd accepted him because Jim Thackeray did. And because he was an excellent gardener, and they were a practical lot.

Robin and Boles were obviously close. They must trust each other one hundred per cent, but Eve was still interested in Boles's motivation for sharing. It sounded as though he was frustrated with Palmer's attitude and keen to hash cases over with a like-minded outsider. Occasionally, Eve had wondered if Palmer himself was corrupt, just like Robin's former colleagues, but instinct told her not. She presumed it would involve effort, which ruled him out.

The DI was energetic about telling Eve to keep her nose out of police business, but otherwise torpid. She shook her head. She was going to have to disappoint him, once again, even without an obituary to write. She wanted to know what had happened to Harry Tennant; she couldn't ignore the horror and injustice of his death.

She finished the last of the Wellington, drained her coffee and got up from the table. 'Gus, I have a plan. How about a walk?'

Her dachshund propelled himself in the direction of the front door as though on springs. Eve donned her fitted chocolate-brown coat, together with the matching knee-length boots. Suede-effect gloves and a faux-fur hat completed her defence against the cold. She bent to put Gus's coat on too: a stylish quilted blue-and-green tartan number. She had a job getting it on him; practical considerations went out the window when he was excited.

Outside the cottage, Gus ran to and fro in the shallow front garden, between the front of the house and the snow-topped privet hedge. She waited for him to calm down, then attached his leash, and was met with an insulted look.

'It's only for a short time. We can take it off again once we're by the river.' She made for Love Lane, at the village end of their byway. It ran alongside the green, and if she turned right, Eve could follow it to the Old Toll Road, which crossed the Sax. There was a path coming off it on the village side of the river which would take her all the way to the mill.

She knew the police would be busy there for hours, if not days, to come. Everything on the far side of the river would be out of bounds, but that didn't stop her strolling by on the near side, on an innocent dog walk.

'I love you very much,' she said to Gus as they reached Love Lane, 'but you are also an excellent decoy.'

The local schools were still on vacation, and it was mayhem on the village green. Her dachshund looked longingly at the children dashing to left and right, but she shook her head. 'I'm not risking a snowball in the face. Not at the start of our walk.' Or, indeed, at any stage, but she might as well let him down gently.

A couple of minutes later they descended from the Old Toll Road onto the riverside track and Eve let Gus off his leash, allowing him to dash ahead. The route took them round the back of Monty's Teashop, past its rear lawn which swept down towards the river. Its grounds were separated from the path by a white-painted wooden gate, set into a low hedge. Beyond, Eve could see Viv's youngest son, Sam, through the teashop's large glazed doors. He was dashing between tables with a heavily laden tray. He and his girlfriend Kirsty were back from university for the holidays and Viv was keeping them busy. ('They love it,' she'd said. 'Wouldn't know what to do with themselves otherwise.' Eve wasn't entirely sure this was true.)

Gus glanced over at Monty's too, and at that moment, Eve saw Viv herself. She plonked the loaded tray she'd been carrying on a vacant table and marched out into the grounds. Eve wondered distractedly which customers were waiting for the tea and cake she'd been transporting.

A second later, Viv had let herself out of Monty's garden and was standing next to them on the path, a frown tracing its way across her face. 'You heard about Harry?' She glanced up the river in the direction of the mill, though it was out of sight from where they stood.

Eve nodded.

'And the rumours? People are saying the fire was started deliberately.'

'I've heard the same.' She couldn't mention that Robin was her source. 'It's unbearable, isn't it?'

Viv's eyes were serious – a rare occurrence. 'Appalling. Are you going to view the scene of the crime, by any chance?'

She couldn't get away with anything. 'I've got to walk Gus somewhere.'

'Hmm. Well, you must tell me everything you find out.'

Eve was due to work a shift at Monty's the following morning. 'As soon as there's a quiet moment tomorrow.'

Viv gave her a severe look. 'News has to take priority, Eve. You know that.'

'As the person in charge of your business administration, I have to tell you that the customer always comes first. I don't have an excuse to get involved this time, anyway.'

Viv batted away her words with a wave of her hand. 'Oh please.'

'You normally worry about me getting mixed up in this kind of thing.'

'I've given up trying to influence you and resigned myself to your fate. I still intend to worry though – just the same as usual.' She turned on her heel and retraced her steps towards Monty's glass doors.

Eve and Gus strode on, past the back of Viv's cottage, which was next to Monty's, and then on by the rear gardens of the other houses that faced the village green.

To her right, the tide was out on the estuary, and a group of noisy redshanks stood on the mud, probing for insects with their orange bills. Up ahead to her left, the majestic edifice of St Peter's had come into view, its spire tall and impressive against the blue sky. They carried on, away from civilisation, towards the mill.

Eve's stomach knotted as they followed the river. In the distance now, she could see a dark smudge against the pale, icy marshes: the remains of Harry Tennant's home. Gradually, as she narrowed the distance, the smudge resolved into details, forcing her to face up to the full horror of what had happened. The acrid smell of smoke still hung in the air.

There was a raised bank on the other side of the river, next to the mill, just wide enough to take vehicles. She could see a scientific support van, a truck with a cherry picker on it, and a patrol car.

As she'd thought, the whole area was taped off. She glanced down at Gus.

'We'd better keep walking, buddy.' She didn't want Detective Inspector Palmer to see her snooping. The less he knew about her interest the better. But the team on the other bank, dressed in their white overalls, paid her no attention, so she was able to snatch a look at the collapsed mill.

Bits of its blackened walls were in place, but the roof had fallen in and the top-most floors had burned or collapsed. Chunks of sail, some little more than charcoal, were scattered over a wide area; they'd come down from such a height. The windows on the first floor had shattered, their lintels and the brickwork above slumping down, giving her a view inside. What was that glinting in the low sunlight? Something that had fallen on top of everything inside, shiny side down, though it was cracked and bits of it stuck up and caught the rays...

She was well out into the countryside now, the buildings on her left few and far between, but almost opposite the mill was the rear of a domestic garage. Between it and a row of densely packed leylandii, she could see a house which backed onto the river and was screened by the trees. It was large, upmarket and twentieth century, with picture windows downstairs. It looked empty, its curtains half drawn.

She walked beyond the mill now. If Palmer was watching – disguised by protective overalls – she wanted to show him she and Gus weren't just there to snoop. But it wasn't long before her dachshund stopped (rather firmly) and gave her an old-fashioned look.

'Had enough? That's fair.' She bent to give him a cuddle. His legs were short and the novelty value of the snow was probably wearing off. 'Let's turn back then, and to heck with Palmer.' She wanted to pay close attention as she passed the mill a second time. What was the shiny, cracked material that had collapsed on what had likely been Harry's bedroom? She couldn't stop her mind straying to what was underneath it too. She doubted the police had had time to move Harry's body.

The return journey settled the matter. A mirror. That was certainly what it looked like. And if it had landed like that, face downwards, with the main walls still standing on that level, there was only one place it could have come from.

Harry Tennant had had a mirrored bedroom ceiling.

CHAPTER SEVEN

Eve didn't want to be narrow-minded. Maybe a whole bunch of people had mirrors on their bedroom ceilings and she was the odd one out. Perhaps Ian had bought one the moment he moved in with Sonia, and Simon and Polly had one on their wedding list.

Both thoughts were horrible.

The mirror made her review her own, limited experience of Harry too: his charm and how she'd warmed to him, confiding more than she might normally. And the way he'd caught her outside the village store to ask after her Christmas.

If he'd survived, would he have carried on being friendly? Might he have asked her round to the mill for dinner? She was sure she'd have said no, but the prospect of mounting the stairs and seeing herself reflected above still spooled through her head.

Did having a mirrored ceiling mean you were more likely to be a lothario than someone who opted for a coat of matt emulsion?

But she needed to take a step back and think what it told her about his death. Harry had only been at the mill nine months, but she guessed the mirror must have been his. She couldn't imagine the previous owner leaving it there to be shown off by the estate agents. And Harry hadn't bought it so he could admire his duvet cover. Unless his lover was from out of town, there was likely someone local who'd be able to help the police with their enquiries. Eve would like to identify them too.

She and Gus were passing the leylandii again, almost immediately opposite the mill, when Eve heard a car pull up, somewhere beyond the trees. As she drew level with the gap before the garage, a white Fiat 500 came into view. A moment later a woman got out of the driver's side. It was Tori Abbott, wife of Hector, from the midwinter open house. Eve watched as she paused a moment and sniffed the air, frowning. If they were arriving home, it explained how the couple knew Harry; they were neighbours, albeit separated by the river.

Gus was keen to carry on. 'Just a second, buddy. This could be useful.' Eve paused, and after a moment Tori glanced up and spotted her. Her eyes widened in recognition and she smiled, but then her gaze drifted beyond Eve's shoulder and her mouth fell slowly open.

Tori walked forward, between the garage and the leylandii, and joined Eve out on the river path. She moved at reduced speed, as though in a trance.

Behind her, Hector had also emerged from their vehicle, a slightly testy look on his face.

Tori was still staring at the mill. At last she turned to Eve. 'What in God's name happened?'

Eve remembered noticing the Abbotts' half-drawn curtains. 'You've been away?'

The woman nodded dumbly.

'I'm afraid there's terrible news. Harry was inside when the mill burned down.'

Tori put a hand to her face and turned away. Hector stepped forward, frowning. 'We've been staying with friends since New Year. We came home early to attend his party tomorrow; he made such a damned fuss about everyone coming along.'

'Good grief, Hector.'

Eve could hardly believe his words either. It sounded as though he resented the wasted journey and a holiday cut short. But it told her something more too: Harry had wanted an audience.

Tori Abbott shook her head. 'Forgive him. I thought I'd married a human being, but it turns out he's more a machine. That's surgeons for you. They're not much use if they allow emotions to get the better of them.'

Eve hadn't known his profession. 'I guess not.'

Tori was still staring at the remains of the mill. 'I-I just can't believe it. He was so young. And for the blaze to take hold like that, before he could raise the alarm.'

'It was late at night, so I guess he must have been asleep. You'd made friends since he moved here?'

Tori looked regretful. 'I hadn't seen much of him, what with the river being in the way. That was why I made a beeline for him at your party. I wanted the chance to catch up with him. Otherwise, our interactions were mostly limited to bellowed hellos, and a cheery exaggerated wave.'

Eve nodded.

Harry's neighbour was shaking her head now. 'If we'd been here, we might have woken and seen what was going on. It could have been so different.'

Eve hesitated. 'A lot of people knew you were going off for New Year, I suppose?'

Tori frowned questioningly.

'Apparently the fire was started deliberately.'

Her eyes widened. 'How horrible.' At last she answered Eve. 'Yes, I suppose plenty of people knew we'd be gone, now I think about it. We mentioned it at your party, and to Moira at the village store.'

In that case, there probably wasn't a single person in Saxford who wasn't aware. And of course, anyone spying out the land in the run-up to Harry's death could probably have guessed too. Eve had thought the Abbotts' house looked empty herself, with its curtains left ambiguously half-drawn.

Eve and Gus walked slowly back along the river, reaching the Old Toll Road at last. 'It's no good,' she said to him. 'I'm going to have to dig into this, even though it's none of my business.' Her resolution was all very well, but how could she interview people for information when she had no excuse to write about Harry?

But within half an hour of arriving home, everything changed. Gus had just settled down by the fire she'd lit in the living room when her mobile rang. It was Portia Coldwell from *Icon* magazine.

'*Eve, I'm so glad I caught you.*' Her ingratiating voice oozed down the line. '*I assume you've heard of Harry Tennant's tragic death? I know he's in your neck of the woods.*'

Eve rallied her mental resources. Why was a national glossy like *Icon* contacting her about the death of a business consultant? 'Yes, I'd heard.'

'*You won't be surprised to know that we'd love you to write his obituary for us.*'

'Of course. I'd be delighted.' She was playing for time. If she bluffed long enough, would Portia give away her reason for asking?

'*Perfect. I have to confess, I only just found out who he was. You knew already?*'

'Erm…'

'*Pippa Longford.*'

'Excuse me?'

'*The* Real Story's *agony aunt was actually an uncle! I'd never have guessed! A friend of mine there tipped me off an hour ago. It's the kind of tale our readers will love. I'll pop you over a contract.*'

Eve put her phone down and went to find her laptop. There was a whole lot more she wanted to pass on to Robin and Greg now.

CHAPTER EIGHT

By tradition, between midwinter and 6 January, Monty's was decorated to reflect the season. Viv's trademark jam jars were currently trimmed with emerald-green ribbon, and contained gold-gilded bay leaves. Meanwhile, Monty's stylishly mismatched crockery, which created a relaxed feel, was Christmas themed: unified by the greens and reds of holly, robins, mistletoe and wreaths. A friend had given Viv a side plate decorated with grinning Santa Clauses the previous year, to add to the collection. ('Unthinkable,' she'd said, shaking her head, as soon as the friend had left. The plate had been banished to the back of a cupboard.)

Between Christmas and New Year, Eve had felt flat, and the décor reminded her of the fact. When a successful celebration was over, it was time to move on. But the morning after the news of Harry's death, she found it comforting. The familiar trappings were something normal and traditional in the face of what had happened. The blackened mill had haunted her dreams the night before.

Monty's was already filling up as Eve entered the teashop. People came together in the wake of bad news – taking comfort from sharing their thoughts. Before Eve had even shut out the cold, she heard Harry's name mentioned.

Scanning the scene, she saw not only Angie, one of the regular student helpers Eve had booked for the day, but also Viv's son Sam again, and his girlfriend Kirsty. *They* hadn't been on Eve's weekly plan.

Sam grinned in response to her puzzled look. 'Mum asked us to step in. Apparently she wants you in the kitchen for some urgent baking.'

'Hmm. Thanks, Sam.' Eve knew what preparation needed doing – that was part of her job. Letting things get urgent wasn't allowed.

In the kitchen, Viv rushed up and put an arm round her shoulders. 'How are you? After seeing the mill, I mean? I thought it would be best if you could lurk back here, rather than joining the melee.'

'Sure you're not just after the latest news?'

Her friend's eyes widened. 'How can you say that?' Eve met her gaze until Viv groaned. 'Okay, it's a fair cop. But my motives are pure. I can't bear the thought of what's happened. And if you're going to try to work out who killed Harry, you'll need me as a sounding board.'

She let go of Eve, who sighed and went to hang her coat up in the office off the kitchen. 'What about Sam and Kirsty? Don't they need a rest?'

'Nonsense!' Viv laughed. 'Hard work is character-building. Besides, they're desperate for the extra cash to fund their disgusting student lifestyles. They'll be back at uni before you know it, with another whole term of clubbing to pay for. And anyway,' she smiled ingratiatingly, 'I want you to be more involved in the baking. Your fruit and peel cakes at the midwinter do were sublime.'

'I can see through your flattery, you know.' Eve hoped the words would disguise how pleased she felt, but Viv grinned knowingly. *Very irksome.*

Her friend's smile faded. 'I'd like to know your thoughts – chip in if I can. If you let me be Watson, I'll unlock the secrets of sloe gin spice cakes for you. Poor Harry. I haven't walked up the river, but I keep visualising the mill.'

The sight of it reared up again in Eve's head. 'It's a harrowing scene.' How could one person do that to another? 'And all right, you win – it would be good to share.' Hashing through her thoughts always helped.

Viv produced the liquor-soaked fruit and they washed their hands and donned their aprons and blue hairnets. Viv had photographed Eve in hers once; there was a constant live threat that it might appear on Facebook.

'You beat the eggs and sugar while I zest these clementines,' Viv said.

'Yes, ma'am!' Eve glanced at the recipe and began to weigh out the ingredients. She was conscious of Viv's eyes on her but took no notice. She wasn't fast, but she was accurate; swapping to a more intuitive method would mean mistakes.

She felt a release of tension as Viv stopped eyeing her and started work.

'I saw the news,' her friend said. 'I can't believe Harry Tennant was an agony aunt.'

'Nor me.' Eve's mind went back to how he'd described himself: a consultant, who tackled all kinds of problems. There'd been hints at the truth, but nothing that allowed her to guess. 'It means I've got a proper excuse to talk to his contacts now.' She explained about *Icon*'s commission. 'The most surprising thing to me was discovering *which* agony aunt he was.' Eve began to beat her butter and sugar.

'How do you mean?'

'You remember Moira told me I should write off for advice about Ian?' She glanced over her shoulder to see Viv's eyes widen.

'It was Pippa Longford she recommended?'

'Weren't you listening?' But Eve already knew Viv used the sight of Moira to remind her to do her pelvic floor exercises. It wasn't a total surprise she'd drifted off. 'Yes. She suggested I offload my woes to Harry Tennant.'

'Blimey.' Viv was turning the clementine as she expertly removed its zest without looking. 'Do you think she knew?'

Eve had asked herself the same question, before dismissing the idea. 'If she did, the whole village would have heard about it.'

'Fair point. But it's still an odd coincidence.'

Too much of one. 'My bet is someone recommended Pippa to Moira in turn. And maybe *that* person knew "Pippa" was local.' Eve explained how Sylvia and Daphne said Judd Bentley from the stables had been asking about Pippa Longford too. 'He said everyone was talking about her. There's got to be a reason for that.'

'It's weird that Judd was asking.'

'Yes, and I've a suspicion it wasn't a casual thing. I saw him buttonhole each new arrival at the get-together; it looked like he had a mission.'

Viv went to rinse her hands as Eve turned to crack eggs for the cake into a separate bowl. The recipe said to beat them before adding them to the butter and sugar, which was good, because she could surreptitiously pick out any bits of shell.

'So you'll want to talk to Moira to see how she first heard about Pippa Longford's column then,' said Viv. 'And to Judd Bentley too, to find out why he was so interested in her?'

Eve nodded. She'd already set up two documents, one relating to Harry's obituary and another to his murder. The tasks Viv had identified were top of her to-do list in the second. 'I can use the article I have to write for *Icon* as an excuse. If there's someone local who knew Harry was Pippa, I've got a legitimate reason for tracking them down.'

As Eve whisked the beaten eggs in with the sugar and butter, Viv sifted the flour and baking powder.

'Anyone else on your radar?'

'I'll need to trace Harry's contacts: relations, childhood friends, the editor at the *Real Story* and so on.' She cast Viv a sidelong glance. 'And then there's his lover.'

Viv's eyebrows shot up, making her hairnet crinkle. 'You've worked fast. I didn't know he had one!'

Eve told her about his mirrored ceiling. 'So I assume he had an active love life.'

'Fascinating…' Viv grinned for a moment. 'As far as family goes, I heard he has an uncle who lives locally.'

Was that why Harry had moved to the area? Maybe the man was frail and needed looking after. 'That's useful, thanks. Any other friends that you're aware of?'

Viv frowned. 'Not sure. Moira's probably your woman for that question.'

She'd be in seventh heaven when Eve asked. After gathering gossip, spreading it was her favourite pastime.

Viv was sniffing the sloe gin-soaked fruit. 'This is going to be a winner, I can feel it. We'll top each cake with sugared plums. I'll save us some; we might need comfort food with everything that's going on.' She shot Eve a look. 'Anything else to consider on Harry's murder at this stage?'

Eve went back to the thoughts that had coalesced overnight. 'It seems the killer picked their moment; Tori and Hector Abbott live right opposite the mill, but they were away when the fire started. Assuming they're telling the truth, that is.'

'You reckon they're lying?'

'I don't suppose so, but I'm not taking anything for granted.' Eve had fallen for a false alibi in the past. 'Anyway, assuming the killer took advantage of their absence, it looks like they're local.'

'Because they knew the Abbotts would be away?'

'Exactly. They could have heard on the grapevine.'

'Moira?'

'Most likely. Or they might have found out by visiting the scene of the crime beforehand. Again, that would imply someone within easy reach of Saxford.'

Viv nodded slowly. 'Unless the murderer was utterly reckless, and didn't worry that a neighbour might raise the alarm.'

Eve considered. 'It's not impossible, but it seems less likely to me. Setting the fire needed careful planning. I don't see the killer as rash.' She prepared to fold the flour into the batter.

'You need to use a metal spoon for this bit,' Viv said. 'And be very gentle.'

'I *know*!'

'If you're tense, it will affect the mixture.'

'Right. Thanks.'

Viv folded her arms. 'You're hell to teach, you know that? A determined perfectionist, with a strong dislike of being told what to do.'

'Sorry.' She relaxed her shoulders and took a deep breath. *Totally calm.* As she finished the folding, she closed her eyes for a moment. 'There's one more oddity to focus on. Normally, you'd expect Pippa Longford's correspondents to be spread across the country: the *Real Story* is a national magazine after all.'

'Makes sense.'

'But with Moira recommending the column to me, and Judd Bentley telling Sylvia and Daphne everyone's been talking about "Pippa", maybe Harry Tennant's inbox contained more local pleas for help than you'd imagine.'

Viv leaned against the worktop. 'All pouring out their private affairs to a man who might guess who they were.'

'Exactly.'

Eve visualised them sending their entreaties, quite possibly from email addresses that gave away their names, assuming they were corresponding with a journalist based in London, who wouldn't know or care who they were.

'If a villager shared a damaging secret, then discovered Pippa's true identity, they might have panicked. And Harry was hinting about surprises at his upcoming party. Maybe the timing of his death isn't a coincidence.'

CHAPTER NINE

Early that afternoon, Eve walked Gus round the perimeter of the village green. The snowball fights were still in full swing; she was looking forward to the start of school term the following week.

On her way home, she paused at the village store, leaving Gus outside, his leash attached to one of the hooks Moira and her husband Paul had installed for dogs.

'Only two minutes, buddy – I promise!' she said in response to his wounded look. Pushing the door open, she was met with the jangle of the old-fashioned bell and the sight of Paul disappearing through an inner door. He hadn't accepted her presence in the village yet. According to the locals it took around twenty years for the magic to work.

Not so with Moira. She'd been keen to chat with Eve on her very first visit to Saxford. Her love of gossip meant Eve's 'two-minutes' promise to Gus would require strict discipline.

'Oh, my dear, Eve!' she said now. 'I suppose you've heard about poor Harry Tennant? What a thing to have happened!'

Eve remembered the admiring glances Moira had sent his way at the midwinter party. 'I know.' She took a basket and chose a packet of cheese from one of the humming fridges. The store was warm and smelled of ground coffee and – faintly – of the bread Toby from the pub supplied. There were only flakes of crust left in the wicker baskets now.

'And to think,' a blush rose to Moira's cheeks, highlighted in the overhead strip light, 'that he was Pippa Longford.' She turned a shade more puce. Had she really never written in herself? She was very red for someone with no special interest in Pippa's identity.

'I know. I only heard when *Icon* magazine called to ask me to write his obituary.'

Moira's mouth formed an O. 'So you'll find out all about his work, then?'

Eve took pity on her. 'I won't have access to any of his correspondence. I'm sure that would go against data protection.'

'Oh, of course. I hadn't thought of that.' There was a note of relief in her voice, but she was still anxious. What else was wrong?

'I wondered, what made you recommend Pippa to me? You said you'd never written in yourself.'

'No,' Moira said quickly. 'That's right, of course.' Her brow furrowed. 'It was Camilla Sullivan who recommended her column. I understand she pointed several people in her direction. Maybe *she* knew Pippa was Harry.' Her frown deepened. 'Though I can't think why he would have confided in her. I wasn't aware they were friends.' She pursed her lips. 'But she did take out a subscription to the *Real Story* a couple of months ago. Very odd, I thought.'

Eve tried to keep up. She didn't know who Camilla Sullivan was, or why that was strange.

Moira was still frowning. 'Before that, she only took the *Telegraph*.'

That explained the storekeeper's previous comment: the two publications had a very different style. Eve imagined most *Telegraph* readers wouldn't be seen dead with a copy of the *Real Story*, and vice versa.

'I don't think I've met Camilla.'

Moira leaned forward eagerly. 'Oh, I assumed you must know her, but I can fill you in. She's rather well known around these parts as a florist. Very experienced: does all the most exclusive weddings.' Her eyes took on a dreamy look. 'Always so well dressed, too. And gracious. There was a time when we could have fallen out.' She frowned. 'It was a little awkward. I'd just heard that her ex-husband had remarried. A twenty-four-year-old, would you believe? Naturally I was horrified, and – out of sympathy – I was discussing it with Molly Walker when Camilla walked in.'

Yes, Eve could see how that would have been 'a little awkward'.

'I sensed she'd picked up on our conversation, though of course we changed the subject the moment she appeared. But she was kindness itself when I made her next home delivery.'

As Eve watched, Moira's eyes opened wider. Light of some kind seemed to be dawning. 'Oh my goodness, it's just occurred to me! Camilla hinted recently that she had a new boyfriend. She didn't say who – she enjoys being secretive.' Her lips pursed in irritation. 'But she did say something about how she might be doing flowers for her own wedding one day soon. Perhaps Harry Tennant was her new man. And if she knew he was Pippa... well, really, I'm quite put out!'

'Though at least it makes no odds, given you never wrote to him,' Eve said, trying to suppress a smile.

Moira blinked quickly. 'Well, of course, that's true. But all the same...' She took Eve's cheese, and the packet of coffee she'd also picked up, and entered the amounts on her old-fashioned till. 'Anyway, I can see you'll want to speak to her. She lives in that beautiful Elizabethan house on Blind Eye Lane.'

It was out near Simon's stables, and shared its name with the local woods. Both had provided smugglers with clandestine routes to move their wares out of the village in olden times. The locals had known turning a blind eye was their safest option.

'Thanks, I'll contact her. You don't happen to know the name of Harry's uncle, do you? He's someone I ought to speak with.'

Moira managed to switch a smug smile into a sympathetic sigh with reasonable speed. 'Tristan Tennant. The poor man. I can't think what he must be going through. He doesn't live in Saxford, but he visits. I saw him with Harry a couple of times.'

And had managed to identify him, naturally. 'Thanks, that's helpful.' Eve would find him.

At that moment, the bell over the store door jangled and Molly Walker, Moira's friend and fellow Saxford resident, walked in.

Eve said hello then turned back to Moira. 'I mustn't hold you up, but is there anyone else you think I should interview for Harry's obituary?'

The storekeeper's smile faded now. 'I really can't think of anyone.' She wasn't meeting Eve's eye. What was going on?

'Thanks anyway. How much do I owe you?'

'Nine pounds ninety-five, thank you.'

As Eve turned to leave the store, Molly Walker stepped forward. 'I suppose Moira mentioned Kerry Clifton?'

Eve glanced instinctively at the storekeeper.

Her face fell before she jacked up a smile. 'Oh, how silly of me! Yes, of course, Kerry.'

'Who is she?' Eve asked.

'A fellow domestic help.' Molly smiled. 'She worked for Harry, and in that position you get to know a *lot* about your employer, take it from me. She lives at the last cottage on the right on Dark Lane, before the turn-off to the stables.'

Five minutes later, Eve and Gus arrived back at Elizabeth's Cottage.

'Why didn't Moira want me to speak to Harry Tennant's home help?' she said to him. It was weird.

She went through to the dining room, booted up her laptop and opened her 'Murder Suspects' and 'Obituary' spreadsheets. She'd started to populate the first as soon as she'd written Robin and Greg's report, and the second after the call from *Icon*.

She entered details relating to Harry's uncle Tristan, his cleaner Kerry Clifton, the florist Camilla Sullivan and the Abbotts on both sheets. Every contact of Harry's was a suspect until she had reason to discount them.

Camilla was only a provisional entry, of course. Moira's boyfriend theory was unproven. The woman might not even have known Harry, let alone realised he was Pippa. But the fact that she'd recommended the agony aunt to multiple people made her worth investigating.

'And her subscription to *Real Story* hints at a connection between them, too,' Eve said to Gus. 'It's not her usual style and she's clearly a recent convert, not a life-long fan.'

Camilla could have been looking out for the answer to a letter she'd sent in, of course, but why write to that agony column if she preferred the *Telegraph*?

Eve googled and the result confirmed what she'd suspected: like most nationals, the broadsheet had celebrity advisers of its own.

'Maybe this afternoon's enquiries will provide some answers.' She stood up and Gus sprang to attention, sensing they were about to head out again. 'Sorry, buddy – I think this has to be a solo mission. Camilla might not welcome impromptu visits if dogs are involved.' Eve had seen her house from the road; it looked smart.

Gus turned his back on her and pottered through to the kitchen, treating her words with the disdain he clearly thought they deserved.

The location of Camilla Sullivan's house was convenient; she could drop a note in at Kerry Clifton's cottage on her way. Eve paused to write it before leaving home, explaining the job *Icon* had given her and providing her phone number. She suggested an interview at the Cross Keys that evening and offered to buy the woman supper if she was free. Moira's weird reluctance to pass on her name left Eve itching to meet her as soon as possible; it might result in something unexpected.

Once she'd sealed the note in an envelope she went upstairs to get changed. Moira said Camilla was elegant, which made Eve want to smarten up, but clothes were important whenever she interviewed for an obit. Dressing neatly showed respect. Eve slipped into a herringbone tweed dress and jacket, then pulled on her woollen coat downstairs, before making her way across the village through the snow.

Walking up Blind Eye Lane felt like stepping back in time. The way was narrow, the day snow-muffled, the only sounds the rooks in the bare oak trees above. The houses were few and dated back hundreds of years.

Camilla's place – a large half-timbered cottage – came into view. Hawthorn House, according to the sign. She walked up the garden path between rows of lavender bushes still heavy with snow.

Through one of the leaded, latticed windows, she could see the glow of a table lamp. It looked as though Camilla was at home.

Eve rapped the lion's head door knocker and heard footsteps a moment later.

The door opened to reveal a woman Eve knew: the shining dark eyes, olive skin and silver hair were all familiar.

It was the woman who'd cannoned into Harry at the midwinter party, and who'd sat next to him in church on Christmas Day.

And on both occasions, they'd acted as though they were strangers.

CHAPTER TEN

Eve weighed up what she knew as she introduced herself to Camilla Sullivan and explained her mission.

She'd seen Camilla and Harry in close proximity on two occasions. Had Camilla knocked into him deliberately at the midwinter party, so she could act out being a stranger and enjoy their private joke? Eve was starting to think so, and that Moira's guess about their relationship might be right. But what had Harry thought? She remembered his split-second look of irritation at Camilla's move. He'd disguised it quickly, but it had been interesting. Not a look of surprise, which would be natural when someone bumped into you, but instant annoyance.

Perhaps he'd been less keen than she was to risk their relationship being revealed.

Camilla blinked and smiled in response to Eve's explanation for being there, but with a look of confusion. 'Why would you want to ask me about Harry Tennant?' She was just as glamorous as Eve remembered. The longline jacket she wore, nipped in at the waist, was in pale stone, which would have drained Eve of colour, but Camilla's skin tone stood up to it. Her complexion glowed and her deep brown eyes had a spark in them. Under the jacket, the loose trousers she wore looked expensive.

Eve took a leap. 'You're the only person I've found so far who knew Harry was Pippa Longford.'

A wry smile crossed the florist's lips now. She stood back in her shadowy hallway. 'You'd better come in.'

Eve followed her through to a thick-walled sitting room where Camilla motioned her to a chair. A chilly light drifted in through the leaded windows, though the room itself was warm, with long radiators and a thick carpet.

'Can I get you a coffee?'

'That would be wonderful. Thank you.' It would combat the chill of the walk over. A moment later, Eve was on her own, and had the chance to observe the living room more closely. The flower arrangements were exquisite, which figured, given Camilla's profession. A beautiful display of white roses, trailing jasmine and gypsophila sat on a side table. The greens and whites looked fresh and clean and echoed the colours beyond the window. If that was an example of Camilla's work, Eve could see why she was in demand.

The roses smelled glorious, but she could detect Camilla's perfume in the room too: Chanel No. 5. It was the scent Eve had wanted for her fortieth birthday, having tried a range of options, but Ian had decided he knew better and bought her his favourite instead. It had made her feel sick.

Next to a Chesterfield sofa sat a magazine rack. Eve had a quick peek, wondering if she'd find copies of *Real Story* there, but there was only the *Telegraph*, *Vogue* and *House and Garden*.

On top of a mahogany bureau sat a silver-framed photograph of Camilla receiving some kind of fancy award. Eve couldn't place the woman presenting it, though she looked familiar. A minor royal perhaps.

Everything about the room spoke of Camilla's success. Her husband might have remarried a twenty-four-year-old, as Moira had said, but there were no signs of any chinks in her armour here. Maybe she'd outgrown him. If he'd chased after someone so young that implied immaturity.

Eve heard movement and went to sit back on the seat she'd been offered: a button-backed armchair upholstered in mistletoe-green velvet. Camilla arrived with a tray and set coffee and associated paraphernalia down on a low table between Eve and a second chair, which she took.

She poured the steaming rich liquid from the white bone-china pot into matching cups. 'Milk? Sugar?'

'Just black, thanks.'

Camilla nodded and added a dash of milk to her own cup. 'How did you discover mine and Harry's secret?' She didn't seem upset by the development. Tragedy aside, Eve sensed the relationship had put a spring in her step and she'd be happy for people to know about it.

'Moira at the village store said you'd recommended Pippa Longford's column to her. She thought I might find it useful too.' Eve sipped her coffee. 'And then I happened to see you and Harry interact at my open house, and again on Christmas Day. When I found out Harry was also Pippa, the facts meshed.'

Camilla gave her an amused look. 'I see.' She'd created both scenes: in church it was she who'd picked a seat next to the dead man.

'I'm so sorry for your loss,' Eve said.

The woman sighed. 'It's one hell of a blow. And people don't generally know that Harry and I were… close friends. That being the case, I've been careful to keep a tight lid on my emotions.' She shrugged. 'I tend to anyway. Upbringing. I warn you now, don't get sympathetic or the floodgates will open.'

Despite her self-control, her hints to Moira about an exciting new relationship said a lot. 'Things were getting serious between you?'

The woman frowned. 'You heard gossip?' She looked torn between amusement and irritation. Maybe she guessed Moira had been the source – which was annoying – but liked being talked about.

Eve didn't reply and Camilla sighed. 'Things were moving forward.' Her eyes sparkled. 'The relationship was intense.'

But that didn't always lead to wedding bells. Eve wondered if the woman's hints to Moira about doing her own flowers had been based on genuine plans made with Harry, or her own dreams for the future. Camilla seemed keen to share; Eve sensed she'd say if Harry had asked her to marry him.

'When did you hear about his death?' Eve wanted to know where Camilla had been when it happened, but there was no way she could slip that question into conversation.

The florist looked down at her lap. It might be an automatic reaction to disguise her upset, but it also robbed Eve of the chance to read her expression. 'I went out early yesterday morning and there was still smoke in the air, in the direction of the mill. I walked straight over to investigate.' She shook her head. 'I was worried about what I might find but I couldn't stop myself. And of course, my worst fears were realised.'

It sounded as though she'd been at home in Saxford overnight, then. And she lived alone, as far as Eve could see; there were no signs of any other presence in the house. The coats and shoes in the hall had all looked like hers.

She could have slipped out and crossed the river on the Dunwich road, just beyond the end of the village, before setting the mill alight. There were few neighbours to see her – especially with the Abbotts away.

Eve put the thought on hold. There was no suggestion Camilla had a motive.

'So, you want to know more about Harry for his obituary, and our connection will come out.'

'Only if you're okay with that. If not, I can quote you anonymously. "A close friend of Harry's said…" That sort of thing.'

Camilla sat back in her chair. 'You can name me. In a village like Saxford, there's no way of keeping a secret like that.'

'But you have up until now?'

The glimmer of amusement came into her eyes again. 'As far as I know. But after the murder, you won't be the only journalist who's all over this story.'

She was right, but you'd think she'd hold back if she minded going public. Eve took her notepad and favourite black pen from her bag.

'Well, thank you for your willingness to speak openly. In that case, perhaps you can tell me how you first met?'

Camilla sipped her coffee, then put it back on its saucer on the table. 'I was in Blyworth around three months ago' – it was the nearest town of any size – 'visiting the wedding boutique there. They recommend my services as part of their package. As I turned to leave, Harry was on his way in. I found out later he was after "something blue" to send to a friend as a wedding-day keepsake.'

Eve knew brides often wore something blue for luck, but had had no idea a whole industry had sprung up around it. She tried not to feel joyless and disapproving.

Camilla picked up her cup again. 'Harry caught my eye that day. We didn't speak, but,' she smiled and cast her eyes down for a moment, 'I had a feeling we might meet again.'

There was a trace of nostalgia in her look, and a wistfulness about her tone, but Eve had seen a spark of excitement at the memory too. She remembered that feeling herself: the promise of something in the offing, that might lead anywhere.

'The next time was in Saxford?'

She nodded. 'I was walking down the lane here, soon after I saw him in town, and he was coming the other way. It was as though it was meant. We recognised each other, stopped to chat and found out we got on rather well.' Her lively eyes were bright. 'He told me the truth about his career within a few days, but I appreciated the secret was sacrosanct. It explained why he distanced himself from the other villagers. We kept our connection quiet to avoid all the questions that would follow.'

It made Eve think of Robin, who kept himself separate for the same reason. Yet Harry's situation had been a little different. Keeping his true career under wraps hadn't been crucial for his safety. Or at least, it shouldn't have been. And he'd been planning a party, something that Robin would never risk. Was it really necessary to be so secretive about his relationship with Camilla, simply to avoid people pressing her for information about him?

'It was good to avoid the village gossip too,' Camilla added, leaning forward. 'You know what this place is like.'

Eve did, but Camilla's reasoning didn't quite ring true. She'd invited talk, with her hints to Moira about a relationship and her mock-collision with Harry.

'Did you recommend the *Real Story*'s advice column to many people in the village?' she asked.

'Oh, several, I should think,' Camilla said. It seemed like an odd turn of phrase. 'I had a great deal of time for Harry, but that magazine isn't everyone's cup of tea. I realised there were a number of people in the village who might benefit from his help without being aware of Pippa's column.'

Eve nodded. 'It would be fascinating to find someone who'd approached him and didn't mind sharing their experiences. Would you be prepared to pass my details on to the people you spoke to, in case they're happy to talk? I have some business cards.'

The woman smiled. 'I'm sorry, but beyond Moira I really can't remember.'

Eve found that hard to believe. Was she being diplomatic? Or holding back for another reason? The people she'd steered in Pippa's direction might not be too pleased with her when they realised she'd known Pippa was Harry.

It prompted Eve's next question. 'Did Harry ever confide in you about the people who wrote to him?'

The woman shook her head. 'Never. We spoke about many, many things, but that wouldn't have been ethical. We both knew it.' Her answer had come quickly.

'So, as far as you know, no one else in Saxford knew Harry was Pippa?'

'That's right. He was very discreet.'

Yet he'd told Camilla within days of meeting her.

'I was approached by someone who thought I might know Pippa in real life, as a matter of fact.' Camilla looked thoughtful as she drank the last of her coffee.

'Really? Who was that?'

'A man called Judd Bentley. He works at Simon Maxwell's stables.'

Eve nodded. 'I know him by sight; he came to my open house. Was that when he approached you?'

She frowned. 'No. It was a day or so later. He came here and knocked at my door.'

That was interesting. Why tackle Camilla at home, rather than at the do? Had he heard about her at the party, then opted for a private conversation for some reason?

'Like you, someone had told him I'd recommended Pippa's services.' Camilla's eyes were on Eve's. 'I'm not sure who. But anyway, he asked if I could put him in touch directly.'

'That's odd. Did he say why he wanted the introduction? Couldn't he just email the column?'

'He said he imagined the inbox would receive hundreds of messages every day, and he wasn't after advice. His sister's a budding journalist and he was hoping a contact on a national paper might help her career.' She shrugged. 'I suppose journalism's very competitive.'

Eve nodded. She was glad Camilla didn't know how much time she spent trying to keep herself in work. Thank goodness for Monty's and her steady employment there.

'But, of course, I didn't admit anything. I apologised for not being able to help, but I told Harry about Judd Bentley's request later that day.'

They could have met, then. 'Do you know if Harry followed it up?'

Camilla frowned. 'He never mentioned it.'

'I see. Thank you.' Eve went on to ask Camilla for her fondest memory of Harry. The answer to that innocuous-sounding question was often telling. People found it hard to lie, and long pauses followed by waffle said a lot.

The woman's eyes glittered and Eve watched her face change, from excitement, to something that made her colour slightly, then finally regret. 'He was a lot of fun.' Eve couldn't help but think of the mirrored ceiling at the mill. 'Because we wanted our privacy, we went for a midnight walk once, in the autumn, soon after we'd met. It was unseasonably warm for late October and we went miles up the track by the river, listening to the owls hoot and looking at the moon.'

It sounded both romantic and adventurous. And if they'd walked from the mill, it also meant she'd be familiar with the route at night: exactly how long it took to reach a road, for instance. Eve had no reason to think she'd wanted to kill Harry, but there were elements of the woman's story that made her curious.

'Camilla, when Harry was at my midwinter open house, he talked about the party he was due to host at the mill. He said to expect some surprises.' She needed to work out how to couch her question. 'I wondered if he was planning on sharing some big news with the village. It might be relevant to my obituary if you happen to know the details.'

She watched the woman's eyes closely. If Harry had accessed compromising information about a villager through his column, she might be aware of it too.

She gave a sphinx-like smile. 'Oh no! I have no idea. How interesting.'

Her tone was playful and Eve cursed inwardly. Camilla either knew, or wanted Eve to think she did, but which? She remembered Moira saying the florist enjoyed being mysterious.

'I presume the police will want to hear all about you and Harry too,' Eve said, as she got up to leave. She didn't want to tell DI Palmer the woman's secrets. It would feel wrong. It made her glad Greg Boles hadn't demanded regular updates after her initial report. At least she could make her own judgement calls. But the idea of withholding something so fundamental as Harry and Camilla's relationship made her anxious. DI Palmer was one of Eve's least favourite people, but what if keeping information back hampered his investigation?

She'd been dreading raising the subject, but Camilla took her by surprise.

'Of course, you're right. I must tell them what I've told you.'

For a second, Eve wondered if she was grateful for her visit. If she had anything to hide, it had given her a dummy run at being quizzed.

The interview had triggered a multitude of questions in Eve's head. Thoughts swirled: Camilla's keenness to be named, and to talk to the police; the way she'd started to take risks with the secret she and Harry shared – hinting at a new relationship and publicising his column for him. Her subscription to the *Real Story*, and Judd Bentley's attempts to identify Pippa Longford.

It was time to fetch Gus for a pre-supper walk and thrash things out.

CHAPTER ELEVEN

Eve and Gus made for the heath between Blind Eye Wood and the sea. It was deserted, and the perfect place for a thinking walk. The sun had set, but despite the deepening dusk, they could still discern the clumps of snow-coated heather at their feet.

The sound of the sea, crashing on the shore, tugging at the shingle-strewn sand, filled the air as Eve let Gus off his leash. He trotted forward, past one of the sporadic gorse bushes, and she followed, hastening to catch up with him.

'Camilla Sullivan's an interesting one,' she said, double checking they were alone. Talking to Gus always helped, but she didn't want people to think she was a complete weirdo. Or to hear her innermost thoughts on the florist, come to that. Not that her words would carry far – the sound of the waves would see to that. 'She claims, loftily, that she and Harry never discussed "Pippa Longford's" correspondence. But how ethical was it to recommend his services, knowing her fellow villagers might unwittingly confide in a man they knew?'

Gus paused and put his head on one side. For a moment, she was convinced he was listening, but as he dashed off, she realised it wasn't to her.

Eve jogged slowly after him, picking her way through the shadowy heather. 'They could each have discovered compromising information about their neighbours. Even if they didn't gossip, Camilla might have identified people from the content the *Real Story* published. And maybe she hinted to Harry about the requests he might expect, too. She could have encouraged him to prioritise locals. She likes fun and intrigue. She probably hoped she could keep track of the advice Harry gave to people she knew.'

Her cover would shortly be blown, yet she didn't seem to care. Eve sensed that was part of the fun: to see the look on her friends' faces when they found out. Of course, the one person Eve knew she'd targeted was Moira, and that could have been an attempt to get even. After all, Camilla had walked in on the storekeeper discussing her husband's new wife.

'Having a joke at her neighbours' expense fits with the way she kept coming into contact with Harry on purpose, while pretending not to know him,' she said to Gus. 'She's the type to enjoy fooling everyone, and taking risks – but maybe being a secret lover was finally wearing thin.' Eve sighed and shook her head. 'I think she wouldn't have minded if people guessed. She was proud to be with him.'

Gus's attention was elsewhere, his nose lifted as though he'd detected some new scent on the breeze.

Eve pressed on. 'But I don't think Harry felt the same.' Harry had been keen to keep Camilla at arm's length and their relationship secret – that was Eve's gut feeling. But why had that been so important to him? Neither of them were married, and the reason Camilla gave, that Harry wanted to avoid the villagers asking her about his profession, didn't seem strong enough. He already had a reasonable cover story. And besides, Eve doubted Camilla would have told, even if they had gone public about their love affair and people had asked. She'd enjoyed the sport of pointing people in Pippa's direction, then watching the fallout. She wouldn't have given that up.

'Of course, now Harry's dead, her fun's over and I think she's already anticipating her next dose of drama: people's reactions when they find out she knew Harry was Pippa all along.' She frowned.

'She's not bothered what other people think and she likes to cause a stir.

'As for Camilla's emotions, I'm sure she found Harry intoxicating, but there was a hint of wistfulness and regret when she talked about him.' She shrugged. 'That might be down to grief, but it would fit if their relationship went sour too. I don't think they wanted the same things.'

She shifted her focus to Harry. Why had he confided in Camilla within days of meeting her? The florist had made their relationship sound romantic, but the mirror on Harry's ceiling put the emphasis on the physical. Not that one should exclude the other. In theory. Could a mirrored-ceiling man also be an adoring, faithful partner? In her experience, even non-mirrored-ceiling men sometimes struggled with that.

Gus was staring at her oddly. She probably looked like she'd been sucking lemons. Or maybe he just wanted to get home. The darkness had intensified and it was bitterly cold.

'You're right. Let's go.'

She attached his leash again as they left the heath, to a look of indignant protest. As they walked up Heath Lane, past the first seaward houses of Saxford, her mobile rang. The woman on the other end announced herself as Kerry Clifton. She must be keen to talk. Eve felt a spark of anticipation.

Safe in the knowledge that Harry's cleaner was happy to meet her a little later that evening, Eve fed Gus, then settled down with her laptop in the dining room at Elizabeth's Cottage. She wanted to record the interview with Camilla and the thoughts she'd worked through with Gus afterwards. The story of the florist and Harry's secret relationship and their moonlit walk up the River Sax would work well in her article.

After that, she googled 'the *Real Story*'. It was time to test her theory that Camilla could have identified friends and acquaintances who'd written in to Harry's advice column. It certainly looked possible: each request for help was accompanied by the initials of the sender, followed by their county. That would be quite a hint if Camilla had a mental list of likely correspondents.

Eve spent the next two minutes scanning the most recent columns, after which she felt both guilty and slightly disappointed. If Moira had written in, it seemed her secrets were safe.

Her mind turned to Camilla's subscription to the *Real Story*. Eve had just proved her own point: looking at the column was irresistible if you thought you might know someone who'd requested help. She imagined Camilla browsing the contents in a leisurely way, for pleasure. And there'd been no copies of the magazine in her newspaper rack. The *Real Story* probably didn't fit with the image she wanted to project, but maybe she was keen to hide her interest in its advice section too.

Although Eve didn't immediately spot any correspondents who might be known to her, one of the letters caught her eye. The heading was 'Pippa says abandon your daughter'. Like every other person who'd spotted it, Eve guessed, she immediately scrolled to read the text.

Please help. My seventeen-year-old daughter already regards herself as an adult. She can't bear to hear my advice, but as her dad I can't bear not to give it. She's drinking and has abandoned her schoolwork. Sometimes I hear her crying. She says it's with frustration because I don't understand her.

Harry's recommendation left Eve dumbstruck.

She's old enough to be left to fend for herself overnight and she clearly believes she can cope. Why not put her to the test? Take off for a long weekend, have a break. If you have other children, take them with you.

Leave your number but don't tell her where you're going. Leave her enough to eat, but not stuff she likes – and no money or alcohol of course. If you're worried you can always ask a friend or family member to drop by to check there are no signs of trouble. But they shouldn't intervene in any way, even if she seems upset.

Children often think they can cope alone, but it's a tough adolescent who's really independent at seventeen. I predict your daughter will be rather more amenable on your return.

Eve swallowed. She could hardly believe the affable man she'd chatted with at the midwinter party had written the response. From the father's letter, there was every chance the girl was in some kind of trouble. She might be coping with a dilemma she didn't know how to share, questions about her identity, or friendship problems. It could be any number of things. Even if her problem was solely her relationship with her dad, how could attempting to make her feel abandoned be a sensible solution?

What Harry had suggested wasn't illegal, but surely it was criminally irresponsible and cruel? There had to be a better way. At the very least Harry could have advised the father to make it clear he wanted to help, despite his feelings of frustration.

Harry hadn't told Eve what he really did, but when he'd said he found people fascinating she'd thought they had something in common. Now, she felt sick. She had to make a living, just like him, but she would never use the information she gathered in such an irresponsible way.

If you were going to involve yourself in people's personal lives, you had to do it with the utmost care, and only for the right ends. Harry's advice had been deliberately provocative. She bet the mag had loved it. It would have created controversy and driven traffic to their website. But what had motivated Harry to be so ruthless and cavalier? The desire to make himself indispensable to the *Real Story*? Or did he truly believe in the harsh methods he'd advocated?

And had his column made him a target for murder? She could imagine his advice might have had awful consequences. It all depended on how obvious the cause and effect was.

It took her a moment to turn back to the calm procedure she needed to adopt to sort through the suspects for his murder. She needed to focus; it was almost time to go and meet Kerry Clifton.

Hastily, she conducted an online search for Judd Bentley's sister. If she was really a budding journalist, she ought to have a presence.

The results took her by surprise. Judd's stated reason for wanting to contact 'Pippa' had left Eve sceptical, but on entering 'Bentley', 'journalist', and 'Suffolk' into Google she got a meaningful result in the first page of hits.

Sally Bentley. She had a piece in the local advertiser. Armed with her first name, Eve googled again and got more results. The first was an article in a student newspaper in Manchester. Further down, Eve found her LinkedIn page, where she described herself as an investigative journalist.

Eve sat back in her chair and frowned. So Judd had been telling the truth after all. But was it really enough to explain the way he'd quizzed the guests at her midwinter party? Sally didn't appear to have advice work as a long-term goal, yet Judd had been so systematic about his search for Pippa. She remembered the intensity in his eyes, and how he'd apparently fought his natural introverted nature to talk to her guests.

She glanced down at Gus. 'I don't like it. I need to find out more, and I think I'll go direct to Sally. As a freelancer her number will probably be online. If I call her without warning, it might be revealing. But right now, I need to get ready to quiz Harry's former cleaner at the pub.'

CHAPTER TWELVE

When Eve entered the Cross Keys that evening, she was taken back to the midwinter party. The woman she'd mentioned in her report for Greg Boles, who looked like Mrs Tiggy-Winkle, was waiting for her. So this was Harry Tennant's cleaner, Kerry Clifton. They ordered their food at the bar and made small talk about the village as they waited for it to arrive. Eve wanted to break the ice with general conversation before getting down to more serious questioning – they had plenty of time and a relaxed atmosphere would help.

They discussed how they'd come to be in Saxford and Kerry told her about her family roots, up in Yorkshire.

'Though I've been in Suffolk so long it feels like home now,' Kerry said, smiling comfortably.

Eve was momentarily distracted by movement at the pub's window as Harry's cleaner spoke. Moira from the store was peering in, her husband Paul just behind her. Her gaze met Eve's, then rested on Kerry, whereupon she ducked back and retreated in a very unsubtle move.

Eve kept half an eye on the door as she and Kerry continued to chat, but Moira and Paul didn't enter. They must have gone home again, which was seriously odd. The pub didn't front directly onto the pavement; you had to cross the forecourt to peer in at the window.

What was going on? Earlier that day, Moira had failed to put Eve in touch with Kerry Clifton. Now, it looked as though she was avoiding her too.

At that moment, Gus pressed himself against Eve's feet under the table. The dachshund's move was a sign that Jo Falconer was on the approach with their meals. Jo owned the pub jointly with her husband and brother-in-law, and put the fear of God into most people, and definitely into Gus. He still hadn't recovered from Jo giving him and the pub schnauzer, Hetty, a telling-off eighteen months earlier. She had impact. Eve had managed to acclimatise to her after ongoing training from Viv.

'This looks awesome,' she said, beaming at Jo for all she was worth as her food landed in front of her. It was game pie with red wine gravy, buttered kale and Parmentier potatoes.

Jo gave her a gracious smile, like a dog owner encouraging good behaviour in their pet.

Eve felt it was her duty to keep the cook happy that evening; there were reporters in the Cross Keys, which always ruffled her feathers. You could tell who they were: they spent their time on their phones, talking loudly about sensitive local subjects and shovelling in their meals as though they were at a fast food joint.

Eve could see Harry's cleaner was familiar with Jo too. She bobbed her head of tawny curls, heavily streaked with grey, and murmured gratitude for her coq au vin with all the reverence of someone uttering responses in church.

Treating an interviewee to dinner wasn't Eve's standard practice; her fee from *Icon* wasn't *that* munificent. She'd made her plan on instinct, hoping to tempt Kerry out. Moira's apparent reluctance for Eve to quiz the woman made her curious. Besides, she likely had useful information and there was a lot at stake.

As Jo turned to walk away, Eve's eyes met Kerry's and she saw a spark of amusement there. It was nice to share the moment, though Eve had become fond of Jo now. The three Falconers made the place what it was, Jo with her straight talking, her husband Matt with his roguish good humour and his brother Toby with calm friendliness.

Gus eased himself off her feet and pottered out from under the table, a questioning look in his eye. His playmate, Hetty, was over by the window, beyond the crackling fire.

'Go on then,' she said. 'But rough and tumble is out.' The pub was packed. 'Fraternise *quietly*, please!' He knew the score. If he didn't want Jo pounding out of the kitchens again, he had to toe the line.

Now the cook was behind the scenes, Eve took her notebook and pen from her bag and set them on the table. Jo didn't approve of mixing work and food, but Eve couldn't risk forgetting crucial details. She'd record what she could now, then add private thoughts and conclusions later.

Kerry Clifton's cheeks were rosy in the warmth of the pub, her eyes twinkly in the firelight. 'This looks lovely,' she said, indicating her meal. 'Thank you for inviting me out; I haven't been in here to eat since my birthday. My son and daughter-in-law treated me, but it was chaotic; they've four children under six, so you can imagine!'

Eve could. Contending with twins had floored her on occasion.

'I come in for a quiet drink with Moira Squires and Molly Walker quite often though. That's normally more relaxed!'

So Kerry was clearly friends with Moira, then. If Moira had written to 'Pippa', Eve could imagine her confiding in Kerry and then regretting it when she realised Eve would interview her. She might worry that Harry's cleaner would share the details. But why avoid her too? If Moira thought Kerry might gossip to Eve, she'd have all the more reason to dash into the pub and break up their cosy chat. Eve couldn't work it out. She filed the thought away for consideration later and focused on Kerry again.

'Thank you for agreeing to speak with me, especially at such an upsetting time. I'm so sorry for your loss.'

The woman cast her eyes down for a moment. 'Thank you. I still can't quite believe it. I kept suggesting he install smoke alarms. I was chatting to Moira about it in the store, only just before Christmas. I think he thought I was fussing, but there was so much wood at the mill, and it's shaped like a chimney. My late husband was a builder; I don't believe it would have stood up to modern safety regulations.'

So Kerry, and quite possibly half the village given she'd mentioned it to Moira, had known Harry had no alarm… on top of anyone who'd visited the mill since he took possession.

The woman smiled sadly. 'Anyway, tell me what you'd like to know – I'm happy to help.' She picked up the glass of Beaujolais Jo's husband, Matt, had recommended to go with her dish. The glass glimmered in the light from the fire.

Eve cut into her pie, the rich aroma making her mouth water. 'I hardly knew Harry myself, so I have very little background on him.' She cast her mind back to the conversation they'd had at the midwinter party. She'd done most of the talking, which had been unusual. Normally, she was the one who listened, but he'd turned the tables on her. Fleetingly, she wondered if he'd shared the details of their conversation with Camilla Sullivan. It left her uncomfortable, even though she had no secrets. She shut the thoughts out. 'The windmill was such a fine place to live, but it was a major move, leaving London for the country. Did he mention what triggered that?' She imagined they must have chatted and discussed his circumstances – when he first took her on, if nothing else.

Kerry relaxed in her chair. 'He said he'd wanted a change of pace; life outside the city. I was curious about his wealth, to be honest.' She gave a sheepish smile and a little shrug. 'Before I took the job with him, just after he arrived in the village, I worked for multiple clients over a wide area. He wanted me five mornings a week, and I was delighted to swap to one local employer, but surprised too. The mill wasn't large. It turned out he wanted more than just cleaning. I'd go in to cook his breakfast each morning, and leave an evening meal to reheat too. I found myself wondering how he could afford daily help.'

'That's understandable.' Eve was curious too; she'd be delighted if Kerry had found out the answer.

'It started to make more sense after what I heard on the grapevine. You know what Saxford's like. His father had made a fortune from a travel company that specialised in tours to remote places. He had a lot of super-rich clients, but then he was killed in a helicopter crash when he was fifty-eight.' She rolled her eyes. 'Luck of the devil up until that point, but it finally ran out. His wife was killed with him, so I assume Harry inherited. He certainly seemed very comfortably off. His father's death was years back now.'

Eve noted Kerry's comment about Mr Tennant senior's luck – did she think the success was undeserved? She'd be curious to find out more about the adventure travel business. It probably didn't relate to the murder, but Eve had learned to pay attention to small details. She always dug deep.

Kerry Clifton prepared a forkful of coq au vin. 'Harry's dad's family were well off to begin with, from what I gather, so he had a good starting point for his venture. It's often the way.' Her look was wry.

'True.' Eve sipped her Barbaresco (Matt had advised her too). 'What did Harry tell you about his work? I wondered how you felt when you found out he was secretly an agony aunt.'

The woman looked up from her plate. 'Oh, I knew what he did.'

Eve was surprised. 'I'm sorry. I had the impression he was very secretive about his job.'

'In general, he was.'

Except for Camilla and Kerry then. So far. Had he liked to make people feel special? As though he'd singled them out for privileged knowledge? Once again Eve's mind ran back to the way he'd charmed her. She needed to focus.

'Did you help him with his correspondence?' That might explain why Harry had let Kerry in on his secret.

The woman picked up her drink. 'Oh no. My role was purely domestic.'

'Oh, I see. I thought that might be how you'd found out.' She couldn't imagine it being pillow talk with Kerry, somehow. She and Camilla must be a similar age, Eve guessed: mid to late fifties maybe, both a little older than Harry had been. But Kerry was a very different type to Camilla: down to earth and homely against the latter's cool elegance.

Kerry put her fork down. 'Oh, I took the odd packet of correspondence to post to the *Real Story*. Errands were part of my role.'

'I see.' But the address on the packets probably wouldn't have revealed his job title; he'd likely confided in her specifically. 'So, you must have been quite close then, if he told you about his work. Did he ever say what he did before he took on the role at the *Real Story*?' Eve was curious. She'd looked, but Harry had no LinkedIn page. Of course, it made sense, given he'd kept his job under wraps.

'No, he never mentioned that.'

'No problem.' Perhaps his uncle would be able to help. 'And what was he like to work for?'

'Oh, very affable,' she said. 'Entertaining. He'd give me his news, and ask after mine.' She paused a moment. 'He always wanted to know what was going on in the village, and to find out more about his new neighbours. He was too busy with his consultancy work to get involved with the locals in person, so I kept him in touch with the latest news.'

It all figured. He'd liked to gather information, mostly at arm's length, via Kerry or his column. Eve wondered again if his planned party had been to pass some of it on...

'As I said, I've been in this neck of the woods for years now,' Kerry went on, 'and he seemed to value my insights. He was generous too.' She gazed into the fire, shaking her head. 'Always giving me little presents: bottles of wine, a knick-knack he didn't want or a book he'd finished.' Her eyes met Eve's. 'You know how charming he could be, I expect. He was always friendly when he first met people. I tried to explain to the police. I can't imagine who would have wanted to kill him.'

Eve nodded. 'What about other friends? It would be great to find more people who knew Harry personally. Did he have many callers at the mill? I hear his uncle lives close by.'

Kerry finished a mouthful of casserole. 'Tristan Tennant. Yes, he was there for dinner, the night Harry died.'

Eve guessed he'd have been grilled thoroughly by Palmer and his team, given that detail. 'They must have got on well then, I presume?' Unless he'd come back later and killed him, of course...

'I assume so.' Her tone was guarded.

'I hear he lives outside Saxford?'

She nodded. 'Somewhere in Blyworth, I think, but I don't have his number.'

'And did you clean for Harry on Wednesday? I was wondering how he seemed.' Had he been looking forward to his uncle's visit?

Kerry nodded. 'I was there as usual.' She frowned. 'He was effervescent, I'd say. Sometimes he shuts himself away when I clean, but on other days he follows me round to chat. Wednesday was one of those days. He was in a good mood.'

Eve sighed. 'Poor man.' What had happened was horrific, however he'd behaved in life. 'Well, I'll track down Tristan Tennant to interview him. It's just as well he's around; I'm short of locals who knew Harry well.'

A twinkle came into Kerry's eye. 'I know there must be others you could speak to.'

Eve matched her tone. 'That sounds interesting!'

'I could tell he had a woman friend,' she said. 'Or rather women friends, plural.'

Eve tried to keep her expression neutral and spoke casually. 'I guess you must have noticed a lot. So he had a series of girlfriends while he was at the mill?'

Kerry chuckled. 'I think it was just a couple of them, but with some overlap. I'd smell one perfume in his bedroom one morning, and another the next.'

The waft of Chanel No. 5 at Camilla's house came back to Eve, vividly. Had Harry two-timed her? It sounded like it. Maybe that explained his motive for keeping their relationship secret: it left him free to lure in other women. An uncomfortable feeling settled in Eve's stomach. She wouldn't have accepted if he'd asked her out – her interests lay in another direction – but she had found him charming. She'd never have guessed…

'I expect it would be enlightening to talk to them,' Eve said lightly. Her mind was racing. 'I don't suppose you're able to guess who they were?'

Kerry shook her head. 'Sorry. I wondered though, believe me!'

CHAPTER THIRTEEN

Back at Elizabeth's Cottage, Eve put her feet up on one of the couches in the living room and flipped open her laptop, working in the glow from a standard lamp. It was too late to light a fire, but she could feel the warmth from the radiator behind her seat, and had pulled a woollen rug over her legs. She tucked one side of it round Gus, who was lying on the floor next to her, and went through her notes from the pub in order, pausing each time she hit an oddity. Half an hour later, she put the computer to one side.

'I got a lot out of Kerry while you were cavorting with Hetty, Gus.'

His gaze met hers. It was probably the mention of the schnauzer.

'I had her down as a comfortable Mrs Tiggy-Winkle-type, but it doesn't do to make snap judgements. That comment about Harry's dad having "the luck of the devil" was interesting.' Eve had googled 'Tennant' and 'adventure travels' and found reviews and comment pieces on Harry's father's old firm, Way Out There. Several journalists reckoned he'd ridden a wave, taking advantage of rich clients with tame lives who'd pay over the odds to feel like pioneers. But wasn't that what business was about half the time, selling an idea? Eve agreed it could be irritating, but it was the way of the world.

'Kerry's tone made her sound resentful. Yet why would she take what Harry's father did personally?'

Gus's eyes were three-quarters closed now, but she ploughed on.

'And then after going on about how lovely Harry was, she proceeded to tell me he was a two-timer.' For a second, Eve's mind turned to Ian. She pushed the thought away and took a deep breath.

'Would she have given him away like that if she'd really liked him?' It had been a pretty personal bit of information to pass on.

'The interview confirmed Harry liked to gather information on the villagers, too.' Gus had closed his eyes completely now. *Ah, well.* 'On top of what he got via his column, Kerry fed him gossip.'

She shook her head. There was a lot more to find out, but one thing looked certain: if Kerry was right, and Harry had had more than one lover, it wasn't just locals with secrets who had a motive for his murder. Camilla Sullivan did too.

Eve thought of the look in the woman's eye as she'd described their moonlit walk up the River Sax. And she'd dreamed of marriage. No one enjoyed being taken for a fool.

Before Eve shut down her computer, she made an effort to track down Harry's uncle. It wasn't hard. Within five minutes she'd discovered Tristan Tennant owned a bar called the Hideaway in Blyworth. Via that, she found a second address for him, listed on the Companies House register. It was also in the market town. Putting the postcode into Google, she found it was in a residential area, and likely his home.

She whizzed off an email to the Hideaway's admin inbox, asking for an interview. If he didn't respond, she'd follow up with a call.

As she got ready for bed, one more query she'd had that evening came back to her: why was Moira avoiding Kerry Clifton?

It was hard to sleep that night. The question circled in her head along with others. Had Camilla Sullivan known Harry was two-timing her, and who was Harry's second lover? Was it a coincidence that the murder took place the night Tristan Tennant had visited the mill – and just before Harry's party? Were Kerry Clifton's feelings towards her boss as friendly as she'd implied?

And what on earth was Judd Bentley up to?

*

A thaw started on Saturday morning and Eve took Gus for a run along the beach. The outing was marginally less painful on her fingers and toes than of late, and the sun, glinting on the North Sea, raised her spirits. Gus was happy too, indulging in half an hour of enthusiastic jumping after black-headed gulls. *Ever hopeful…*

Back at home, she planned her call to Judd Bentley's budding journalist sister, Sally. She'd managed to find her mobile number on a website devoted to freelancers. She wanted to take the woman by surprise – it was the best way to get her unguarded reaction to the story Judd had told Camilla. With a page of notes in front of her, sitting in the dining room, she dialled.

'*Sally Bentley.*'

'Hello! My name's Eve Mallow. I'm a journalist like you but I specialise in obituaries. I gather your brother Judd was trying to put you in touch with Pippa Longford, the advice columnist, as a useful national media contact. I'm writing about the man who wrote as Pippa – Harry Tennant – for *Icon* magazine, so I'd love to talk to you. What was it that you admired about the column? I assume you were a fan if you hoped to contact Harry.'

'*I… that is to say, I didn't…*'

Eve waited. She wasn't going to help. She needed to know if Judd was telling the truth.

It was several seconds before Sally continued. '*Sorry. I was deep in an article I'm writing. Of course, yes. It was very good of Judd. I wasn't particularly an admirer of the column, if I'm honest. It was just that my brother got the idea "Pippa" was local and she was a big name. He thought the connection would help me.*'

There was a definite note of relief in her voice as she finished her sentence.

'Ah, I see. That makes sense.' Eve paused. 'But presumably you familiarised yourself with Pippa's column if you thought you might be in touch with her. What did you think of the advice?'

Sally Bentley was stuttering again. '*I… well… I'm no expert in these matters.*'

She sounded totally at sea, and Eve pressed on. 'But I assume you have an interest in advice work, if you wanted to network with Harry?'

'*I, er… it was more just to get some kind of national contact.*'

'I guess the *Real Story* sells a lot of copies. I can understand why you'd target them.'

Sally laughed nervously.

'And did you ever get to meet Harry?'

'*No, sadly. I was waiting on Judd. He called me with an update only last Wednesday, but he never found out who Pippa was.*'

Called her with an update? Simon must be wrong about them living together then. Was she telling the truth? It was the first time in the call that she hadn't stumbled over her words, but maybe she'd hit her stride.

'Ah, well, thanks anyway. I'll keep working through my potential interviewees.'

'*Sorry I wasn't more help.*'

Eve ended the call and turned to Gus. 'Oh boy, did she sound relieved to get me off the phone.' She stood up. 'She's covering up for her brother; I'm sure of it. But why is another matter.' After fetching a coffee she settled down to google Sally Bentley more extensively.

It wasn't long before she found an article the woman had co-written with a journalist whose name she recognised: a regular contributor to the *Guardian*.

'That clinches it,' she said, as Gus looked up at the sound of her exclamation. 'Sally didn't need a national newspaper contact; she had one already, who worked in her field. I need to speak to Judd Bentley.'

CHAPTER FOURTEEN

Eve called Simon to see if Judd was working at the stables that day. It might make sense to talk to him on neutral territory with others close at hand, just in case.

'*Sorry*,' Simon said when he understood what she wanted. '*He's got the day off, and I know I claimed he never shares information, but I overheard him tell one of the other grooms he was heading to Ipswich.*' He paused for a moment. '*But if you want to speak to him somewhere public, why not try after church tomorrow? He usually comes along.*'

'Good thought, thanks.'

She felt more settled now she'd got a plan, and sat down to review her schedule for the day ahead.

Robin had texted to suggest they 'bump into' each other on the estuary path later and had promised updates from his police contact, Greg Boles. As usual, their meet-up would be surreptitious, to avoid the questions it might otherwise provoke. Eve knew how curious the villagers were about his history. Jim Thackeray's willingness to vouch for him was constantly discussed and dissected. Luckily, the vicar was good at being inscrutable when required. He offset it with a mischievous smile, which let him get away with most things. It was nice that one other person in Saxford knew Robin's secret. She could be unguarded with Jim.

Before the meeting with Robin, Eve was due to work a shift at Monty's, but she had the morning free.

She'd bought a copy of the *Real Story* from Moira on her way back from walking Gus and opened it to look at the coverage of Harry's death. They'd produced several pages about his murder, despite the lack of actual news. The paper also carried its own, short obituary: a print version of an article Eve had read on their website on Thursday evening. It was full of praise for Harry's 'selfless dedication' to his correspondents, but thin on detail, especially when it came to his career. It left Eve frustrated; she still wondered how he'd entered his profession.

There was a quote from Rollo Mortiville, an old school friend of Harry's, who said his secret career hadn't come as a surprise, without explaining why. Maybe the *Real Story*'s obituary writer hadn't asked…

Eve shook her head, put 'Rollo Mortiville' into Google, then emailed him at the accountancy firm where he worked.

'Lots of people to follow up with, Gus,' she said, as he pottered in to join her in the dining room. 'I think I'll go and try my luck with Tori and Hector Abbott first.' She thought back to her brief conversation with them opposite the mill. 'The River Sax separated them and Harry, but they knew him well enough to chat to.' She wanted to know if they'd been aware of his 'secret' career, just like Camilla and Kerry.

She bent to give Gus a cuddle. 'Sorry to leave you out, but they're more likely to invite me in if I don't come with the promise of muddy pawprints.' The track along the river would be slushy by now.

Half an hour later, Eve was nearing her destination. The Abbotts' brick-built garage and army of leylandii came into view – along with what remained of Harry's mill to her right, still shocking against the pale-blue sky. It was deserted now, and makeshift barriers had been erected round it, with signs warning the public to keep out.

For a moment Eve imagined what it must have been like for the CSIs, picking through the man's remains, painstakingly putting together their grim package of evidence.

She drew level with the gap between the garage and the trees and glanced down at her knee-length chocolate-brown boots. They weren't too bad – just wet from the melting snow. She was quite presentable, whereas Gus would have dashed into a ditch or two by now, and be covered in dirt.

She walked through the gap, onto the Abbotts' gravel driveway, past the shiny Fiat 500 she'd seen previously, then skirted round to the front of the house and rang the doorbell. As she waited, she sized the place up: it was around fifty years old, she guessed, and probably architect-designed. Most of the windows were high and wide, to match the expansive feel of the building. She caught movement to her right, but missed a glimpse of whoever was home. Tori would be ideal; Eve imagined she'd be chattier than grumpy Hector.

Whoever it was, they'd been in the kitchen. The window there was higher than the others, but she could see the curve of an elegant mixer tap over a sink, and a dresser on the opposite side of the room. That one view told her the Abbotts had a place for everything, and everything in its place. Eve liked to have things shipshape too, but her preference was for a well-ordered cocoon, not a regimented laboratory.

A moment later, Tori Abbott appeared at the door, with a frown-cum-smile. The woman recognised her, but was unable to account for her presence, Eve guessed.

She stepped forward. 'I'm sorry to bother you, Mrs Abbott.'

'Tori, please!'

'Tori. Thank you. I never explained when we met at the midwinter party, but I'm a freelance obituary writer. I had an unexpected call after we bumped into each other on Thursday: *Icon* magazine want me to write about Harry.'

Comprehension dawned in Tori's face. 'Because he was the agony aunt on the *Real Story*?'

'That's right. You were aware that was his real job?'

Her eyes opened wide and there was a snap of annoyance in them. 'No, I wasn't. I daresay I'm old-fashioned, but the way he lied about his work has made me quite cross. He was a friendly man, and I took him at face value.'

Join the club... But Eve ought to have known better; assessing people was her job. It made her determined to get to the bottom of Harry's true character now.

Tori stood back in her spacious hallway. 'Please, come in if you'd like to ask me about Harry. Not that I have much to tell.' She hastened to close the door after Eve – it was still cold outside and her house was wonderfully warm.

'Underfloor heating,' Tori said. She glanced at Eve's boots, as Eve had known she would.

'Would you like me to take them off?' She reached for the zip, but Tori shook her head.

'Good heavens, no. Just use the mat. Pam will be in again on Monday to clean.'

Eve wanted to take her boots off now, for Pam's sake, but it would look pointed.

'Let's go into the kitchen,' Tori said. 'I've made a pot of coffee; perhaps you'd like a cup?'

'Thank you. Just black.'

Tori nodded and Eve followed her through and took the high stool she was offered at a breakfast bar.

As Tori poured the coffee, Eve took out her notebook and pen. 'Leaving aside Harry's lack of honesty about his profession, it would be great to know what he was like as a neighbour.'

Tori put her shoulders back, blinked and sighed. Was she finding it hard to shelve her more negative thoughts? Perhaps falling for

Harry's lies had made her feel foolish. It would explain the pursed lips. 'On the whole, we liked him.' She sounded grudging. 'He was affable. And thoughtful, in fact. When Hector's car conked out on the way into work one day, Harry called him a taxi, then waited for the garage people to turn up. I was away overnight, or I'd have done that, obviously.' She sighed again. 'But then people are kind to surgeons, and Hector could hardly miss a shift at work.' She shook her head. 'But yes, he was a good neighbour, I suppose.'

'Did you ever socialise with him?'

'Not really. We knocked at the mill to introduce ourselves when he first arrived, then invited him round quite early on, but he said he had a prior engagement and time slipped by. You know how it does. But, of course, we were due to attend his party.' It would have been the previous night. 'People were starting to comment about his lack of sociability. I thought perhaps he'd organised the get-together to counter that.'

Would he have worried about public opinion? Eve couldn't imagine it; he'd seemed too self-possessed.

'I suppose you're after people who knew him better, and finding it hard because he kept himself to himself?' Tori sipped her coffee. 'I'm afraid Hector's out at the moment, but he won't know much more than me.'

Eve nodded. 'No problem. I'm aware of his uncle, and I hope I'll track down some of his friends and contacts from childhood, too. But it's true, I'd like to find some more recent connections.'

Tori hesitated, running her forefinger round the rim of her coffee cup. At last she glanced up and caught Eve's eye. 'He had a girlfriend, I think. At one point, at least.'

Had Tori found out about Camilla? Or might she know about the other woman Kerry had mentioned? Eve tried not to look too eager. 'Speaking to her could be helpful. I never pressure anyone into talking with me; I'd only pursue the lead if she was happy to chat.'

Tori nodded thoughtfully. 'I don't have a name, I'm afraid, but the person I'm thinking of is very distinctive to look at. I happened to catch sight of her from one of the upstairs windows. She was over at the mill. Also on an upper floor.' Tori's eyes met hers. 'It was very early in the morning.'

'I see.'

'She was standing in the window – I couldn't avoid seeing her – and she looked like Botticelli's Venus.'

Not Camilla, then.

'Her hair was almost as long,' Tori added. 'Waist-length, certainly. And she was just as shapely, too. She was a good twenty years younger than Harry.'

A different type, but just as striking, by the sound of it. Of course, Harry had been good-looking too. But handsome is as handsome does, as Eve's father always said. Harry had been friendly and affable, but also, Eve had to accept, an amoral two-timer to whom lies came easily.

'When did you see her?'

Tori frowned. 'Last year, back in the late summer? Or it might have been early autumn. I think they split up a short while later. I overheard some upset one afternoon, when I was setting out for a walk along the river. There was a lot of shouting, and the woman I'm talking about came out of the mill in tears. She looked beside herself.'

She was Camilla's predecessor then, by the sound of it, but they'd overlapped, judging by the perfumes Kerry had smelled. Maybe Harry's 'Venus' had found him out, hence the split.

'The description might help me track her down. Thank you. I won't mention you put me onto her.'

Tori shrugged. 'She wasn't hiding herself away. Though I think people forget our upper-floor windows. The leylandii give the impression of a screen but they're not full height yet and of course there are gaps at the top where they taper.'

Eve imagined the woman in Harry's mill had felt safe. Just one relatively distant house, beyond a bank of trees – and no one else in sight. The nearest dwellings beyond were Simon's house and Camilla Sullivan's place. Luckily for Harry, hers was well out of sight. He'd had a fighting chance of keeping the two women from seeing each other.

Eve paused a moment. 'I'm sorry to ask, but could I use your bathroom before I head back? I think it's the cold and the coffee.'

Tori nodded. 'The closest is at the top of the stairs. Turn immediately right.'

Eve stepped out into the hall. On the upper floor, she found that the bathroom faced the mill. Looking out she could see how Tori had seen Harry's Venus. Between the trees she could still just glimpse bits of the mill herself, though it must have lost a third of its height in the fire. She made her visit to the bathroom as quick as possible, then stood on the landing and listened. The sound of clinking china came from the kitchen; she guessed Tori was clearing away her cup and saucer. The position of the bathroom had presented an unexpected opportunity, and Eve decided to take it.

Thankfully, the Abbotts weren't the sort to close every door. Having a house as warm as toast probably helped. She peeked into each of the upstairs rooms that faced the mill. One was a study, another a workroom, set up with a sewing machine and a dressmaker's dummy. The third must be a guest room. There was a coverlet over the bed, but it wasn't made up.

Within a moment she was walking briskly back downstairs again.

'Thanks so much for your help.' She handed Tori her business card. 'I'll let you get on with your day.'

The woman nodded and moved into the hallway to show her out. 'If I think of anyone else you might approach, I'll let you know.'

Back at home, Eve cut herself a hunk of Toby Falconer's crusty farmhouse white. She'd bought it that morning, at the same time as the *Real Story*. Eating it with farmhouse cheddar and tomatoes for lunch was one of life's purest pleasures. She'd need to write up her notes from the interview with Tori later, after her shift at Monty's. The Botticelli woman was a promising lead. There couldn't be many people matching her description in the whole of Suffolk, let alone Saxford and the surrounding area.

'And she's crucial,' Eve said to Gus. 'If she's one of the two women Kerry Clifton was aware of, she has to be another suspect for Harry's murder. She and Camilla could each have killed him in revenge for his infidelity.' She frowned. 'The timing is interesting, though. Assuming Harry's betrayal triggered the split with "Venus", she didn't act immediately if she's guilty.' But of course, she might not have found out about Camilla back in the autumn; their love affair could have ended for any number of reasons. Maybe she'd only recently realised Harry had two-timed her. Or it could have been Camilla who'd just found out about "Venus". The blonde woman might be in Harry's past, but knowing he was sleeping with her while their romance got under way would still be painful.

Or, of course, neither of them might be guilty.

'I'm glad I got a look at the Abbotts' upstairs rooms.' She'd swear there was a judgemental look in Gus's eye. 'I know. It went against my principles, too, but it was important to investigate. If Tori got wind of Harry's private affairs by looking out of her window, the same could be true in reverse. If she or Hector have secrets, Harry might have found out and become a threat. They said they were away when the fire started, but I've only got their word for that.' But what kind of wrongdoing could they be involved in? The only thing she could imagine being visible from the mill was infidelity, just the same as for Harry.

Gus had turned his back now and was pottering off. Perhaps he didn't buy her excuses. All the same, it had been worth looking at the set-up. Unless Tori or Hector had been indulging in clandestine romps around his study, her sewing room or the rather small and spartan spare bedroom, the chances of Harry seeing something compromising were far-fetched.

CHAPTER FIFTEEN

'Come out the back for a break,' Viv said, when there was a quiet moment at Monty's that afternoon. 'Sam and Angie can cope for ten minutes and you've got to try one of the sloe gin and spice cakes.'

Eve turned her back on the Saturday crowds, and the misted windows, and followed Viv through to the kitchen. Her friend took a couple of cakes she'd reserved from the fridge.

Viv had topped them with the glazed plums after Eve had left. They looked rich and sweet: perfect to offset the winter chill.

'Wait.' Viv put out a hand. 'We need tea alongside too, for the full effect. Assam?'

'Sounds good.'

'So,' Viv took a teapot over to Monty's water boiler, 'how's the investigation going? What did Moira say?'

'She insists she never wrote to Harry herself.'

They exchanged a look and Viv's eyes twinkled. 'I'd so love to know if that's true.'

'Judging by her blush, I'd say not. But we may never know.'

'So frustrating!' Viv took the teapot to the central counter in the kitchen and motioned Eve to take a stool.

'But she was helpful when it came to researching Harry's obituary. And investigating his death.'

'That's Moira: a goldmine of information.' Viv poured their drinks and offered Eve one of the cakes.

The fruit inside was heavy with the liquor, the spices warmed her and the sugar from the plums was good too. It seemed she'd created something edible again. It was starting to feel like a pattern.

She tried to feign nonchalance, but Viv gave her a knowing look. 'You did a good job on the cakes but you must stop feeling smug now and focus on the case. Tell all!'

There was a lot to pass on, from Camilla Sullivan and Harry's second, mystery lover (whose description meant nothing to Viv), to Judd Bentley's suspicious behaviour and Eve's impressions of Kerry Clifton. She lowered her voice automatically as she relayed her interview with Harry's former cleaner. Kerry was in the teashop at that moment, chatting with Molly Walker at a table by the window.

Viv met her update with round-eyed appreciation. 'So, two definite suspects, in the form of Harry's lovers, and other oddities to investigate as well. Next steps?'

'Multiple. But this afternoon presents an immediate opportunity. Moira seems to be avoiding Kerry and I want to know why. I need to do some digging.'

Eve headed back to the main room of Monty's. Angie had to leave at four, so Sam would need a hand. It was also an excellent excuse to chat with the customers…

Kerry Clifton and Molly Walker were still over by the window, surrounded by crumb-filled plates and empty cups. Sam was on his way to their table but another group was vying for his attention too.

'I'll see to Kerry and Moira.' She grabbed a tray so she could clear for them.

He grinned at her. It was weird to see Viv's eyes looking out of a nineteen-year-old man's face. 'Thanks.'

'Hello! Can I get you some more tea? Or another plate of cakes?' She smiled and took her notepad from her jeans pocket.

Molly Walker sighed. 'I'll pop if I eat one more blondie. But I wouldn't say no to another pot of English Breakfast. Kerry?'

The woman smiled at Eve. 'Yes, why not? It's been an odd week.'

Molly patted her hand. 'You're bound to feel out of sorts after so much upset.'

Eve hesitated, but then went for it. 'I thought you might have Moira with you. I noticed Paul was minding the store just after lunch.'

Kerry didn't reply but Molly leaned forward. 'Is he? That's odd. I asked her to come, but she said she'd be working.'

Interesting, but frustrating. The information didn't get her any further. 'She'd probably just popped out for a moment when I nipped in.'

Molly nodded. 'I expect that's it.'

'I'll be right back with your tea.'

Eve stacked their used crockery and went to the kitchen to prepare them a fresh pot. By the time she returned, the atmosphere had changed.

Camilla Sullivan had appeared, along with a gust of ice-cold air. She was standing over Molly and Kerry's table.

'Something tells me she hasn't come for cake,' Sam said, under his breath.

Eve stood back, still holding the tray. She wanted time to take stock of the situation. Camilla was talking to Kerry Clifton, her voice low, but her flushed cheeks hinted at the nature of their chat.

Kerry leaned back in her seat now, away from Camilla, but not as though she was cowed. It looked more like she wanted to distance herself, out of disgust.

Eve and Sam weren't the only ones to notice the rise in tension; most of Monty's clientele had gone quiet. Kerry's voice was suddenly loud in the room. '… absolutely none of your business!'

Camilla drew herself up tall. 'I'd gone round to check you were all right. I wondered what you'd do now you're jobless. I'd even thought of offering you a position, but that's out of the question now, obviously!'

Kerry's face was red. Not embarrassment, but fury, Eve decided. 'Of all the condescending… I'll have you know I've already been taken on five mornings a week at Seagrave Hall.' It was where Molly worked. Maybe she'd put in a good word. 'So I won't be needing your charity anyway.'

She was half out of her seat now.

'Do they realise the sort of person they've hired?' Camilla spat out the words.

'Sort of…?' Kerry's chair scraped back. Eve knew she should do something, but it would be hard to intervene without offending both women. Besides, the longer she let the scene run, the more she might discover. 'We got on well together!' Kerry was standing now. 'And Harry Tennant was a big-hearted man – or are you suggesting otherwise?' Then a look of realisation came over her face and she stood up straighter. 'Though your level of knowledge is very interesting. Harry never mentioned you, but I assume you're one of the women he had on the go!'

'One of?'

'And, now I think of it, I recognise your scent from his bedroom.'

Viv had arrived from the kitchen now. 'My, this is interesting,' she whispered, slipping behind the counter as though no one would see her staring from there.

'I don't believe a word you say!' Camilla had stepped back slightly. 'He despised you!' She put a hand over her mouth suddenly. She'd gone further than she'd meant, Eve guessed. She might not be too bothered about Kerry's feelings, but she had a business to run. Yelling insults in a public place wasn't great in PR terms. Although she was certainly getting herself noticed.

'He did not!' Kerry's eyes were wide, nostrils flaring. 'It sounds as though he treated me better than you, but that's not my fault!'

Eve wanted to hear every minute of the conversation, but things were getting out of hand, and there were the other customers to consider. With a feeling of regret, she stepped forward. She was still holding the tray with Kerry and Molly's pot of tea.

'I'm sorry…' She let her sentence hang.

Camilla glanced at her, snapped her mouth shut and turned to stalk out of Monty's door, setting the bell above it jangling.

'I'm so sorry,' Eve said again. 'I wasn't sure whether to intervene, or…'

Kerry waved aside her apology. 'Not your fault. I'm sure everyone here can see who was out of order!'

Eve had fully expected her and Molly to leave without their tea after all, but Kerry sat back down, said 'I ask you!' (loudly) and poured for the pair of them as Eve retreated to the counter. Viv was busy being busy, now there was no more to see.

She turned to Eve and whispered. 'Could Kerry have been another lover of Harry's, do you think? You might have to add her to your list of suspects!'

'Hush!' She glared at Viv, who pulled a face.

'I'm just making sure you were paying attention! This is serious.'

'No kidding!' But Viv had a point. Eve had been sure Kerry wasn't Harry's type, especially after hearing about the Venus woman, as well as glamorous Camilla. But it might depend on what had motivated him: simple desire, or something more complicated.

Eve would certainly have more notes to add to Kerry's section of her spreadsheet.

CHAPTER SIXTEEN

It was dark by the time Eve and Gus went to meet Robin, and the temperature was dropping again. Eve pulled her woollen coat tight around her, knotting its belt securely, and adjusted her scarf to keep out the breeze.

The detective-turned-gardener had suggested meeting by the old mooring block, adjacent to the remote track that ran alongside the estuary. It was a clandestine rendezvous they'd used before.

Eve and Gus walked down Haunted Lane and onto Elizabeth's Walk, the narrow path, pressed in close by gorse bushes, that led towards the marshes. At its end was Saxford Water, where the estuary widened out at a turn in its course, before narrowing again, and finally meeting the sea. A moment later they'd joined the track that ran between the Sax and the marshes on one side, and a ditch and fields on the other, dotted with leafless oaks and ashes, stark against the moonlit sky.

The damp on the muddy path beneath Eve's booted feet was already freezing, the shallow puddles cracking as she walked. Gus was almost skating. From his demeanour, she wasn't sure he liked it. For once he seemed too distracted to notice the wildlife: a pale outline of a barn owl, flying slowly over the fields, scanning the ground for prey.

The old mooring block was a chunk of concrete buried in silt, and in the moonlight, Eve could only locate it thanks to her prior knowledge; it was mostly hidden by reeds and mud. When they neared the spot, Robin's silhouette came into view.

He raised a hand and stepped forward, his eyes glinting. She could just see his smile in the shadow. 'Thanks for all the info you sent through. I had a look before passing it on to Greg. It was interesting to have your impressions of Harry.'

Eve felt herself flush as she realised how little she'd understood the dead man, just two days previously. She wondered what else would come out. 'I've got a lot more to tell you now, though I'd appreciate it if you didn't pass it onto Greg. I'll send stuff through to the police as usual when I'm sure of my ground, but I'm feeling my way at the moment.' She couldn't work freely if she was duty-bound to give the force a running commentary of her thoughts. Besides, the police had their own tools and methods – they wouldn't appreciate gossip. They'd uncover information by following procedure, or at least, Greg Boles would. She trusted him, even if Palmer was useless.

'Understood.'

She caught Robin's smile in the moonlight and tried to switch off the memory of Viv saying he was easy on the eye. Eve hadn't been able to react to him normally since, though their relationship had been odd from the start. When she'd encountered him initially, he'd seemed downright suspicious, and had even featured on her first ever suspect list.

She dismissed the memory and explained what she'd learned so far, adding the argument between Kerry Clifton and Camilla Sullivan to the developments she'd discussed with Viv.

'Fast work!' Robin said, folding his arms. 'I'm not sure if I'm impressed or worried that you sneaked round the Abbotts' upstairs rooms.'

'It felt right to make the most of the opportunity.'

'Hmm. Just stay safe, okay?'

He was right. Any of the people she interviewed could be the killer. 'It seems like Tori and Hector were on friendly terms with Harry, though Tori was mad at him for lying about his profession.

Do you know if their alibi checks out? I saw them arrive home the morning after the fire and they said they'd been away.'

Robin nodded. 'They vouch for each other, and their friends confirm they were staying with them over New Year; Greg asked as a matter of routine, to tick them off the list. But if you find they had a motive I'd still consider them. He mentioned their hosts live in a large house just outside Darsham, so no distance by car. And it sounds as though their dinners featured plenty of drink and chat. I'm imagining rich people with large beds and cars parked on a sweeping driveway, well away from the house. With a household sleeping soundly, it's possible one or other of them could have slipped out.'

'Thanks, I'll keep that in mind. What about Camilla and Kerry Clifton? Have their alibis been checked?'

Robin nodded. 'Camilla went to the police of her own volition. Unfortunately, she mentioned you'd suggested it, which I gather set Palmer's hackles rising. I guess he might have words with you sooner or later.'

'Oh, joy.' He was always keen to put her in her place; she knew she made him look bad. She smiled for a moment. When she'd first been involved in a murder investigation, Ian, her ex, had said she must be hampering the police's enquiries. Since then she'd helped solve three murders. Her desire for justice was strong, but proving Ian and Palmer wrong was almost as big a driver.

'Camilla was home alone the night Harry died,' Robin went on. 'And what about Kerry?'

'The police spoke to her as a matter of course, knowing she cleaned for him. She lives alone too, and the same applies.'

'Has Boles passed on any other information?'

'Some forensic stuff. The fire was started with petrol-soaked rags: a sort marketed to polish cars. There were microfibres left on the outside of the letterbox. The mill had exposed wooden floorboards, and some petrol dripped through onto the joists below, so it didn't burn. The killer didn't do a perfect job of covering their tracks, but the fire itself was deadly effective. There was a window right by the front door. The curtains must have gone up very quickly, along with the contents of Harry's coat stand, apparently, and a wooden chair where he'd sit to take off his boots. The contents of his hall acted as kindling. Either the killer knew the layout, or they relied on the curtains, and used plenty of fuel.'

Eve shivered and Gus reacted to her movement, pressing himself against her legs.

'Harry died in bed of smoke inhalation. It shows he was alive when the fire started, but asleep by the look of it.'

'Do they know yet if he was drugged?'

'Toxicology's found nothing. And from what was left it looks as though he made the standard preparations for bed, so he was in control. The front door burned away, but the mortise lock was found in the secure position. And he'd put out the recycling from dinner that evening before making his way upstairs.'

'I hear he had company.'

Robin nodded. 'His Uncle Tristan came for a boozy meal, so Harry probably slept soundly after that. They haven't found any trace of a smoke alarm.'

'That figures.' Eve filled him in on what Kerry had said. 'It sounds like multiple people would have known he hadn't installed one – not just those who'd visited the mill.'

'That's interesting. Speaking of Kerry, other than Tristan, she was the only person Harry saw the day he died, as far as the police can make out. It seems he stayed home all day.'

Eve nodded. 'She said he was around when she cleaned. I've tracked down the uncle; he runs a bar in Blyworth.'

'Damn. You're always one step ahead of me!'

She couldn't suppress a smile. 'He's agreed to meet me there tomorrow, before he opens for the evening trade.'

She heard Robin's intake of breath. 'Just be careful, Eve. Greg says he lives alone and he has no alibi. He was at the mill the night of the fire and, last but not least, Harry died intestate. As his only relation, Tristan stands to inherit everything. He's top of Palmer's list of suspects at present – he's going after him hard.' He gave her a look. 'Which means you don't need to. He's covered, so there's no reason to take risks. I trust you, but Palmer's got the benefit of backup on call.'

She swallowed. 'Message received, loud and clear. But Tristan Tennant's a key interviewee for my obituary. I'll make sure we sit in the main bar, so we're overlooked. He's on the High Street.'

'Good.' His shoulders went down a fraction. 'And Eve?'

'Yes?'

'If you're planning any interviews where you can't take precautions like that. Or any more explorations round a suspect's house…'

'Uh-huh?'

'Call me. I can be there to keep an eye out. You know how I miss my old work.'

Eve saluted and grinned. 'You got it. I wouldn't want to deprive you.'

He laughed, but only for a moment. 'I'd also like to watch your back.'

Eve felt much warmer on the way home than she had on the walk out to the marshes. She'd just let herself back into Elizabeth's Cottage when the text came. Ian. How lucky he was there to dampen her mood.

Arriving Saxford Sat 11th for one night. Staying Cross Keys. Booked table for two at 7 p.m.

The man was such a jerk. She considered texting back to say she'd check her diary, but in reality she knew she was free. Instead, she made an effort to ungrit her teeth. At least he was only staying for twenty-four hours.

CHAPTER SEVENTEEN

It snowed again on Sunday morning. Through St Peter's latticed windows, with their ornate stone tracery, Eve could see huge, soft flakes drifting down. She turned her gaze back towards Jim Thackeray, who had ended the Sunday service with a tribute to Harry Tennant and was now leading the final hymn. 'Lord of all Hopefulness' was one of the ones guaranteed to get a reaction from Gus. Despite Jim's welcoming attitude towards animals – including vocal dogs – Eve couldn't help feeling a tiny bit self-conscious at her dachshund's 'singing'. Moira kept turning round and staring, her lips pursed.

'She ought to concentrate on her own performance,' Viv hissed. 'Gus is far more dedicated.'

'You're right, but currently I don't think that's an advantage.' She instantly felt disloyal and bent to ruffle his fur, which seemed to encourage him.

After the hymn, the vicar gave the congregation his parting blessing and the organist started on Widor's Toccata. Eve, Gus and Viv shuffled out of their pew towards the nave, then walked to the back of the church. Jim Thackeray was waiting there to say hello to the villagers. Already the crowds were bunching up as they waited to talk to him, and chatting amongst themselves. Beyond him, those who'd already had a word were forming into groups and exchanging news. Eve heard Harry Tennant's name mentioned.

She ran her gaze over the parishioners and caught Simon's eye. 'Looks like you might be on,' Viv said. 'Good luck!'

Simon nodded towards Judd Bentley, who was standing to his right, then turned to say something to him as Eve approached.

Judd shifted his dark-eyed gaze to her as she neared the pair. He looked stern. 'Simon says you'd like a word?'

Viv's brother had removed himself tactfully now, and she and Judd were a little apart from the nearest villagers.

'That's right. It'll only take a moment.'

Judd frowned. 'Weren't you at Elizabeth's Cottage on the solstice?'

She nodded. 'It's my house.'

He unbent a little. 'I'm sorry. There were so many new faces there. Simon pointed you out, but along with a lot of other people, and I lost track.'

'I didn't get to speak with everyone either. There's no need to apologise!'

He shifted his weight from one foot to another. On edge, Eve decided.

'Why did you want to see me?'

Honesty seemed best. 'I'm an obituary writer and *Icon* magazine have commissioned me to write about Harry Tennant.' The moment the words were out something in Judd Bentley's face shut down. What was he hiding?

'I didn't know him.'

'Ah. I wasn't sure if you'd met.'

The groom's brow furrowed. 'Why would you think we had?'

'Camilla Sullivan knew him well.' Had he heard that gossip? Was he aware she'd held out on him, and known Pippa's true identity all along? His eyes told her he was. And there was a flicker of anxiety in them. 'When I interviewed her for the obituary, I was also looking for others who might have something to say, either about him or his work. Camilla mentioned you'd asked for an introduction to Pippa, so I guessed you had an interest in the column. Of course, she couldn't pass on Harry's details; it wasn't her secret to tell. But what made you think Camilla might know "Pippa" personally?'

His gaze drifted down towards the floor. 'I spoke to several people who said she'd been recommending her, but she doesn't look like the sort to read the *Real Story*. It made me wonder…'

Eve had followed a similar line of reasoning.

'She told you why I wanted an introduction, I suppose?'

Eve felt like a diver, about to take a leap into a deep pool. 'She did, but your reason doesn't stand up. It made me curious.'

His eyes darkened and colour came to his cheeks: an angry red. 'What do you mean?'

'I happened across an article by your sister, co-written with a journalist who contributes regularly to one of the nationals. Sally didn't need an advice columnist as a contact.' She paused, but then went for it. 'I called her too. I thought she and Harry might have met, but she seemed confused by my questions.'

It was several moments before Judd Bentley spoke but at last his words came in a rush. 'She's working on an article. An exposé, looking at ethics in advice columns. She had concerns about Pippa Longford's approach.' His voice was tight. 'She thought she might be able to get some inside information out of her – or him, as it turns out – if she could only arrange a meet-up.'

If that were true, you'd think Sally Bentley would be ready with a cover story to explain her interest in Pippa. Eve's inner response was instant. He was lying again; she was sure of it. 'When's the article due to publish?'

Judd had already been shifting away from her, his eyes not meeting hers. At last he glanced up at her again, but he was chewing his lip. 'It's on hold. Under the circumstances.'

Very convenient, if the entire project was fictitious. Eve felt a rush of adrenaline as she watched Judd Bentley edge towards the church door, not waiting to speak to the vicar. Where did she go from here? She'd have to find out more; there'd be a clue somewhere.

'Frightened him off?' Simon said, arriving at her elbow.

'I'm afraid so. Story of my life.'

He laughed. 'Hardly. Was it any use, talking to him?'

She nodded. 'Yes, but there are more questions than answers.'

'Always the way.'

'Speaking of which,' Eve turned her thoughts to another big question mark in the investigation, 'you don't know anyone with waist-length blonde hair, do you?'

Simon's eyes widened. 'Interesting question. I'm afraid not.'

She shook her head. 'Not to worry.'

The church was still full of people. Maybe someone else would be able to identify Harry's 'Venus'.

CHAPTER EIGHTEEN

Eve surveyed the parishioners amassed around her. Weaving a query about a curvy woman with waist-length blonde hair into conversation would take some thought. Not everyone was as discreet as Simon and she didn't want to set tongues wagging – especially after the very public row between Camilla Sullivan and Kerry Clifton. It wouldn't take much for people to work out the blonde was another of Harry's lovers. It was lucky that Camilla herself was absent that morning; there was no chance she'd overhear Eve's enquiries.

She found herself next to Moira. Gus was rightly stand-offish after her cruel looks during the service, and pottered over to Toby Falconer from the pub. It left Eve free to extract gossip. Her earlier feelings of disloyalty mounted as she apologised for Gus's singing. She hoped he wasn't listening.

'Nonsense, Eve!' Moira said, with a quick glance at Jim Thackeray. 'I'm a huge animal lover. You must have noticed mine and Paul's RSPCA collection box at the shop!'

Hmm. 'It's good to know he didn't bother you.' Jim caught her eye over Moira's shoulder and winked. 'Moira, this is going to sound like an odd question, but do you know anyone with fair, waist-length hair?'

The storekeeper frowned with concentration, as though Eve had just presented her with a difficult crossword clue. 'This isn't to do with the amateur dramatics society, is it? I'd heard they were considering *Rapunzel* for next year's panto, but I'd no idea it had been agreed. Deidre Lennox might have told me!' Her indignant tone carried across the crowds and Eve saw Mrs Lennox glance up and frown. 'Anyway, the group has some very good wigs, you know.'

'Ah, no, it's nothing to do with that.' Eve tried to produce a relaxed smile. 'I just heard there's a woman who's been asking to speak with me, but I don't have her name. The description's so distinctive I thought it was worth mentioning her to you.' She crossed her fingers inside her coat pocket. Protecting the woman's privacy seemed more important than being strictly honest. Gus glanced over and gave her an appraising glance, as though he knew what she was thinking and was minded to disapprove.

'Oh, I see.' Moira was still frowning, and at last she gave in. 'I'm sorry, Eve, I can't think who she could be, and we serve all the villagers. I don't suppose there's a single one I wouldn't recognise.'

Eve could believe that, and if Venus wasn't a neighbour, most Saxfordites would probably say the same as Moira. After a moment's thought, she made for Toby Falconer from the Cross Keys. The pub drew in visitors from further afield; it was possible he'd be able to help. She repeated the description she'd given Moira.

'Between ourselves, it's in connection with a job,' she said, modifying her excuse for her audience. She knew Toby would be discreet.

Matt, his brother, leaned in at that moment, looking curious, but Toby only repeated the description, not Eve's reason for asking. She shot him a grateful smile.

'Not been in,' Matt said decisively. 'I'd remember.' He gave a broad grin.

Jo, Matt's wife, was talking to Moira now. She hadn't overheard. Matt would know about it if she had. Toby shook his head too. 'Joking apart, I think I would as well. The hair sounds so distinctive, though I suppose if she'd put it up in a bun or something…'

'Have to be a massive bun,' Matt said.

'Fair point.'

'I'd better dash and get ready for the afternoon punters,' Viv said, appearing at Eve's side and plucking at her coat sleeve. Monty's only opened after lunch on Sundays. 'I'll see you tomorrow!'

Other people were drifting out too, but Jim seemed to pick up on her thwarted expression. 'Anything I can help with?' he said, his friendly gaze meeting hers from underneath his thick grey eyebrows and thatch of hair.

'Maybe.' He was always as forthcoming as his conscience allowed, and of course he might know people from outside the village too. The Christmas and Easter services drew incomers.

She repeated her description and the explanation she'd given Toby, but he shook his head. 'I'm sorry, but I don't think I can help. You're writing about Harry Tennant?'

She nodded. 'But I'm keen for people not to connect the two.'

He smiled. 'I understand perfectly.'

'Did you know Harry?'

'Not beyond welcoming him as a new parishioner and passing the time of day after that.' Jim hesitated. 'He was always very charming, but occasionally I found our conversations… awkward, professionally.'

She frowned. 'I don't suppose you'd like to tell me more?'

'He tended to steer the topic round to my life rather than his.' Jim smiled. 'And of course, much of what I do is confidential, so I can't pass it on. But when I tried to ask him about himself instead, he didn't like it.'

Eve thought back to her party. 'He kept the focus on me too, when we talked, though I didn't get the chance to try to draw him out.'

'Who knows? You might have succeeded where I failed.'

Eve watched his eyes. He doubted it, she could tell. 'Well, thanks for your input.'

Jim smiled, raised his hand in farewell and turned towards the vestry.

Eve walked back across the village green with Gus, deep in thought. Jim's insight into Harry's character was interesting. It fitted with his habit of keeping people at a distance. If he engaged, it looked like it had to be on his terms, the information flowing only one way. But not because he was reserved like her; there was nothing reserved about his advice column or his mirrored ceiling. Was it because he knew divulging personal information could leave you vulnerable? Had he really been amassing details to use against her fellow villagers? New Year's surprises…

He'd enjoyed people-watching, just like Eve. Now she needed to prove to her neighbours that you could be interested in people for positive reasons. She wished she understood Harry's motives. What would he have revealed at his party, and why?

For a second her mind flitted to Camilla, and her sphynx-like smile as she denied knowing the secret Harry had up his sleeve. Eve was still convinced she'd wanted her to think he'd confided in her. She hoped he hadn't. It might be dangerous knowledge, and the reason he was killed.

'Oh my goodness, Gus,' she said, as they crossed Love Lane. She felt hot all over, despite the winter chill. 'Whether or not she really knows is irrelevant. If she's been hinting to all and sundry that she does, she could be in as much danger as Harry was. I need to pay her a visit.'

CHAPTER NINETEEN

As before, Eve dropped Gus off at home before going to see Camilla. The visit was urgent and private; she didn't want to risk being kept on the doorstep.

As it was, the florist invited her in immediately.

'You've been at church? I didn't feel like it today; all those prying eyes.' But people would probably gossip more about her if she hid herself away, and Eve sensed that was just as she liked it.

'Let me get you a sherry.' The florist led the way to the sitting room where they'd talked before. The windows overlooked the road but it was deserted and suddenly Robin's warning came back to her. Eve was concerned for Camilla, but she was still a suspect too. She'd seemed shocked when Kerry Clifton mentioned Harry had another lover, but she might have been acting. And what if she'd wanted him to marry her, and he'd made it clear that was never on the agenda? If he'd led her on, then let her down, it *could* have pushed her over the edge.

Eve needed to keep her wits about her.

At that moment the woman reappeared with two glasses of pale amber liquid. 'Tío Pepe.' She handed Eve one and raised her own to her lips. 'To poor old Harry. You've thought of more questions you want to ask?'

Eve wondered how to approach the matter. She didn't want to anger the woman.

'Honestly, Camilla, I'm worried.'

Her hostess raised her eyebrows. 'Why so?'

Eve took a deep breath. 'I realise when we spoke last there were certain things you didn't feel able to tell me.'

A frown crossed the woman's face.

'Like the names of the people you recommended Harry's column to. You were protecting their identities and I understand that.' Except that Eve had only suggested Camilla hand them her card, in case they were prepared to talk. But even that had been a step too far. Camilla had wanted to keep her secrets to herself.

'But what if one of those people killed Harry?' She held up a hand when her hostess opened her mouth. 'Perhaps one of them gave away personal information – like an affair or something – which wouldn't have mattered if they were writing to a faceless journalist down in London, who'd never guess their identity. But it became a problem when they realised they'd written to a local who might reveal their secret.'

Camilla took a sip of her sherry, her eyes amused. She wasn't taking the suggestion seriously enough.

'If Harry took you into his confidence' – *or you snooped of your own accord* – 'then you could be in danger too.'

Eve wondered whether to mention Judd as well. Eve was sure he'd lied, but she had nothing concrete. 'I still think it's odd that Judd Bentley was so desperate to get to Pippa too,' she said at last. 'I'm not sure his excuses hold water.'

Camilla actually laughed. How could Eve get through to her? 'I doubt Mr Bentley ever found out Harry was Pippa. I'm sure Harry would have mentioned it if he'd ended up making contact with him.' Then, suddenly, she looked angry. 'As for the locals imagining either of us would use their secrets – the suggestion's laughable! I assume you're implying Harry or I might stoop to blackmail. But I'm not short of money, as you can probably see. And he wasn't either. He wouldn't get involved in anything so grubby and I resent your thinking otherwise.'

Eve had guessed previously that Harry would regard blackmail as beneath him, and it was true that he and Camilla were both wealthy.

'I'm sorry you're upset; that wasn't what I meant. But the fact remains, Harry wanted the whole village to know he had something to reveal at his party.' She hadn't imagined that. 'And it's not so much what you would or wouldn't do.' She kept her voice calm. 'It's the sense of threat Harry's correspondents might have felt, even if they had no cause to worry. If they were scared enough, maybe they got violent – and perhaps they will again.'

Eve could see from her eyes that Camilla was still really angry. 'You seem to forget, I never read the correspondence Harry received. I don't know any secrets!'

Eve sighed. 'I had the impression you knew what Harry was going to share at his party. When I asked you, you denied it, but your smile was knowing.'

Suddenly, Camilla's shoulders went down, and she shook her head. 'I was pretending. It was fun. But I've no idea what he would have said, so you can relax.'

She was missing the point. 'You haven't hinted to anyone else that you were in on Harry's secret?'

'I really don't think so. You're blowing this out of all proportion.'

But Eve wasn't comforted. Camilla was enjoying the notoriety of having been Harry's girlfriend and she'd encouraged everyone to think they might marry. Locals would probably assume he'd confided in her, and Eve bet she'd do nothing to dispel the idea.

'I wondered—'

But Camilla held up a hand. 'No more! Wonder all you like, but don't come to me with any more questions. I regret inviting you in now.' She picked up Eve's half-drunk sherry from where she'd set it on the occasional table and stood up.

Eve had no option but to follow her lead. And as she left the house she felt tenfold more anxious than she had on entering.

She'd burned her bridges with Camilla Sullivan and been cut short before she could ask about the row with Kerry Clifton. She could only hope her words might give the woman some sense of self-preservation, but she was worried she'd blown it.

CHAPTER TWENTY

After a late lunch and a consoling chat with Gus, Eve set off to find the Hideaway, Tristan Tennant's watering hole in Blyworth.

On arrival, she found Tristan shared the good looks that Harry had enjoyed. Eve guessed he might be around sixty-five, with iron-grey hair, which was darker on top than on the sides. His eyebrows were still dark grey too, the same colour as his irises. Eve took all this in as he greeted her at the glass front door of the Hideaway, but underlying the face-value impression was Robin's warning. *He lives alone and he has no alibi. He was at the mill the night of the fire and, last but not least, Harry died intestate. As his only relation, Tristan stands to inherit everything.*

The bar had a wide window that faced onto one of Blyworth's main streets, but on a snowy Sunday afternoon, the road wasn't busy.

'Thanks so much for meeting me.'

Tristan's handshake was firm. 'My pleasure. This is such a sad business. I like the idea of talking about Harry – and of you celebrating his life in *Icon*.' Tristan put his hand to his face. 'It's against the natural order that he should go before me.'

'I gather you've suffered much loss as a family,' Eve said, thinking of Harry's father, Tristan's brother, who'd been killed in the helicopter crash along with his wife. 'I'm so sorry for what you've had to go through.'

Tristan sighed. 'Thank you. There have been some dark times. I'm lucky I have my career to distract me.' He gestured around the bar. 'My passion for business has kept me going many a time.'

'It's a beautiful place.' It looked like something from a 1930s grand hotel. The wooden bar was dark and highly polished, with a beautiful grain. Art deco lights were fixed on a mount overhead, and rows of glasses sparkled under shelves of spirits.

His face lit up. 'Thank you. Would you like to sample the wares? I can get you something soft if you'd prefer a clear head?'

Eve definitely wanted to stay sharp. She always did when she was working, plus Tristan was an unknown quantity, and she was driving. The bus from Saxford didn't run on Sundays, so she'd braved the snowy lanes. She opted for a lime and soda and Tristan had the same.

'So,' he said, sitting down at one of the leather upholstered bar chairs alongside her, 'how can I help?'

'Perhaps we could start with the loss of Harry's parents? That must have been incredibly hard on him. I gather he was quite young when it happened?'

'His parents?' Tristan's dark eyebrows went up.

'I understood his father and mother were killed in a helicopter crash?'

'Ah.' The bar owner pinched the bridge of his nose. 'No. In fact, it was my brother Darius and his *second* wife who died that day. Harry's mother, Petronella, she…' he rubbed his chin, 'she walked out of the family home some years before that, and she and Darius divorced.'

Not an easy upbringing. 'How old was Harry when all this happened? I'm sorry to ask – it's just that such dramatic life events are bound to have influenced him.' She knew the answer would be on public record, but Tristan was likely to put a personal spin on the information. It would tell her more about his relationship with his nephew.

He took a deep breath. 'I understand. He was seven when his mother left, and fourteen when my brother, his father, died.

Petronella was a dress designer. She went off to work in New York and married a billionaire banker. She died five years ago, but it's been more than a decade since they saw each other.' His tone was full of bile, which she could understand. He was likely to take his brother's side and for any parent to go to another continent like that, leaving their child…

Eve thought of her mom and dad, back in Seattle, and how dearly she loved them. The thought of either of them abandoning her when she was tiny for an exciting new life abroad gave her a physical pain in her gut. What must Harry have gone through?

'I wonder, was your brother away from home a lot, with his travel business?'

'Oh yes.' Tristan's tone was weary now. 'When he started Way Out There he led most of the adventures himself.'

'I suppose it would have been hard to afford guides at the beginning.'

'He never gave up the Far East tours. He'd go to and fro between the family home in Surrey and wherever the next "adventure" was taking place. His second wife, Mary, had a wide circle of friends. She was happy occupying herself with liquid lunches, house parties and the like. And periodically she'd go out and join Darius at the end of a tour for a luxury break. She wasn't so keen on the trekking side of things. It was on one of those visits that they were killed.'

'Harry attended a private school?' Who the heck had looked after him?

'That's right,' Tristan said. 'He boarded, of course. Anything else would have been crazy given my brother and Mary's availability. Or lack of it. He often came to me during the holidays.'

Eve wondered how that had played out. Tristan only looked around fifteen years older than Harry had been. He'd been young to take on the care of a child. 'That sounds like a lot of work for one person on their own.'

'I had a long-term girlfriend who helped.' He produced a smile, but it didn't look genuine. Eve wondered what had happened to the girlfriend. 'Only we lived in a flat, so it wasn't ideal. Not so bad as Harry got older, but younger children have so much energy.'

Eve held up a hand. 'I have twins. I know what it's like.'

Tristan nodded then frowned. 'Of course, Harry was an amazing boy. He had problems when he was younger – didn't speak for a week after Petronella left, but he got over it.'

Did anyone really get over something like that?

'He was very precocious,' Tristan went on.

'In what way?' As an obituary writer, Eve was used to people employing euphemisms to describe her subjects. He might mean gifted and talented, but a pain in the rear was another possibility.

'Sometimes I'd almost forget he was in the room, but then he'd inject some dry, sharp little comment into the conversation my partner and I were having.'

Pain in the rear, then.

Eve sensed Tristan had read her expression. 'He turned into a wonderful adult.'

'All credit to you, I'm sure.'

The man gave a hollow laugh. 'I don't know about that.'

'Did you know he was Pippa Longford?'

'Oh yes. And he was always free with his advice, ready to give his input. He had *lots* of ideas.'

Eve could hear the bitterness in Tristan's voice, however hard he fought to hide it. She wondered what recommendations Harry had given him, and how it had felt, receiving them from a man fifteen years his junior. It sounded irksome.

'How did Harry get into the agony aunt work? It was a pretty unusual career.'

Tristan nodded. 'He did a degree in psychology.' His gaze drifted beyond Eve for a moment, his look faraway. 'I sometimes wondered if he chose the subject to try to understand himself. After he'd finished, I don't think he was quite sure what to do. For a while he worked as a management consultant.'

That must be why he'd chosen 'consultant' as his pretend career.

'But he got sick of it and went for a complete change of direction. He saw a job advertised, tutoring two young children who'd been bullied. Their parents wanted someone to homeschool them until they were old enough to start their secondary education, so it was a nice two-year package. He didn't stay the full course, though.'

'No?'

'The father of the boys was the editor of the *Real Story*. He offered Harry the agony column nine or so months into his contract. Harry always said the family had their ups and downs, and he helped. That and the psychology degree were what got him the role as "Pippa", apparently.'

There had to be more to tell, surely? Now she knew the background, she wanted to speak with the editor of the *Real Story* and his family too. A simple phone call wouldn't do. She made a note to follow it up.

'Do you know what triggered his move to Suffolk?'

Tristan glanced down into his drink. 'No. I'm based here, of course, and I'm the only family he had. But on the whole I think he'd just had enough of London, and the mill was idyllic.' He shook his head. 'Or at least, it seemed to be.'

It was sensitive territory, but Eve couldn't omit her next question. 'I gather you had dinner with Harry, the night he died?'

Tristan nodded. 'It's an odd feeling: to have seen him in such good spirits, not knowing what lay ahead.'

'Was he always upbeat?'

'Mostly, outwardly at least. Life amused him.' He paused. 'I'm not saying he didn't have difficult moments. He had a short fuse at times.'

'With you, you mean?'

He shrugged. 'Not often. Not as an adult. But we weren't in each other's pockets. He let rip at his cleaner, Kerry Clifton, when I dropped in on New Year's Eve. She broke a glass and he went – well – ballistic is how I'd put it. Poor woman. But I suppose she was used to it. It wasn't the first time I'd seen him go at her like that.'

Eve felt her skin prickle. Kerry had specifically said what a good boss Harry had been. Affable. Generous even. He'd given her bottles of wine and odd knick-knacks he didn't want. Apparently. Had that all been invented? Or had he given her presents to try to make up for his awful behaviour? To persuade her to carry on working for him, maybe? Either way, Kerry had deliberately controlled Eve's impressions of their relationship.

After she'd finished interviewing Tristan, Eve went to find her car in the side street where she'd left it. Dusk had turned to darkness, but the snow made everything glow in the streetlights. A further sprinkling had fallen while she was inside and she went round the Mini Clubman with her scraper, clearing the windows. Part of her felt like driving straight back to Saxford, given the conditions, but she still had Tristan's home address noted in her phone. He'd told her he was staying on at the Hideaway to do some paperwork before opening up. If she wanted to snoop, now was the perfect time, and seeing where he lived might tell her more. Google Street View had given her an idea of the area, but it was no substitute for a proper look. Context was always good.

Ten minutes later (she'd taken the journey at a very sedate pace), she pulled up outside the address that was listed at Companies House – '7, The Laurels', turned out to be flat seven in a characterless block above some local stores on the outskirts of the town.

She set off for Saxford, her thoughts whirling. She needed to shelve them for now and keep her mind on the road, but that was easier said than done. Each time she pushed away hunches about Tristan, other disparate bits of information floated into her brain.

Why had Harry been killed? That was the question. If not by his uncle, keen to inherit, then had it been a letter writer who'd given away more than they'd meant, or a furious girlfriend who'd been betrayed? And who was his other lover?

It was as she walked back up Haunted Lane that she realised she had one more Saxford connection who might know Harry's 'Venus'. It was a long shot, but inaction felt intolerable. She needed to try every avenue.

She gave Gus his supper, then took him along to Hope Cottage, which looked like the centrepiece of a child's snow globe in the moonlight.

It was just on six o'clock, and Eve had an ongoing open invitation to join Sylvia and Daphne for gin and tonic.

CHAPTER TWENTY-ONE

It was just possible that Eve's neighbours might be able to identify Harry's 'Venus'. Sylvia was a photographer. She did family portraits, covered events and more besides. Just like the vicar and the local business owners Eve had already tried, she might have come across Harry Tennant's mystery lover.

A minute after Eve had knocked, she was inside Hope Cottage, being offered refreshments by Daphne, as Sylvia motioned her to take a seat on their peacock-blue couch. The room was cosy, a fire lit, the dark-gold shot-silk curtains drawn tightly closed.

'Daisy Irvine,' Sylvia said, taking the bowl of cashew nuts Daphne had brought in and putting them on the occasional table in front of Eve. 'Sounds like, anyway. I haven't come across anyone else with hair that glorious.'

'She's a beauty,' Daphne added, nodding.

'You've met her too?' Eve hadn't really expected to strike lucky; she was just being thorough. She'd never have slept, having thought of a lead without following it up.

'Sylvia's the real connection – through work. But I've seen her on the odd occasion, when we've dropped in at her shop with promotional material – that kind of thing.'

Daphne passed Eve a gin and tonic and they all sat together. Eve was grappling with the partial information she had. 'Thanks. So what's her line?'

'She manages an upmarket wedding boutique in Blyworth: A Bicycle Made for Two. Twee, I know. It sells dresses and the most bizarre range of accessories brides never knew they needed.' Sylvia gave a wry smile over the top of her tumbler, then took a sip, the ice cubes clinking, the cut glass catching the firelight.

'I don't think you should be so sniffy,' Daphne said, then turned to Eve. 'Sylvia gets a lot of business through them.'

'They recommend me as the swankiest photographer in the neighbourhood. And it's true, their clients tend to pay well, but they're always utter pains in the—'

'I get to hear all about them, naturally,' Daphne said, with a small smile. 'And Daisy includes my ceramics in the "exclusive" section of her recommended-present list, too. I understand it all sounds a bit precious, but it does help with sales.'

'It's all right for you,' Sylvia said. 'Handing over a purchase doesn't involve extended interactions with the happy couple.'

Eve always enjoyed their banter, but her mind had zoned in on Daisy Irvine's business and Harry Tennant's murder. 'Do you know, is there more than one wedding boutique in Blyworth?'

Sylvia put down her gin and tonic and laughed. 'Hardly! It's not exactly a heaving metropolis.'

'It ties in with another element of the research I've been doing.' Eve's mind was crawling over the details, making connections.

The photographer's intelligent eyes met hers. 'We heard Camilla Sullivan's been publicly linked with Harry Tennant, and of course Camilla's associated with the boutique too. She's their go-to florist, just as I'm their go-to photographer, ready to "capture treasured memories".' She raised her eyes to heaven.

And not only that, Daisy Irvine, Harry Tennant's Venus, worked at the store where Camilla Sullivan first met Harry.

He'd told her he'd been shopping for a present, but if so, it probably wasn't the only reason he'd been in. Not given he'd been sleeping with the owner.

*

Back at Elizabeth's Cottage, Eve let Gus out for a scamper round the garden where he chased snowflakes by the light of the kitchen window. He seemed to enjoy it; they were easier to catch than seagulls.

With her mind still full of Harry's 'Venus', she set about making supper: a heartening bolognese with plenty of red wine. As she let the sauce simmer, she poured herself a glass of Shiraz and closed her eyes for a moment, picturing Camilla Sullivan bumping into Harry Tennant for the first time as she entered A Bicycle Made for Two.

She said he'd been buying a present for a friend. Something blue. Eve had the impression she'd believed him, and if so… if so, that meant she hadn't known about his affair with Daisy. It would fit with her shocked reaction when Kerry let on Harry had had more than one lover and it threw her motive for the murder into question.

But Daisy might have known about Camilla. According to Tori Abbott, she and Harry had a major row, not long after Tori had seen her in the mill window, which had been in late summer or early autumn. And Camilla mentioned she'd started seeing Harry around the beginning of October. Meanwhile, Kerry said Harry had two women on the go at one stage, and one of them had been Camilla; Kerry had recognised her perfume. The disparate facts didn't prove anything, but the timing was suggestive… Daisy and Harry might well have split up because she discovered he was two-timing her.

Gus had appeared at the back door, having had enough of his winter sport. She ushered him in and he went to his basket by the radiator, which was kicking out a comforting wall of heat.

'I need to meet Daisy,' she said. His look in response told her he didn't care what she did, so long as he could settle down and warm up.

Just before supper, Eve emailed Harry's editor at the *Real Story* to request an interview. After that, she settled down to her meal, but kept her laptop next to her on the kitchen table as she ate. Between mouthfuls, she googled 'A Bicycle Made for Two'. They were open every day except Sundays. 'I'll head over there tomorrow and see if Daisy Irvine will talk with me.'

Making the plan didn't quell her uneasiness. Daisy was a work contact of Camilla's and that made a difference. Camilla probably trusted her. But even if the florist would hear Eve out, was it right to tell her Daisy had probably been Harry's lover?

The muscles in her shoulders were knotting. It was no good. What if Camilla was guilty after all, and Eve's information put Daisy in danger? Camilla might have killed Harry because he'd let her down: told her the last thing he wanted was marriage. She might suspect he still held a flame for Daisy once she knew about her, and go on the attack.

And even if Eve was sure Camilla was innocent, how could she wade in and pass on such sensitive information? She knew nothing about Daisy, the possible circumstances of the affair, or even whether it was definitely true.

She'd just have to find out more the following day, and then decide how to act.

Resolutely, she turned her attention to Tristan Tennant. She needed more context to make the most of what he'd told her.

The results of her searches were interesting. She couldn't find any record of him having married, so either formal commitment wasn't his thing, or his relationships hadn't worked out. She found publicity shots of him opening the Hideaway, and two previous bars as well. None of them featured anyone who looked like an 'other half'. Yet he'd had that long-term girlfriend, back when Harry was young.

She took another sip of wine, then went back to the computer to check when Tristan had launched his various ventures. Comparing them with Harry's dates was enlightening. Tristan hadn't opened his first bar until Harry was twenty-one. Before that he'd worked as a teacher in a state secondary school, according to LinkedIn. It was quite a change of direction and she wondered if the timing was significant. Had Tristan felt duty-bound to keep a steady job with academic holidays until Harry no longer needed a bolthole? Eve could imagine that.

And then had come Tristan's ventures into the hospitality sector. His first bar had closed after eighteen months, but he'd had another go eight years later, with a café-bar in a village. That had lasted for four years before he went bust (according to local news reports). And now he had the Hideaway. The banks must still be lending him money… unless he'd financed the latest bar by downsizing his home. The flat he currently occupied looked small, and the area wasn't great.

So although Tristan had talked up his expertise, his career path had been shaky at best. And how well was it going at the Hideaway? It had only been open six months. Eve visualised the bar. It was smart, but old-fashioned. And recreating the scene in her head, she realised the bottles of spirits had all been full. It had been like walking in on opening night. How many people went to drink there? Was it significant that the bar had been shut that afternoon, instead of open all day? Maybe Tristan couldn't justify the staff and the heating, given the low footfall.

She tried to imagine how he might have felt about his uber-successful brother, Darius, who'd had 'the luck of the devil', as Kerry put it. And who'd then, apparently, bequeathed his sizeable fortune to his son, leaving Tristan with nothing but a duty to fulfil. A wannabe bar owner, stuck in teaching, trying to keep a relationship going while caring for a precocious and emotionally demanding boy.

It hadn't been a recipe for family harmony. But surely Tristan wouldn't have killed Harry. He'd cared for him on and off from when he was small.

Time enough for resentment to build up, a small voice whispered in Eve's head, leaving her uneasy.

And Tristan was due to inherit all Harry's money. If his current venture was struggling, that might save him.

She thought back to Robin's update: Palmer was going full steam ahead in pursuit of Tristan. She shook her head; knowing the DI's success rate, that probably meant Harry's uncle was innocent. But if he was guilty, Greg Boles was on the case too. He'd find any evidence there was. All the same, Eve intended to feed in anything concrete she discovered. But for now, she ought to turn her attention to someone the police were ignoring, as far as she knew: Judd Bentley.

Her gut told her there had to be some extra link between him and the Pippa Longford column – the real reason he was trying to get at the journalist behind the name. Whatever was going on, it was personal. Judd's intense, burning gaze filled her mind's eye.

After Eve had finished her last mouthful of bolognese and stacked the dishwasher, she settled down to google both him and his sister. She still doubted Judd's story about Sally's advice column exposé, but it was a place to start. She put the woman's name into Google in quotes, alongside Pippa Longford, also in quotes, but the only results were for pages listing contributors to different publications, and didn't show any connection between the two. There was no reason to suppose Sally had known Pippa was really Harry Tennant, but still she went through the same process again, this time with Sally and Harry's names. After that, she repeated the exercise for Judd, but again she drew a blank.

Eve stretched and became conscious of Gus's snoring. *It's all right for some. I still have work to do…*

If Judd had a personal grudge against Harry as Pippa, it was possible he or Sally or one of their close friends might have been badly affected by the *Real Story*'s advice column. She looked up the relevant web page, scanning all the letters Harry had answered there, starting with the Saturday before the midwinter party, then going back in time.

She reviewed letters sent the previous fall and summer, noting all Suffolk correspondents, but there were no JBs or SBs. She took a deep breath. It was a seriously long shot, but she could use Facebook to try to identify Sally and Judd's close friends, then see if she got a match for any of them.

She started with Judd, since tracking down Pippa seemed to have been his obsession. He'd been careful with his Facebook privacy settings and she could only view his cover and profile pictures, going back through time. After fixing herself a coffee, she trawled through them, searching for inspiration.

At last, she found one that made her pause. It showed Judd and Sally, whose image had appeared in Eve's Google searches. But there was a third woman in the photograph too. She was a similar age to the others, and shared an unmistakable family resemblance, like enough to Sally to be a twin.

Eve felt a shiver snake its way up her back. Simon had said Judd lived with his sister, so she'd been surprised when Sally Bentley mentioned him calling her with news. Why had Eve never thought he might have another sibling?

She shook her head. She needed to find the woman's first name. She wasn't tagged in Judd's photo, or listed under family in his 'about' section, but Eve could view his friends. She trawled through them, feeling grateful that Judd wasn't the gregarious sort.

Even so, he had seventy-two. At last she found the missing Bentley sibling: Melody.

In an instant Eve had clicked through to her page. There wasn't much to see, but someone called Lottie Briggs had posted: 'Miss you, Melody' on her wall.

Eve scanned the list of initials she'd made, belonging to requests for Harry's advice in the *Real Story*'s column.

There was a letter from an MB, Suffolk, back in early December. She called it up and read the contents.

The headline for the letter was 'Humiliate your Bully'.

I feel embarrassed, contacting you, but I'm being bullied at work. It's become so bad I tried to get another job. After count-less applications and a handful of interviews the rejections are making me feel even worse. I'd already lost confidence and I've reached rock bottom now. My employers know the woman who's victimising me is a tyrant, but they'd rather turn a blind eye than tackle the problem. Please help. MB, Suffolk.

Harry's reply had begun sensibly:

For a start, you need to stop feeling embarrassed.
It's estimated that nearly a third of people are bullied at work. It's not your fault. That said, it's wise of you to recognise that you are the person who needs to tackle it and you're already one step closer to being free of the person who's mistreating you.

They're probably taking out their feelings of inadequacy on you; and may secretly envy you for being good at your job. The key is to show them that you're not afraid. Fight back. Act as though you're in charge. Call them out. Show them up. Humiliate them as they've humiliated you. You mention your management

team aren't keen to intervene, but in all honesty, it's probably
best you tackle it yourself. It's an old-fashioned viewpoint, but
there's a reason it's endured all these years.

Best of luck and be strong, Pippa.

What happened to the employer's duty of care? Surely it couldn't
be wise to tell 'MB' to go it alone without understanding the person
they were up against? Eve googled for advice from official sources
on how to tackle bullying at work. It recommended keeping a
careful record of the incidents that took place, talking to HR or
an independent colleague, and being aware of the laws that were
there to protect you.

But instead of being cautious, Harry had pushed the correspondent to do something dramatic.

Had they done it? And if so, what had happened next?

Eve checked, and found the woman who'd posted on Melody's
Facebook wall, Lottie Briggs, worked at an estate agents in Blyworth.
There was no mention of Melody on their website but when she
googled the woman's name in quotes, together with the firm, she
found references to her on one of their press releases, six months
previously.

Lottie and Melody had been colleagues, and not long ago. Then
Melody had, potentially, written to Harry about problems at work
and been given dubious-sounding advice. And now she was no
longer employed at the estate agents.

If Eve wanted to find out more, she'd probably have to ask
point-blank.

She messaged Simon.

Sorry to disturb. May I ask what time Judd's due to start work
tomorrow? (Will explain all in due course.)

Simon replied with a laughing face emoji and a message:

Just as well I trust you. Assume you're not planning to burgle his cottage while he's out. His shift starts at seven.

She messaged back her thanks. She wasn't planning to rob him, but speaking with Melody while he was out sounded like a plan.

CHAPTER TWENTY-TWO

Eve was too full of adrenaline to sleep well that night. What had happened to Melody? And her visit to Daisy loomed large too…

She got up early the following day and filled the time after a dog walk and crack-of-dawn breakfast by taking the decorations off the Christmas tree. She'd meant to do it the night before, but her research had taken over. She dragged the spruce through the house, showering the place with needles, then dumped it in the back garden. Robin had said he'd take it for recycling when he was round next. After that, she swept up before Gus impaled himself. Finally, she used a stepladder to take down the holly and mistletoe, regretting her lack of height. Once the work was complete, she breathed a sigh of relief. There was a newly spacious feel to the dining room, now the six-foot tree had gone.

At last, it was a reasonable hour to visit Judd Bentley's cottage. He'd be at work and with any luck, Melody would have switched her dressing gown for jeans and a sweater.

Gus looked at her hopefully and she bent down to hug him. 'I know it's going to seem like I'm using you, but you can come this time!' He often worked wonders if she had to deal with someone out of the blue. People tended to trust Eve when she was accompanied by an enchanting dachshund.

Fifteen minutes later, with butterflies dancing in her stomach, Eve knocked on the door of the house she knew to be Judd Bentley's. She almost gave up, the place seemed so quiet, but after she tried a second time, and waited another minute, she heard movement inside.

She was over-optimistic to assume Melody Bentley would have changed out of her dressing gown. In fact, Eve wondered if she ever did. She looked exhausted and hollow-eyed, her hair lank and in need of a wash. She'd kept the chain on the cottage door and her eyes met Eve's through a six-inch crack, as she began to close it again. She only paused because Gus had snuffled forward, his tail wagging. His nose was in danger of being squashed.

'Did you think I was the post?' Eve said.

The woman nodded slowly.

'I'm so sorry to bother you without warning. My name's Eve. I work at Monty's – the teashop in Saxford. Though I don't think I've seen you there.' Melody didn't look as though she'd been outside in months. She was pale and seemed to flinch slightly at the daylight.

'No.' Her voice was croaky. 'I only moved in here recently. With my brother. He's putting me up for a bit. Did you want him?'

Eve shook her head. 'It was you I came to see, in fact.'

The woman looked confused, but Gus was paying her such attention that she undid the chain on the door and bent to pet him. It was a good start.

'As well as working at Monty's, I moonlight as an obituary writer,' Eve said, 'and that's why I'm here. I've been asked by *Icon* to produce a feature on Harry Tennant.'

Eve knew this moment was crucial. Thank goodness Melody was still petting Gus, or she was sure Judd's sister would have shut herself back inside the house. As it was, she started and half rose to her feet. She *was* 'MB', then.

'Melody, I just need to understand more about him and the way he worked. I'm sure there will be plenty of people who'll sing his praises. I've emailed his editor to request an interview. But I can't write only half the story. Some of the advice he gave horrifies me. It surely doesn't meet the professional standards people have a right to expect. If it backfired, I'd like to be truthful about that in my piece. I don't need to name individuals or go into details,' she added quickly. 'I just need to know I'm basing my report on verifiable truth. His old paper won't challenge it. It would be far more damaging for them to make a fuss and have the criticisms become headline news.'

The woman was chewing her lip. There were tears in her eyes. She was at the end of her tether, Eve could see. Too little sleep, misery, drink maybe. Something had gone wrong in her life and Eve was willing to bet it was down to Harry.

'How much do you know already?' Melody said at last.

'I know you were being bullied at work and that you wrote to Pippa Longford for advice. She said to stand up to your bully: call them out. Humiliate them. You no longer appear on the website of the estate agents where the problems took place. And I saw your colleague, Lottie, wrote on Facebook that she missed you. Do you want to tell me what happened? It can be off the record if you prefer.'

The woman's shoulders sagged.

'I'm a good listener, if it would help to talk.'

At last, she nodded. 'Do you want to come in?'

The cottage itself was tidy. Judd must be keeping the place going for the pair of them. Melody motioned her to take a seat and sank into an armchair herself, tucking her dressing gown round her legs.

She put her head in her hands. 'The bullying had been going on for ages. I kept thinking that if I just took it, the woman – Patsy, my line manager – would get bored eventually. But it didn't happen. I felt as though I'd run out of options. I was desperately unhappy.'

'I'm not surprised – it sounds dreadful. And work's such a massive part of our lives. If it goes sour it taints everything.'

Melody nodded. 'I felt as though I was treading water but gradually sinking. So I took "Pippa Longford's" advice and told Patsy to back off. It took a week to pluck up courage to do it, but in the end I said my piece in front of witnesses. They all knew

Patsy's behaviour had been unforgivable: name-calling, humiliation, unfair blame. You name it.

'But I couldn't control my emotions as I spoke. Trying to stop myself crying made me sound fierce and angry, when I'd wanted to be measured and reasonable. I ended up spewing personal insults as well.' She glanced down for a moment. 'Everything I'd bottled up for the last couple of years came pouring out.'

'Totally understandable. I'm sure I'd have been the same.' She should have had support – someone independent to mediate. What had her work been thinking of, not listening to her problems in the first place?

Melody pulled a tissue from her dressing gown pocket and blew her nose. 'One of my colleagues called out "Well said" from the back of the room, but I was suddenly afraid the whole thing would backfire. There was pure hatred in Patsy's eyes.'

Melody's gaze was unfocused, as though she was back in the moment.

'A few days later, Patsy accused me of stealing a bundle of department-store vouchers. The firm gives them out to house buyers as part of a promotional deal. They turned up in my bag, right after Patsy suggested they might be there.'

'She planted them?'

Melody nodded. 'I think most people at the firm guessed what she'd done. The trouble is, even the management are scared of her. And you hear them say things like: "Well, she does get results." When I had my appraisal last year, one of them said to me, "Really, Melody, Patsy can't do anything right as far as you're concerned, can she?" They put the blame on me because it's easier. Lottie says Patsy's found a new person to pick on since I left.'

It was horrendous, how one mean-minded sociopath could effectively control an organisation. 'Do you still have any records that show the way Patsy behaved towards you? Could you put information together to present to your former employers, or take to a lawyer even?'

Melody shook her head. 'I know Patsy deserves to pay for the way she behaves and other people ought to be protected from her too, but work have made it impossible for me to do anything. They said if I left quietly they were prepared to write me a decent reference. Whereas if I fight what happened and lose, I might never get another job.' She let out a sob. 'Only I'm not making the best use of the "chance" they've given me. I've been so down, I haven't felt like applying for anything.'

Eve's blood was boiling. Maybe she could contact Lottie and find out about Patsy's latest victim. This couldn't keep on happening.

'You must be furious with Harry Tennant for advising you badly.' But as Eve said it she could see it wasn't true. Melody was broken and exhausted. Fury required fire in your belly, something Judd, her protective brother, probably had.

'It was my decision to follow his suggestion.' Melody's tone was despairing. 'I wish my gran had never suggested I write in. She was addicted to the column, but it's one thing finding it entertaining, another relying on it to solve your problems.'

Eve hesitated. 'Your brother was very keen to find out who Pippa Longford really was. I can understand he was hurt and angry on your behalf.'

The woman was so low, Eve didn't think it had even crossed her mind that she and Judd had a motive for murder. Now, the faintest flicker of anxiety showed in her eyes. 'He was angry. I think he'd have liked to tell Pippa what he thought of her, but although he had the impression she was local, he never found out who she was. And he wanted justice. You don't get that by killing someone. That wouldn't right a wrong. Anyone who thinks Judd's guilty just doesn't know him. Take it from me.'

She sounded honest, and almost too tired to act out a lie, but Eve couldn't be sure, and if the police found out, they wouldn't be either. Melody was Judd's sister; he'd taken her in when she lost her job and had been fighting her corner ever since. She was hardly likely to admit he might be a killer.

CHAPTER TWENTY-THREE

After dropping her car back home, Eve left to work her shift at Monty's. As she walked through the bright white world a feeling of renewed determination gripped her. She must find out who had killed Harry. Melody had suffered a huge amount already, some of it down to his ill-thought-out advice. Now she'd suffer again, if she and her brother ended up being questioned by the police for murder. She didn't want to tell Palmer about them; she'd no proof Judd had ever identified Harry as the author of the column. But she could only justify holding the information back if she found the real culprit to put them in the clear.

Deep down, she wanted to succeed for her own sake too, out of professional pride. And Harry was a fascinating mix. His charm hid a dark side, but the interview with Tristan showed the situation was complicated. She was still analysing what had made him tick, but his harrowing childhood must have had an effect.

Thoughts about the case were wiped from her mind on entering the teashop.

The school vacation was over and Viv had exchanged Monty's Christmas décor for a fresh New-Year theme, with spring-green tablecloths and early snowdrops in the jam jars. Despite the return to normal life, the teashop was unusually busy. Several of Saxford's more senior residents seemed reluctant to wave goodbye to the holiday atmosphere.

Eve was part way through her shift when her mobile started to vibrate. Her hands were full and by the time she pulled her phone from her pocket there was just an on-screen alert. A missed call from Robin. She caught her breath. It must mean news.

Glancing up, she saw two tables were vying for her attention. Angie had come down with a cold, and Kirsty was late, thanks to the weather playing havoc with the buses. Viv was helping front of house – sporting her new green hair, to match the tablecloths – but she'd disappeared to fetch a pot of Earl Grey and dark-chocolate cranberry cakes for a couple sitting in the window.

Eve dashed between the tables, noting orders, her mind half on Robin's call.

It was only after she'd delivered refreshments to three more tables, passing Viv at speed – the flash of a grin and a streak of green hair – that Eve paused long enough to pick up on a conversation at a table near the counter.

It sent the hairs on the back of her neck rising.

'… when they found her.' The face of the woman speaking was pale, her eyes glassy.

'Really?' Her companion put her head in her hands. 'I can't believe it. And so soon after Harry Tennant. Are you sure it's true?'

Eve was setting a vacated table. She placed the silverware down carefully, all her attention on the conversation.

'Certain, I'm afraid. My daughter's best friend works as an administrator at the station.'

'Do they think the two are connected?'

The first woman's eyes widened. 'I'd guess they'd have to be, wouldn't you? I mean, two murders within a week in one small village?'

Her companion looked down into her tea. 'No, you're right. Of course…'

Another table called Eve over to order more refreshments.

It had to be why Robin had rung. Eve was desperate to listen to his voicemail. Her legs felt like jelly, her heart going like an out of control sewing machine. What the heck had happened?

A moment later, when Kirsty arrived, Eve practically hugged her. At last she'd be able to escape. 'Thanks so much for stepping in, Kirsty!'

Viv's son's girlfriend gave a wide smile. 'No problem.' She switched to an undertone. 'I spoke to Angie earlier and she sounded horribly snotty. Probably best not to inflict her on the customers. Sam'll help tomorrow if she's still off.'

Eve knew Viv's son was doing a last-minute assignment for uni and an all-nighter was forecast. Sometimes you could tell he was his mother's son.

Once Kirsty had her coat off, Eve went into Monty's office to listen to Robin's voicemail. There was no detail; he just said to call him.

'You all right?' Viv poked her head around the door.

'Sorry, yes. Just a missed call.'

'No worries. Why don't you take five, now Kirsty's arrived?'

Eve's mobile was burning a hole in her pocket. 'Thanks. And then I'll cover your break.'

Viv grinned. 'Deal!'

Eve didn't dare call Robin from the teashop. Instead, she slipped on her coat and left Monty's via the side door. A moment later she was walking alongside the village green, the crows cawing in the stark snow-covered oak trees. She kept her gloves off to make her call, her fingers numb in the frigid air.

'Robin? Sorry – I was at Monty's and it was crazy in there this morning. I heard one of the customers talking. There's been another death?'

She heard him take a deep breath.

'*Camilla Sullivan.*'

CHAPTER TWENTY-FOUR

Eve could hardly take in the news Robin had passed on.

'Camilla…' The woman's bright eyes, beautiful olive skin and high cheekbones filled her mind. Her commanding presence, the feeling of her power and success. But then her loss of control at Monty's when she'd let rip at Kerry Clifton. And now this. It was unthinkable.

'*She was found this morning,*' Robin said, '*but killed sometime last night, the pathologist reckons. She never went to bed.*'

Seeing her so recently brought home the awful reality. 'I called on her yesterday, just after church.'

'*I heard. Someone saw you and told Palmer, according to Greg. I expect the police will be round to see you soon – especially as it was your second visit to her house. What made you go back?*'

It was too awful to contemplate. 'I wanted to warn her – and to press her for more information. I knew she was holding back at our first interview.' Games. She'd enjoyed making Eve wonder – and the other villagers too – but it had ended in tragedy.

'*Did you get anywhere?*'

Eve's heart sank at the question. 'I messed up and made her angry. She got the impression I thought she and Harry were in cahoots, with a plan to blackmail someone who'd written in to his column.'

'*Is that what you think?*'

'Not exactly. As Camilla pointed out, neither of them needed the money. And she said it was beneath them in any case. Grubby. And I can believe that too. But they liked to make mischief. Her behaviour means half the village may have assumed she knew more than she did. That could be why she's dead. And if either of them had a hold over one of Harry's correspondents it might not have been financial gain that motivated them. They played with people; it amused them.'

'*A dangerous pastime.*'

'Absolutely.' Eve's mind was running over recent events, putting the latest murder in context. 'The timing of the killing is interesting. Up until the row in the teashop, most people didn't know Camilla and Harry were close enough to swap secrets, but after that, the killer could have seen her as a threat. Not just because she might share his knowledge. The more intimate she was with him, the more likely she was to guess the murderer's identity too.'

'*True. The killer could have talked to her to gauge what she knew.*'

'Yes.' Eve shivered. 'And then acted to protect themselves, on the back of her playful hints.' She tried to order her thoughts through her horror. 'I guess loathing and revenge *could* be a motive too, if one of Pippa's correspondents felt Camilla and Harry had been laughing at them secretly.'

'*Maybe, if it was somehow the final straw. I suppose there's a chance there are two killers: a jilted lover for Harry, say, and a humiliated friend for Camilla. But I'm not sure I buy humiliation as a sole motive. It's not as though the whole village is gossiping, so I guess people haven't matched an embarrassing plea for help with one of the locals. If someone's been made a fool of, it sounds as though they only lost face in front of Harry and Camilla.*'

'That makes sense. So maybe it's a single killer then, and the pair of them possessing damaging information about a neighbour is a likely motive. That or the jealous lover angle. I've identified Harry's "Venus", by the way.' She explained the background. 'I'm planning to visit her store later. I'll let you know what I find.'

'*You know the way to a man's heart.*'

Despite the awfulness of the moment, she felt a blush come to her cheeks, though she knew he was only joking. *Ridiculous.*

'*Was anything else said on your visit to Camilla?*'

'I warned her I didn't trust Judd Bentley.' Where did the florist's death leave him and his sister? Eve explained the latest developments and her interview with Melody.

Robin let out a long breath. '*So she not only lost her job, but her peace of mind by the sound of it. Judd had a prime motive to kill Harry, and Camilla too, if she guessed what he was up to.*'

'That makes sense, in theory. But I've a hunch he never found out Harry was Pippa.' A memory brought her up short. 'I caught Harry watching Judd in church on Christmas Day and he looked nervous.' She considered the timing. 'That would have been just after Camilla passed on Judd's request to meet him.' She closed her eyes for a moment, working it through. 'I believe Harry knew Judd meant trouble – maybe after hearing him ask every guest at my party if they knew who Pippa was – himself included.' She recalled seeing their stilted conversation on the solstice. 'And he was nervous because he didn't want to be found out. Which means there's no way he'd have met with Judd.'

'*But Judd could still have discovered Harry's secret another way,*' Robin said.

'True, though I can't see how.'

Eve heard a quiet laugh. '*You don't want Judd to be guilty because of Melody.*'

'I feel sorry for her, and the more I think about it, the more she and Judd don't fit the bill.'

'*You might have a point. There was no sign of forced entry at Camilla's place. It seems she wasn't wary of her killer.*'

Eve paused for thought. 'That's interesting. She didn't seem to take my warnings about Judd seriously, but I doubt she'd have actually let him in. Melody, maybe, but she's not even well enough to get dressed and wash her hair at the moment.'

'It's all right, I agree – they're unlikely. But don't write them off altogether. Judd could have identified Harry somehow. He was hellbent on that task, and if he killed him, Camilla had enough clues to guess at his guilt. And Melody could have attacked her. The drive to protect Judd might have overridden her listlessness. Maybe her apparent frailty stopped Camilla seeing her as a threat.'

Eve had been feeling confident, but his words made her pause. 'Yes, that's true. Thanks for the self-preservation reality check.'

He laughed, but it sounded like relief rather than amusement. *'And what do you think about Tristan Tennant, in the light of your interview and Camilla's death?'*

Eve explained how Harry had probably made his uncle's life difficult in multiple ways. 'Whatever the truth, I think Tristan will find Harry's bequest useful.

'And if he's guilty, I could imagine him seeing Camilla as a threat. He was a regular visitor to the mill, so he might have discovered her and Harry's affair weeks back. On the back of that, he could have visited her last night to find out if she knew anything, while ostensibly offering his condolences. She wouldn't have let him in if she was worried, but maybe he made her suspicious once he was there. He's not good at hiding his feelings.'

'Interesting. Nice work, Eve.'

'Thanks.' He sounded genuinely impressed, not patronising. She found his words as warming as a cup of Viv's hot chocolate.

'He's still top of Palmer's list too. But they're interested in Kerry Clifton now, as well.'

Someone must have mentioned her row with Camilla already. Eve pictured the woman. 'I find it difficult to imagine Kerry as a murderer. She's the sort to tackle resentment immediately: she didn't hold back at the teashop. And would she kill when she'd made herself an obvious suspect?'

'*If she talked her way into Camilla's house to continue their row she might have been overtaken by jealousy – or the need to keep her quiet if Camilla suddenly realised she was guilty.*'

'True. Tristan says Harry treated Kerry like dirt.' She sighed. 'It looks like she lied to me about how affable he was – unless it's Tristan telling untruths. Anyway, if Palmer thinks Kerry's easy prey he'll be disappointed.'

Robin gave a soft laugh. '*I got that impression too.*'

All the same, it was another driver for Eve to unearth the truth. Harry had meddled with a lot of lives and had a long reach, even after death. So many damaged contacts, all under suspicion.

'*The police will be checking alibis and conducting interviews,*' Robin went on, '*so I'll keep you updated. Speaking of which, good luck with yours…*'

'Thanks. I'll gird my loins.' Would she get Palmer himself? He sometimes sent a deputy – which was certainly more appropriate – but she knew he enjoyed putting her down in person.

'*And Eve…*'

'Yes?'

He took a deep breath. '*Apparently Camilla was beaten to death: a rounded weapon according to the pathologist. Take good care, won't you?*'

Eve swallowed. 'I will.'

Back at Monty's, Viv met her in the kitchen, her face pale, blue eyes wide.

'There are people out there saying Camilla Sullivan's been killed.'

As usual, Eve found acting hard when she was dealing with Viv. 'Really? Heck – how horrible. What happened?'

She managed not to slip anything Robin had said into conversation, and in the next hour more people drifted in with similar news delivered in ever more lurid detail.

Eve was almost glad when her mobile went and someone from the police team asked if she'd be free for an interview at Elizabeth's Cottage in half an hour. The feeling fizzled away when she heard it would be DI Palmer who came.

Viv gave her a bolstering pat on the shoulder. 'Give him hell. Oh, and Eve?'

'Yes?'

'Cross Keys tonight. Seven. Food. Wine. We need time to talk.'

'All right.' When Viv had that look in her eye there was no point in arguing. Besides, she might have more information on Daisy Irvine by then. Food and chat would help her think.

CHAPTER TWENTY-FIVE

Gus had excellent taste, so it was no surprise he'd never taken to Detective Inspector Nigel Palmer. He'd been reluctant to let him into the cottage and had done lots of bold sniffing of his shoes and trouser legs as the detective inspector stood on the threshold, a look of disdain in his piggy eyes.

Why couldn't he have sent Greg Boles? Or DC Dawkins. She was good.

Palmer was sitting on one of her couches now. She was sure they lost around three months of useful life each time he came; he put their springs through a thorough stress test.

'It's interesting that you went straight to interview Ms Sullivan after you were commissioned to write Harry Tennant's obituary,' Palmer said, his voice full of mistrust. 'Yet Ms Sullivan wasn't known to be a friend or even acquaintance of Mr Tennant's. It seems you were focused on both murder victims for your own reasons.'

Eve frowned and Gus gave the DI a fierce look.

'There's nothing odd about that. I can't write about Harry Tennant without focusing on *him*. And I knew Camilla Sullivan had been recommending the *Real Story*'s agony column around the village. When it turned out "Pippa Longford" was local, it seemed like a big coincidence, so I went to ask her if she'd known her true identity.'

'It seems like a leap, if you had no inside knowledge yourself.'

Well, it would seem like a leap to you, you noddle head… 'You wouldn't have thought it a coincidence?'

'Ms Sullivan talking to her friends about an agony aunt wouldn't strike me as odd. Lots of women busy themselves with such things.'

Eve wondered if he could hear her teeth grinding. 'Agony columns are popular with lots of people, but I've never come across one that's the talk of the town before. In any case, it struck me, and that's why I visited Camilla.' *I wasn't secretly plotting a killing spree…* 'And of course, as soon as she confirmed my hunch, I suggested she call you.' *Rather suggesting I'm on the level.*

Palmer's left eyebrow rose higher than Eve would have thought possible. 'But then you visited her again, just yesterday. The day of her death. Were you going to mention that?'

Eve took a deep breath. 'Yes, naturally. During my first interview with Camilla she hinted at a couple of things without being specific. She told me she'd recommended Harry Tennant's column to a number of people, but not who, for instance. She also gave the impression she might be in on some kind of secret Harry was keeping. I went back to try to fill in the blanks.'

'You were playing at being a detective.'

'Inspector, my job *involves* detective work. To write a good obituary I need to look for clues that will reveal Mr Tennant's true personality.' That was all true, as far as it went.

'And what did you discover, on your visit yesterday?'

'Nothing. Camilla assured me Harry hadn't shared his secret, and I still don't know who she advised to write to his column.'

'It's interesting that she was so uncooperative. Perhaps she objected to your methods.'

Eve said nothing.

'I must ask you, Ms Mallow, where you were between eight and midnight yesterday evening?'

Eve mentally noted the time of death. She'd add it to her spreadsheet later. 'I was here. I'd been into Blyworth to interview Harry's uncle at the bar he runs, and then to visit my neighbours, Sylvia

Hepworth and Daphne Lovatt, for a drink at six. But by eight I would have been at home, having supper. After that I went to bed.'

'And no one can vouch for you, I suppose?'

Eve took a deep breath. He always asked, and the answer was always the same. 'That's correct.'

'I understand you went upstairs with Mr Tennant, during an open-house event you hosted on midwinter's evening.'

Seriously? He must be doing this to wind her up. 'With two other people, the Abbotts. And there were around forty more guests down here.' She hadn't managed to suppress an eye roll.

'Can you think of anyone who would have wanted to kill Mr Tennant and Ms Sullivan?'

Eve's mind ranged from Tristan and Daisy to Kerry and Judd Bentley. But Palmer already had Kerry and Tristan in his sights and she still felt the Bentley siblings were highly unlikely. Forcing Melody into the centre of a murder investigation might be the final straw. As for Daisy, Eve knew next to nothing about her at present. It wasn't as though they'd even met.

'No.'

'And what can you tell me about the argument between Ms Sullivan and Kerry Clifton at Monty's Teashop? I understand you saw the whole thing.'

He made it sound as though she'd taken her job purely to witness local drama. She objected to his tone, but she couldn't hold back in good conscience. She gave him the facts and knew what he'd conclude. Even to her ears it sounded as though the women had been arguing over Harry, and which of them he'd valued most.

Her mind ran back to Kerry's claims that Harry had been kind, overlaid by Tristan's story of him yelling at her. She needed to dig deeper. There was more going on than the row at Monty's implied.

'So there's nothing more you can tell me?' Palmer's eyes bored into hers.

'Nothing.' Gus got to his feet and glared at the DI with a 'stick that in your pipe and smoke it' look.

Spot on, buddy. She bent to ruffle his fur.

'Very well.' Palmer got to his feet. 'I need hardly tell you, Ms Mallow, that we don't require your "help" with the investigation. I shall be making enquiries, and if I find you've been interfering I can promise you I'll take action. Murder isn't a game.'

It was because it was so serious that Eve planned to ignore his instructions. (Though her desire to put one over on him was a powerful motivation too.) She managed to keep her temper until she'd ejected him, then stomped around the cottage until the fury was out of her system.

At last she turned to Gus. 'Sorry, buddy. Let's go and run somewhere.' It was a good Palmer antidote.

CHAPTER TWENTY-SIX

Hurling stones into the sea gave Eve some relief from the after-effects of DI Palmer's visit.

By the time she set off for Blyworth, taking the car again because the buses were still on a go-slow, it was almost dark. She was following her plan to arrive late in the day, in the hope of catching Daisy Irvine alone.

In town, store windows glowed from buildings still laden with snow. Navigating the pavements was a treacherous business, but Blyworth looked beautiful in its winter guise. The streets were unusually quiet and the scene resembled a stage set, the lighting stark in the white landscape.

A Bicycle Made for Two was on a side street lined with sixteenth-century timber-framed buildings: the sort of road Eve loved to walk down, purely for the historic architecture. The boutique's windows were appealing, too. The store was double-fronted, and the gowns on display were in warm ivories, offset by trailing greenery, with mother-of-the-bride outfits in jewel colours, sewn in rich taffeta. Eve felt a quiver inside: a long-buried memory of the excitement she'd experienced when she and Ian had decided to marry. It had been fun at the time. He'd changed. Or she had. She wouldn't alter a thing though; their twins were everything to her. She shook away the memory and approached the glass door, pushing it open to send a bell jangling. A lot of the stores in the area had them: an old-fashioned clapper setting off sweet notes against a metal ring.

The woman who stood inside, talking to the only customers, had to be Daisy Irvine. She fitted right in with the store's fairy-tale atmosphere. Her hair was just about long enough to sit on. It shone in the light from the crystal chandeliers hanging from the ceiling.

'… though really, for a June wedding, you might prefer something sleeveless,' she was saying. 'It's so hard, buying now. I can barely imagine feeling warm again!'

She was talking to a young woman who might be in her twenties, and a second who Eve took to be her mother.

'Be with you in just a moment,' she said, turning to Eve.

'No hurry, I'm just browsing.' She wanted the woman to finish serving the other customers before paying her any attention. She couldn't speak freely until they were alone.

Eve made an awkwardly detailed inspection of the gifts section until the pair left. They'd only looked at one sleeveless dress when the mother's mobile rang and they announced they'd have to go.

'Take your time. Have a think,' Daisy said. 'It's not something to rush into. You can come in at any stage to have another look.'

She had the perfect low-pressure sales technique. Now, she turned to Eve. 'How can I help?'

'You have a beautiful store. The way it's laid out is really attractive.'

A smile lit the woman's face. 'Thank you so much!'

'But in fact, I actually came here to speak with you. I didn't want to begin until you were free.'

A look of puzzlement crossed her pretty features. 'Oh, I see.'

'My name's Eve Mallow, and I've been asked by *Icon* magazine to write Harry Tennant's obituary.'

Eve watched her expression change again. A flash of anger.

'I'm sorry,' Daisy Irvine said, 'but I'm not sure what that's got to do with me. I mean, I've seen his name in the paper, of course. A local man leading a double life is more than enough to get the *Blyworth Advertiser* excited. But why seek me out?'

'I'd heard you two were close, but if you don't want to talk to me, I completely understand. There's no pressure.' Like Daisy, Eve preferred a softly-softly approach. Pushing was against her principles, and the alternative often worked better anyway.

'Who told you we knew each other?' The woman lifted her hand to rub the back of her neck. The diamond on her ring finger, next to a wedding band, caught the light.

Eve took a deep breath. She'd promised she wouldn't give Tori away. 'A villager in Saxford mentioned they'd seen you together.'

'Me specifically?'

It had to be. She was a perfect match for Tori's description. 'Yes.'

Daisy's lips were white. 'Well, they must have been mistaken. I'm sorry you've had a wasted journey. Now, if you'll excuse me, it's time for me to close.' She went to turn the sign over on the door, and remained in place to hold it open so Eve could leave.

Eve hesitated for a moment. She wondered whether to mention Camilla too, and express her sympathy. She was desperate to know if Daisy was aware that the florist had been her rival, but it seemed too low. She might not even know of Camilla's death yet. Unless she'd killed her…

'I'm sorry to have bothered you,' she said, preparing to exit. As her gaze met Daisy Irvine's she was sure the woman realised Eve knew she was lying about Harry. She took a business card from her bag and left it on the inside windowsill. It seemed unlikely, but maybe she'd have a change of heart.

Eve went back to her car and let herself in. She was parked just up the street from Daisy's store. Was she really going to drive off and leave it, when she knew the woman was holding back? One of Harry's contacts was a killer, and a double-crossed lover seemed a likely prospect.

Principles were all well and good, but Eve realised she might have to modify them when a potential interviewee was also a murder suspect. Daisy wore a wedding ring. Assuming her husband was alive, that made her home life of interest, and him a possible suspect too. There was only one way Eve could think of to glean more information. It was freezing cold, but if she waited just a few minutes…

A quarter of an hour later, the lights in the boutique window changed subtly, to a slightly dimmer setting. Two minutes after that, Daisy appeared outside and stood, locking up, her long golden hair trailing down the black velvet coat she wore.

Eve watched as Daisy strutted stiffly along the pavement. The compacted snow was freezing hard now. When she reached the street corner and turned left, Eve started her engine and followed slowly. The conditions meant driving at a snail's pace wouldn't attract attention.

By the time she made the same turn Daisy had, the store manager was getting into a VW Polo. Eve was far enough back to let her pull out and follow from a safe distance, past stores shutting for the night, bars opening up, and then into the suburbs.

Before long they were out in the countryside, heading to the north of Saxford. A thirty-mile-an-hour speed limit came into view, together with a sign announcing they were entering the village of Wessingham. Eve followed Daisy through and out the other side. Just beyond the main settlement, the woman turned right into a driveway.

Eve slowed her Mini and pulled in by the gate to a field, just before the turn. She shut off the engine and stepped out. It took her a minute to scramble along the snow-covered grass verge, but after that she was shielded from Daisy's view by a yew hedge that bordered her property. Unfortunately, it meant Eve couldn't see Daisy either. She stumbled into the field that lay on the other side of the hedge, thankful for the darkness.

In a moment, she was trying to peer through the dense vegetation. She wanted to get an idea of the woman's home set-up. She could only see the glow of an outside light and some vague shapes, but it looked as though Daisy had company.

'About time!' A man's voice. 'Thought you were going to finish early.'

'I had customers, Dan.'

The man swore. 'What the hell's wrong with people, tramping round in this weather looking at wedding dresses? I can't believe you manage to sell that rubbish.' His tone was as cruel as his words. 'Oh, except I bet you didn't, did you? Sell anything, that is? Go on – tell me I'm wrong! Those "customers" of yours – did they buy one of your ridiculous dresses? Or even a trinket to give to some poor blighter as a present?' He gave a derisive laugh. 'Thought not. Just as well my work pays the bills, isn't it?'

It was horrible to listen to him, demolishing her life. Eve had no way of knowing what sort of money the boutique made, but it was a beautiful place, put together with panache.

'Well, at least you're here now,' the man went on. 'I need supper early. I said I'd have a beer with Steve tonight.' Then he laughed. It was wholehearted this time, and sent a shiver down Eve's spine. 'You promised you were prepared to work at our marriage, remember? I'm just giving you the chance to do that.'

No wonder Daisy hadn't wanted to talk about her love affair with Harry. If it had been a terrible mistake – an act of disloyalty committed during a loving marriage – she'd refuse to comment, of course. But this was something else. A dangerous man who took no prisoners. Did he know she'd had an affair? Was that behind the comment about making the marriage work?

The man spoke again. 'You ought to be grateful that I—'

He stopped abruptly. Eve had been so deep in thought that the sudden scrabbling sound on her side of the hedge made her jump too.

What the heck was it? There were countless creatures that roamed the countryside after dark, but this one had the potential to expose her. She stood absolutely still, hardly daring to breathe.

The noise continued and Eve saw a shape. A cat. She willed it to go away. It was watching her, its eyes gleaming in the moonlight, and a second later it let out a yowl. She stood there, surrounded by snow and ice, the heat building under her collar.

'Shut up, you mangy animal!'

If Eve had been the cat she'd have run a mile in response to his tone.

'She's probably caught another mouse,' Daisy said, her tired voice getting nearer. 'She must be just the other side of the hedge. Sooty!' Eve could visualise her, crouched down, looking through the yews for the cat, seeing more, where the foliage was sparser… 'Supper time!'

At that moment, the cat abandoned Eve and shot through the hedge towards its owners. She stood stock-still, her shoulders taut, breath held. She wouldn't feel safe until they were inside.

At last, she heard the couple's front door open and close again. She began to creep back along the hedge, pressed in close, desperate not to give herself away.

Only when she reached the end did her breathing return to something like normal. Using the cover of the thick yews, she risked peering down Daisy Irvine's drive. There was a truck parked next to her VW with the branding of a local garage on it, just visible in the moonlight.

Andy's Autos.

Overhearing the conversation left Eve feeling powerless. She intended to find out more about Daisy Irvine's husband. If only there was some way to help.

But the set-up left her uneasy too. Dan sounded like the kind of man who enjoyed being cruel. The sort who practised demolishing people's self-esteem as though it was a sport. If Daisy had embarked on an affair, despite the dangers, Eve could only imagine she'd gone into it with high hopes – for a lasting relationship maybe. She'd probably been devastated when Harry let her down. Such powerful emotions in someone at the end of their tether might have drastic consequences.

CHAPTER TWENTY-SEVEN

Eve was five minutes early for supper at the Cross Keys that evening. After returning home she'd spent some time soaking in a hot bath. Standing behind the Irvines' hedge had left her chilled to the bone, but it was almost getting caught that had the most lasting effect. She hadn't been able to stop shivering.

Her more-than-prompt appearance at the pub was especially unnecessary, as Viv would be at least five minutes late. Still, there was no point in fighting her own Type A personality. Besides, the extra time would be useful. She had lots to hash over with Viv, so getting her thoughts straight was essential, and working in the Cross Keys was always a pleasure. She loved its cosy atmosphere: the tables with their tealights, the bookcases and slouchy sofas, and the huge chimney breast with its heartening fire. Paintings hung on the walls under the glow of picture lights. The whole place smelled of woodsmoke and delectable food.

Eve stood at the bar as Gus trotted over to say hello to Hetty. Toby was serving and laughed as his schnauzer and her dachshund greeted each other. Their mismatched sizes made their ecstatic meetings comical.

Eve asked for a glass of Pinot Grigio.

'Coming up.' Toby's friendly eyes met hers as he unscrewed the bottle and poured her drink. 'You and Viv are on table nine. I'll put the wine on the tab.'

'Perfect!' The table was in a corner – shielded from draughts and away from the hubbub – ideal for a discreet chat.

She was crossing the room to take her seat when she saw Moira was in the pub. She must have decided to drag her husband Paul out again, after her abortive attempt to visit the previous Friday. Eve knew Paul only ever ate fish and chips at the Cross Keys, despite Jo Falconer's extensive menu. Matt was constantly trying to persuade her to batter something else, to trick 'the cantankerous old idiot' into trying something new, but Jo said it would be a waste of her talents. Thankfully, Moira was too thick-skinned to notice any undercurrents. The storekeeper gave Eve a smile and a little wave.

Once she was seated, Eve bent to reach her notepad from her bag, ready to list the items she wanted to discuss with Viv. When she righted herself, she came face to face with Moira and jumped.

'Paul's just nipped to the bathroom, so I thought I'd come and say hello!' Paul hardly spoke at all, so she was likely after an outlet. 'You're waiting for someone?' She glanced at the chair opposite Eve, a look of relish in her eye. She probably hoped this was a date and she'd be the first to get the details.

Eve smiled. 'Viv's joining me, but do take a seat. She'll probably be another couple of minutes. How are you?'

'Very well.' Moira slipped into Viv's place. 'Though I'm still trying to come to terms with the deaths in the village, of course. Poor dear Harry. It's unthinkable. And as for Camilla...' She sighed but then pursed her lips suddenly, one wave of emotion rushing over another. 'I still can't believe she knew all along that he... But anyway, that's all in the past now.'

Eve was still convinced Moira had written to 'Pippa' on the back of Camilla's recommendation. 'What news from the store?'

Moira frowned for a second, as though searching for the most interesting nugget she could provide. A moment later she leaned forward, her eyes bright. 'As a matter of fact, Tori Abbott came in. Now, she's been hoping that Hector will take retirement in the New Year. He works long hours and of course the pressure must be terrible, what with him being a surgeon. She said he'd promised her he'd finally "hang up his scrubs" as she put it, but he's reneged, once again. She was rather put out. In all honesty,' her voice dropped to a whisper, 'I think she's a little bored. All those hours on her own…'

She'd thought of something juicy to pass on; Eve could see it in her eyes.

'Though she's had *some* company. I saw her a few weeks before Christmas with a very good-looking young man. *A lot* younger than her.' She glanced down at her lap, then up at Eve again. 'I happened to be dropping off a large order of wine and spirits for them in our van, and I saw him through the window of her and Hector's house. Hector was out, of course…'

Eve imagined Moira checking the garage and drive for his car, then pressing her nose up against the Abbotts' window.

'The interesting thing was that he ducked out of sight when I knocked at the door. He was rather dashing, I must say. He looked almost like a pirate, with a pointed beard and an earring. And I thought I heard suggestive laughing… Though of course, I'm certain there's an innocent explanation.'

Yeah, right. And what did 'suggestive' laughing sound like?

'So as I say,' Moira gave Eve a knowing look, 'I think she's been finding ways to fill her time. And if Hector doesn't see sense and take some time off, well, he'll only have himself to blame… Oh!' She glanced up, and following her gaze Eve saw Viv had arrived. 'I'd better free up your seat!' She rose, smiling. 'See you both later.'

As she crossed back to her and Paul's table, Eve saw her exchange a friendly word with Kerry Clifton, who'd just come in with a young woman Eve didn't recognise.

Moira wasn't avoiding her any more, then. That was interesting.

CHAPTER TWENTY-EIGHT

The Cross Keys was filling up, and the background noise of laughter, chinking glasses and clinking silverware filled the air.

Viv slid into the chair Moira had vacated, and Gus trotted over and graciously allowed her to tickle his tummy.

'What would you imagine if someone talked about a "suggestive laugh"?' Eve said, when she looked up.

'Sid James.'

'Who?'

'Oh, you! Google him and "laugh" and you'll see. Weird question, anyway. What's Moira been saying?'

'Let's order first.' Eve was ravenous and she'd think better over food. 'Then I'll tell you.'

Eve went for chicken in a cream, tarragon and mustard sauce and Viv for sausages in red wine gravy. While they waited for their food, Eve relayed Moira's tale, keeping her voice down.

'Blimey.' Viv sipped the Shiraz she'd requested at the bar. 'Remind me to be on my guard when Moira's in a five-mile radius. What do you think of her story?'

Eve frowned, looked over her shoulder and lowered her voice still further. The hubbub in the pub was useful cover. 'Although she's a gossip, I've never known her to make something up. And it's interesting, in relation to the murder investigation. It occurred to me before that if Tori saw Harry misbehaving the reverse could also be true. It was just speculation, but now...'

'You think Tori could have killed Harry to hide an affair?'

'I suppose it's not impossible. She struck me as quite hard underneath her socially smooth veneer. And she has a nice lifestyle; she might be loath to lose it. If Harry crossed her, I could imagine her anger building up.' She shook her head. 'He might not have wanted money, but he thought he had all the answers. What if he advised Tori to confess her infidelity and reignite her marriage? Maybe he gave her an ultimatum: tell or be outed.' She sipped her wine. 'Harry helped Hector when his car broke down. That favour – from a man who didn't mix much with the villagers – suggests he had time for him. Perhaps he couldn't resist interfering when he saw him being duped.'

'Maybe. And she'd have to have murdered Camilla too?'

'I could see her finishing them both off, under the right circumstances. It has to be worth investigating her "young man". The question is, how to find out more without mounting a full-blown stake-out of her house?'

At that moment, Jo appeared with their food and they sat back and made appropriate reverences as Gus tensed against Eve's legs.

'How did it go with Daisy Irvine?' Viv asked, as Jo retreated.

She was gleeful as Eve admitted following her home, but turned serious when she heard about the woman's husband.

'He sounds vile. You think he knows about her affair with Harry?'

Eve prepared a forkful of chicken. 'Maybe. It would fit with what he said. I was able to dig for more information on him. He had a truck branded "Andy's Autos" and I found him on their website.'

She took out her phone, called up the garage's 'Our Team' page and showed Viv the photo of Dan Irvine. He had large biceps, an angular face and stubble in the picture.

'Mean looking.'

That had been Eve's thought too, though she'd worried she was being influenced by what she'd overheard. She needed to be objective. If he'd recently found out his wife had been having an affair, maybe he was being uncharacteristically cruel. But his tone told her otherwise. He'd been enjoying himself.

'He had a prime motive for killing Harry if he knew about him and Daisy,' Viv said, taking a sip of her wine.

'True.' Eve had been down that avenue. 'And if Irvine was the mechanic who attended to Hector's car then they might even have met, albeit briefly. But there's Camilla too. I can't see why he'd kill her unless she'd found him out – or he thought she might have – and that seems unlikely. It's possible she was vaguely aware of him, as Daisy's other half, but if she never discovered Daisy's affair with Harry, she'd have no reason to think he had a motive. He doesn't live in Saxford, and beyond that, I guess he'd have found it hard to insinuate himself into her house. My hunch is he probably didn't even know she existed. He's not the sort to socialise with his wife's work contacts.'

'Fair point.'

'But although I don't buy him as the killer, Daisy's top of my list of suspects since this afternoon. My bet is she went into her affair with Harry risking everything for another chance at happiness. If she found he'd moved onto another woman secretly, before he'd even ended their affair, her fury with him and Camilla could have pushed her over the edge.'

The shakiness Eve had felt earlier was making a comeback. 'Daisy could have talked her way into Camilla's house. If the love triangle was out in the open, she could have said she wanted to clear the air. But I don't think Camilla ever knew about Harry and Daisy, so it would have been even easier. She could have pretended she'd come about work.'

'What about timing?' Viv said. 'You think Daisy only recently found out Harry dumped her for Camilla?'

Eve wondered. 'Maybe. But even if she discovered months back, when Tori heard them rowing, I think it could still work. Camilla hinted to Moira that she had a new man and that wedding bells were on the cards. I'm pretty certain that was her own wishful thinking, but what if she made the same comment to Daisy when she visited on business? We know she liked to get people talking.'

'You think Daisy hoped her affair with Harry would lead to marriage? And hearing Camilla was about to get what she'd wanted tipped her over the edge?'

'It's possible. Dan's so mean – taking a lover at all must have felt like a huge risk. And to go that far, only to be two-timed and passed over for someone Harry *was* willing to commit to…'

'I see your point. So Camilla's tall tales might have led to her death, one way or another?'

'It seems horribly likely.'

'What about other suspects?'

'Tristan's my alternative top candidate.' She reiterated the thoughts she'd gone through with Robin, then updated Viv on the Bentleys too. 'They're well down the list as far as I can see. Kerry Clifton's more interesting though. I'm sure she's hiding something; I just need to find out what. Along with looking into Tori Abbott's affairs.'

'In all senses of the word.'

'Quite. But that research will have to wait; I have appointments in London tomorrow. Harry's editor got back to me, and I managed to track down his old school friend, Rollo Mortiville, too. He was mentioned in the *Real Story*'s so-called obituary, which was otherwise fact-free.'

Eve was pinning her hopes on Rollo. The more she understood Harry's relationships, the better she might guess who'd wanted him dead.

CHAPTER TWENTY-NINE

Eve felt pleasantly full after Jo's spectacular cooking and decided she'd benefit from an extended walk home. She circumnavigated the village green, then took Gus for a sniff around the moonlit, snow-covered ruins of the old church that still sat on St Peter's present-day grounds.

The tumbledown stone walls looked like something from a stage set, bright in the reflected moonlight. She'd been mentally running through the questions she might ask Harry's editor and school friend the following day, but now her mind drifted back to her evening at the Cross Keys. It came to rest on Moira and Kerry, who were clearly on friendly terms again. But what had caused Moira to avoid Harry's cleaner in the first place?

The issue continued to circle in her head as she let Gus back into Elizabeth's Cottage. They sat down in the cosy warmth of the sitting room, lights aglow.

'I wonder if the timing's significant. Could their issue relate to Harry? It was in the aftermath of his death…' She closed her eyes for a moment. 'And just after it came out that he was Pippa Longford.' Moira had blushed and Eve had guessed she'd been mortified to discover the agony aunt was someone she knew. Probably because of the troubles she'd shared. But also… 'Oh my goodness.' She got up suddenly, making Gus jump.

'What if Moira recommended the Pippa Longford column to Kerry, just like she did with me? After all, they're good friends.'

Her dachshund put his head on one side and followed Eve with his gaze as she paced around the small room.

'If Kerry was discreet, Moira likely had no idea she was aware of Pippa's identity. She's probably been worried ever since, in case Kerry went ahead and wrote in, revealing private information to her own boss. That could be why she's been so awkward around Kerry. It's not Moira's fault – she couldn't know – but I'll bet she felt embarrassed.'

Eve walked through to the kitchen to make herself a decaf coffee. Gus followed and, with a surreptitious look at her over his shoulder, got into his bed.

She eyed him resignedly. 'You're not going to leave me to work this out alone, are you? I think so much better with you as my sounding board.'

His eyes were half closed as she poured hot water onto the grounds in her mug.

She wasn't even conscious of her background thoughts as she took the drink to the kitchen table. It was only when specific words of Kerry's came back to her that she realised doubts were surfacing.

Had Harry's cleaner *really* known about his advice column? She fetched her notebook from her bag and flipped back through the pages until she found the record of her meeting with Kerry. At one point, Kerry had said Harry was too busy with his 'consultancy' work to get involved with the locals.

Eve sat back in her chair. At the time she'd focused on what that said about Harry's attitude towards his neighbours, but now a different element came to the fore. Kerry hadn't referred to his *advice* work, or counselling, or whatever she might call it. Automatically referring to his cover story suggested she was still getting used to the idea of his agony-aunt role.

She sipped her coffee and glanced at Gus, who was snoring lightly. *Am I making too much of this?* she asked him, silently.

But as she reread her notes, other snippets of conversation leaped out at her. Kerry had talked about posting Harry's correspondence to the *Real Story*, but who sent things by standard mail these days? Even legal documents like contracts could be managed electronically. Had Kerry made that up, to make her story more believable? Right now, it was having the opposite effect.

So, what if Kerry had lied? What if she'd had no idea Harry was Pippa until after her boss's death?

Then she might have written to the agony column after all, if Moira had suggested it…

What might her problem have been? But even as the question formed, an answer came.

Kerry said Harry was a great boss: generous, chatty and friendly. But Harry's uncle Tristan had painted a different picture. He'd talked about Harry having a short fuse: losing his temper completely when Kerry broke a glass.

What if Kerry had unwittingly written to Harry about Harry?

Heck. That could have led to a serious row. He might have threatened her with the sack… And Kerry had good reason to pretend she'd known Harry was Pippa all along – that there was no way she'd have written in. Anyone suspecting the opposite would guess there'd been a massive row between them as a result. And people who'd had a major falling out with Harry would leap up the police's suspect list.

And Eve's…

She found it hard to sleep that night as well. She tried to rationalise her feelings: she'd gone a long way on speculation; she needed facts before making too much of this. Besides, Kerry killing Harry because he'd threatened to sack her made no sense. She'd still have ended up jobless, and be guilty of murder as well. Hardly an improvement on her original situation. But of course, if she'd been mistreated for months, she might not act rationally.

The thoughts went round in her head until she got up and decided on a firm plan. She'd talk to Moira as soon as the store opened and ask her point-blank if she'd suggested Kerry should talk to Harry.

Eve wasted no time heading to Moira's store the following day. They were alone, so she was able to ask her question straight away.

'How did you know that?' Moira's eyes were wide.

Eve stood at the counter with a decoy bottle of milk – her excuse for coming in. 'I noticed you looked uncomfortable around Kerry for a few days after it came out that Harry was Pippa Longford. It made me wonder.'

Moira put her hands to her cheeks. 'Well, yes – you're quite right, I did recommend Pippa to Kerry. When I found out what I'd done and how awkward it could have been, I didn't know what to say! I mean, it was Harry's behaviour that was upsetting her, so you can see why I was anxious.' She leaned forward and lowered her voice as though Kerry might spring out from behind the magazine rack. 'The fact was, I never saw Harry's "dark side", as she called it. He was always ever so charming when we met. But even if she was overreacting, I thought writing to the agony column would get it off her chest.' She shook her head. 'I wanted to explain that I'd had no idea Pippa was Harry, and to apologise, but I was worried she might not believe me. I thought she might think I was making mischief.' She paused, then added in an embarrassed whisper: 'She can be quite fierce sometimes.'

Eve remembered the woman's row with Camilla Sullivan. 'I believe you.'

Moira took a deep breath, her ample bosom rising and falling. 'But thankfully, when I finally did mention it, and explained, she was ever so nice about it. And it turned out it was all right! She knew Harry's secret all along. She didn't tell me, of course; it would have been unprofessional.' She looked regretful for a moment and shook her head. 'But as it happens, she says Harry had turned over a new leaf anyway. Really mended his ways and started to treat her better, so the situation resolved itself.'

Very convenient, and not what Tristan says he saw on New Year's Eve. Eve went to fetch Gus from outside the store and they walked back across the green towards home.

In the kitchen, Gus applied himself to his breakfast and Eve did the same, her mind still on Kerry Clifton.

So either her relationship with Harry had miraculously improved, or, more likely, she knew it was in her best interests to claim that it had.

It raised questions about Kerry and Camilla's row in Monty's, where Kerry had continued to claim she'd got on well with her boss. Eve had typed up everything she could remember from the episode as soon as she'd returned home on Saturday. She fetched her laptop from the sitting room now, so she could review her notes as she ate her toast.

Camilla had been to look for Kerry at her home. ('I wondered what you'd do now you're jobless,' she'd said. 'I'd even thought of offering you a position, but that's out of the question now, obviously!')

What had caused her to say that? At the time, Eve had focused on the two women comparing the way Harry had treated them. It made her wonder if Kerry had also had a relationship with Harry, but the thought had always jarred. And it didn't explain that comment of Camilla's.

It sounded like Camilla's visit to Kerry's house had triggered her outburst. What on earth could she have seen, to make employing Kerry 'out of the question'?

Then, when Kerry said she'd already got a new job at Seagrave Hall, Camilla had asked if they knew the 'sort of person' they'd hired. Eve had thought she'd meant someone who had improper relations with her employer. But perhaps not... She couldn't think of anything Camilla could have seen at Kerry's house that would have hinted at an affair.

She scrolled down her notes, feeling her way. Kerry had referred to Harry as 'big-hearted'. Generous. 'Or are you suggesting otherwise?' she'd said to Camilla, inviting her to criticise the dead man, which she wouldn't. And Kerry said Camilla's level of knowledge was interesting.

What had the cleaner been referring to?

Then Camilla said Harry had despised Kerry, which would fit with what Tristan said. And Kerry mounted a counter-attack. ('It sounds as though he treated me better than you, but that's not my fault!')

Eve tried to make sense of it all. So, the row had been triggered by something Camilla had discovered at Kerry's house, from the outside. Something that made Kerry claim Harry had been 'big-hearted', and that he'd treated Kerry better than Camilla. (Though it sounded like that could have been a lie.)

Eve's talk with Kerry at the Cross Keys came back to her. She'd mentioned Harry giving her little presents: bottles of wine, knick-knacks or a book he'd enjoyed.

Big-hearted...

Was *that* what this was about? Gifts from Harry?

Gus, who'd finished his breakfast in short order, pottered up to her and put his head against her leg. 'Maybe Camilla spotted something in Kerry's house that had once belonged to Harry,' she said to him. Her heart was beating faster. 'Kerry commented on Camilla's "level of knowledge", then made the leap to her being one of his lovers. That implies she needed to have seen something upstairs at the mill, and then – maybe – that same something through a window of Kerry's cottage.'

It made sense. Goosebumps rose on Eve's arms, despite the warmth in the cosy kitchen.

Tristan said Harry treated Kerry badly, and Camilla said he'd despised her. And Moira's information backed them up. It seemed unlikely he'd habitually given her presents. Yet Kerry had been at pains to claim that he had.

Was she covering her back? Did Camilla think Kerry had stolen from Harry? Was that what she'd meant by 'the sort of person' Seagrave Hall had employed?

Eve glanced at her watch and got up, causing Gus to move back and do a giddy scamper as he sensed action.

'I'm sorry, buddy, but I'll need to be stealthy on this particular walk. I'll have to go alone.'

Kerry said she'd been given work at the hall five mornings a week. With luck, she'd be over there now. If she had any sense, she'd have moved the item Camilla had seen, but there was a chance Eve might spot it if she looked through a rear window…

For a second, Eve thought of Robin. He said he'd watch her back, but he might try to stop her altogether. She wasn't sure he'd approve.

CHAPTER THIRTY

As Eve crossed the village green for the second time that morning, she wondered what the heck she was doing.

Snooping at Kerry Clifton's cottage in broad daylight felt like madness. For a second she'd wondered about waiting until after dark instead, but by that stage Kerry would likely be home; it would be riskier still.

As she crossed to reach the top of Dark Lane, a fluttery sensation hit her stomach. The pavements were seriously treacherous now – in places the snow had compacted into sheet ice. She felt all the more conspicuous, slip-sliding along, just managing to keep her balance.

Eve opened Kerry's front gate and walked the short way up her garden path, glancing in through the window as Camilla must have done when she'd visited with her offer of work. Knocking gave Eve the chance to double-check Kerry was out. What could Camilla have recognised from the mill? Eve planned to look for anything that seemed out of place amongst Kerry's belongings.

She continued to scan the woman's front room as she knocked a second time. Hopefully it would look like she was checking for signs of life. Multiple people might have seen her walk down the lane; there was no point in trying to hide this part of her visit.

The front room – Kerry's living room – was tidy and unclut-tered, which helped. There was a green vase on the mantelpiece made of glass. She was fairly sure she'd seen something similar in John Lewis, so she guessed that hadn't caused Camilla's out-burst… Otherwise it was just a bookcase, though between the paperbacks there was the odd ornament: a glass paperweight, a pair of ceramic cats and a china figurine. She glanced over her shoulder. The lane was quiet – no flicker of movement from any of the houses. Robin lived across the way; she was especially conscious of him.

Quickly, Eve pulled her camera from her coat pocket, lifted it to the window and took a photo of the bookcase. Using her phone would have been more subtle, but she'd need a decent picture if she was going to research the ornaments later. She assumed the item Camilla had seen must be moderately valuable to have sparked her reaction. The figurine or paperweight were possibilities, but nothing in the room really shouted at her.

She guessed she was right, and Kerry had hidden the item from prying eyes. It made her job more difficult.

The positioning of Kerry's cottage was something to be thankful for. It stood on the corner of Old Yard Lane, the road that led towards Simon's stables, Blind Eye Lane, Camilla's house and the Abbotts' place. It meant the cottage was accessible on two sides.

Eve turned into the lane, keeping close to the perimeter of Kerry's property. There was no pavement and the way was rough and rutted, which made it easier not to slip. Kerry's garden was separated from the lane by a high wooden fence, with a gate set into it. Eve tried it, but it was stuck fast – bolted on the inside, she guessed.

She looked up at the fence. There was no way she'd make it over without a ladder and someone might come along and spot her anyway. It was out of the question.

She walked to the back boundary of Kerry's garden. The fence continued round the corner, but it was bordered by a narrow pathway, which meant she could follow it.

How far should Eve go? Having made her plan, she was loath to give up without at least understanding her options. Glancing over her shoulder to check the lane was still deserted, she slipped past the cottage that stood side-on to Kerry's garden, ducking to make certain she wasn't seen.

Eve walked on until she was behind the house next door to Kerry's on Dark Lane. That plot had thickly planted holly bushes along its rear boundary. She strained to see what was beyond the spiky leaves. It looked as though there were also holly bushes between that garden and Kerry Clifton's – at least in that far corner.

Eve took a deep breath. Pushing herself through wasn't an appealing prospect – and making such a concerted effort to access Kerry's garden felt worse than if she'd slipped in via the gate. But getting a look for herself, to try to see what Camilla had seen, had to be better than reporting her suspicions to Palmer and letting him wade in with all the tact of an angry rhino.

Morally, she thought it was justified, and the lesser of two evils. She couldn't just do nothing. It seemed pretty clear now that Kerry had lied about the state of her relationship with a murdered man.

Taking a deep breath, she pulled on her gloves and tugged a thick cotton beanie she'd had in her pocket down low on her head. Peering through the dense holly, she identified her best route. She ought to be able to cut through diagonally without emerging until she was at the rear of Kerry's house. Cut would probably be the operative word… She ducked her head low, so the hat would bear the brunt of the sharp leaves, and went for it.

As she emerged, she wondered what impression she'd make on her way back home. She'd felt the holly's prickles through her hat, but the sleeves of her coat didn't look damaged. That was something.

From Kerry's garden, she glanced up at the neighbours' windows. They were blank and dark. She could only hope they were out at work. She kept close to the hedge between Kerry's house and theirs as she edged her way up the garden.

At last she neared the rear of the cottage. Kerry's bedroom windows were dormers, set into the red-tiled roof; there was no way she'd get a peek up there. But downstairs, the upper portion of the panelled back door was glazed, and there were two other windows besides. She could see the swan neck of a kitchen mixer tap and a series of leafy geraniums through the first she approached. Inside, the kitchen was as tidy as Kerry's living room. There were rows of Kilner jars on a shelf over a worktop, full of flours and sugars. Kerry must be fond of baking. In Viv's book that should immediately strike her from Eve's suspect list.

To the left, if Eve craned her neck, she could see a clock over the door. It looked old, like something reclaimed from a station. It probably wasn't valuable, even if it had once been Harry's, but Eve pulled her camera from her pocket and took a photo anyway, just in case.

After that, she moved to examine the contents of the house's rear lobby through the glazed back door. It contained a rug, a pair of wellington boots, some garden clogs, and not much else.

Eve glanced at her watch and tried to steady her breathing. Ten. If Kerry worked mornings Eve ought to have plenty of time, and her train to London didn't leave for a couple of hours. But her body refused to be calmed.

She was already anticipating her return journey through the holly, with nothing to show for her efforts, when she approached the final accessible window. It gave her a view of Kerry's dining room. An oval wooden table with four dining chairs sat at its centre, and there was a matching sideboard against one wall. The room had a 1950s feel about it, right down to the retro three-ring light shade.

There was a corner dresser to Eve's left, laden with cut glass, and a fireplace dead ahead, with a fifties-style mantel clock above it.

Moving as far left as she could, to see the right-hand side of the room better, Eve caught her breath. Some shelves had come into view. They were adorned with various objects: a pot plant, a couple of vases and a pitcher. But on the eye-level shelf was a pair of candlesticks. They were silver – ornate with scrolls and some kind of detailing. To Eve, they looked rather ugly, but they were certainly unlike anything else on display. The angle was difficult, but at last she managed to get a shot that she could enlarge later, for a proper look.

At that moment, she heard a voice from the next-door garden. Then someone else shouted something about a dustbin.

Eve's heart beat on overdrive as she crept back along the garden's border.

She waited at the corner of Kerry's plot until she heard a door close, then plunged back through the holly again.

CHAPTER THIRTY-ONE

On the journey from Darsham to Liverpool Street, Eve focused on preparation for her interviews in London. The silver candlesticks in Kerry Clifton's house were high in her mind, but they would have to wait. Careful planning for the day was essential, and her excursion that morning had squeezed the time she had available.

Harry Tennant's editor at the *Real Story*, Max Keller, had agreed to meet her at his apartment, so she could speak with the whole family. It meant Eve could get their reaction to the dead man, both as a tutor and a columnist. After that, she'd quiz Harry's old school friend, Rollo Mortiville, over an early evening drink. She'd googled his picture to help her recognise him in the pub; he had a rugby player's build and the ruddy looks of someone who enjoyed their liquor.

Before she headed back to Suffolk, she'd arranged a quick meet-up with her twins too. They were London-based, and travelling to the capital without seeing them left her feeling robbed.

Viv's son Sam was going to look in on Gus, take him for a walk and give him some supper, so she was free not to rush back.

Eve thought through her objectives. She wanted to know why Keller had offered his children's tutor the columnist's job. The thought of interviewing the editor triggered a rush of adrenaline. He'd aided and abetted Harry as he'd played fast and loose with his readers' lives.

And from Mortiville, she wanted to know what Harry had been like at school, and how family issues had impacted his early life.

She developed an exhaustive list of topics to cover and, after changing trains at Ipswich, made further notes. It was only as the train rattled through the outskirts of London, past rows of terraced houses, their roofs still laced with snow, that she took out her phone and began to google antique silver candlesticks.

She found an online store where the most expensive pair, dating back to 1800, were advertised for fifteen thousand pounds. It was a lot of money, but as she sat, staring out at the blur of high streets, takeaways, bookmakers and laundrettes, she found it hard to imagine Kerry Clifton killing for that amount. There were no signs she was in trouble financially, and she had a new job already, at Seagrave Hall.

Yet – assuming the candlesticks had once been Harry's – Kerry's own claim, that he'd been generous and given her 'knick-knacks', didn't ring true either. That description hardly covered them, and why give such a generous gift if their relationship had been poor?

She went back to the idea of theft again. That seemed less far-fetched, on the face of it, but how would it have worked? If it was the candlesticks, Camilla had clearly known they were Harry's. That meant she'd seen them at the mill, so they were likely on display, not hidden away in a cupboard. Kerry couldn't have hoped to kill Harry before he noticed they'd gone.

It was a puzzle, and continued to occupy her mind as she walked from Liverpool Street Station to the address Max Keller had given her in trendy Shoreditch.

Eve found it hard not to goggle at Max and Samantha Keller's home. It was a loft-style penthouse apartment in a converted factory with a great sweeping living area, accentuated by the long varnished floorboards which spanned its entirety, from a space at one end with slouchy sofas and a pool table, on past a dining area and partitioned kitchen, through to a second, more formal seating area with enough space for two couches and several armchairs.

She bet there was a wet room with floor-to-ceiling marble and a swanky roof terrace too.

It was Max Keller who'd buzzed her up and ushered her in. He looked less shiny than his apartment: in his fifties, Eve guessed, medium height, comfortably weighty, smiling, his eyes crinkling behind almost-round glasses. He had a neat grey beard and short, tufty slate-grey hair that was beating a retreat towards the rear of his head. It suited him. If she'd had to guess his occupation, she'd have said an academic.

'Thank you for seeing me.'

'It's a pleasure, though I'm sad about the circumstances. We at the *Real Story* feel Harry's loss keenly.'

Eve imagined he'd drawn readers in droves, thanks to his controversial advice.

An elegant woman of a similar age to Max appeared from a room off the main living space. She wore loose stone-coloured trousers and a chocolate-brown roll neck which went well with her wavy chestnut hair. The tresses gleamed in the overhead LEDs.

'Most of the staff didn't know him well, of course, as he worked remotely,' Max was saying, 'but he was like a member of our family at one time.'

The woman shot him a quick sideways glance; Eve sensed she might have a different take on Harry.

'This is my wife, Samantha.'

She stepped forward and shook hands as Eve introduced herself. 'Please, come and have some tea.'

A moment later she'd produced a pot and was pouring their drinks, sorting out milk and offering sugar.

Max Keller had taken a seat on a high-backed chair, upholstered in red velvet, and had his tea brought to him. No wonder he looked so genial.

His wife seemed to float to and from the kitchen. She reappeared with some buttery teacakes. They'd been warmed and smelled great, but they wouldn't mix well with note-taking. Samantha handed Eve a plate.

'Please' – Max smiled again – 'let us know how we can help. I'd like to pay tribute to Harry in *Icon*. We've run our own article, of course, but it's only right that people should read about his contribution more widely.'

It was all publicity for the *Real Story*, but Keller might not smile quite so broadly if he knew some of the home truths Eve was planning to highlight.

She picked up her cup and took a sip. She needed to cover non-contentious subjects first, while Keller was still feeling cooperative. 'Maybe we could start off with Harry's transition from tutor to advice columnist. Could you tell me the order of events, and how everything came about?'

Max nodded at his wife. 'Samantha can tell you about the tutoring. And the boys are in their rooms, if you'd like to speak to them.'

Eve nodded her thanks.

'Jon and Jacob had been having trouble at school,' Samantha said, her hair falling forward as she leaned towards Eve. 'A horrible case of bullying that the staff failed to tackle. The culprits ought to have been expelled, but one of them had a parent on the board of governors and it was swept under the carpet. I decided to withdraw them until they started at secondary school. It involved a year's home teaching for Jon and two for Jacob.'

'You advertised the job?'

She nodded. 'And Harry seemed ideal: upbeat, with an excellent all-round education. And he'd had broad experience too. He'd worked as a management consultant for a number of years. He said he wanted a change of pace – and to do something more meaningful. I was taken with the fact that he had a psychology degree. I wondered if it might help him address the boys' problems after the bullying, but of course, I've realised since that you need specialist training for that.'

She seemed to have masterminded the arrangements. Maybe Max hadn't been home much, what with his long hours as an editor. Eve had looked Samantha up too, and found she was a lawyer, but clearly she'd made time.

'And how did it work out?'

'He was a great success, wasn't he, darling?' Max said.

Eve caught a look of reserve on his wife's face. 'The boys took to him. They were thick as thieves.' She sat forward on the white couch. Tense, Eve thought. 'I came home at lunchtimes as often as I could to check in on them. Sometimes I almost felt left out.'

Max raised an eyebrow. 'But as I said at the time, it was good that he managed to bond with them so strongly.'

Samantha said nothing.

Eve sympathised. She'd always been close to her twins; someone like Harry coming in and changing that would have been hard to take. Befriending his charges shouldn't have meant distancing them from their mother.

Eve nibbled her teacake, then made a note on her pad, leaving a horrible smear of butter behind. The lack of napkin wasn't helping. How did the Kellers' couch stay white?

'He had a way with people,' Keller said, 'that became clear early on. He was compelling, and that's what I needed for the Pippa Longford column. The readers have to be spellbound.'

The way he put it sounded unhealthy.

Keller laughed suddenly. 'But of course, he had to be a talented adviser too, and he was.' It was as though he'd read her mind. 'He saved our marriage.'

That was quite a statement. 'What happened?'

The newspaper editor sighed and leaned back in his chair. 'I was working too hard – long hours away from home. Harry could see Samantha and I were drifting apart. At last, he convinced me I needed to take matters in hand, and I've been forever grateful. I thought I was putting family first by working to keep the magazine financially stable. It gave us security, but I was forgetting the other half of the equation: the need to be a proper part of the household.

'The help he gave us enabled me to big him up when I introduced him as Pippa to the *Real Story*. Readers love a personal touch!' He was laughing again. 'Not that I gave away his true identity, of course – or any of the details.'

Just the fact that their marriage had been on the rocks… A flush came to Samantha's cheeks, and Eve wasn't surprised. It was a very personal thing to have shared with their vast readership. The success of the magazine was clearly more important to Keller than his wife's feelings and Harry had marched to the same tune.

Keller smiled as Samantha poured him another cup of tea.

Eve tried to relax her shoulders; she was finding him tension-inducing. She changed topic and asked if she might contact the people who'd written in to pay tribute to Harry. She'd love to know what their real feelings were.

Max promised to find a couple who were willing to be quoted in her article, giving him full editorial control…

After that, he told a series of innocuous anecdotes about Harry during the time he'd spent at the *Real Story*. All carefully selected, Eve imagined.

'I'll go and give the boys a shout,' he said at last, and walked off across the vast floorspace towards a staircase leading up from one corner.

Eve turned to Samantha. 'Do you think Harry knew you felt cut out as his relationship with the boys developed?'

She took a deep breath. 'I think so. He enjoyed it when people turned to him, and if it was in preference to someone else, I think it gave him a boost. I expect he revelled in his role as Pippa.'

'I can imagine.'

Samantha gripped her teacup tightly. She was probably still furious with Max for sacrificing their privacy in return for sales, which Eve could well understand.

'It must have been hard to have your marriage problems publicised.'

A bitter smile crossed Samantha's lips. 'It was. But despite the name of his blasted magazine, Max never had the real story…'

Eve held her breath. She could see how mad the woman was, and how tempted to offload. 'I can keep what you say private, if you'd prefer. Confidential reports are still useful; they help put on-the-record interviews in context.'

Samantha gave her a long, assessing look and glanced at the staircase her husband had ascended. Voices came from above. It sounded like the boys weren't keen to come down and be interviewed.

'Harry didn't just talk to Max about our problems, he spoke to me as well.' She shook her head. 'The "long hours at the magazine" weren't about editing. Max was chasing after his deputy. Just one in a long line of women at his office. He had a string of affairs; that was painfully obvious to me and to Harry too. I was already down, and Harry annexing the boys' affection made it worse. It was as though I was being rejected all round. It was only later that I guessed that had been part of Harry's plan.'

'How do you mean?'

'He wanted me low. It meant I was easier to manipulate when he gave me advice.'

The thought made Eve shiver. 'What did he recommend?'

'He said I should give Max a taste of his own medicine. He offered himself up for the job, as a matter of fact.' Her face was pale and drawn. 'It never went that far, but I was stupid. I'd lost all my self-esteem and I let him kiss me, one day in the kitchen, when the boys were playing pool during a break. They could have seen us. I've never forgiven myself.'

'He took advantage of the situation – it sounds unforgiveable.'

'It only felt that way later, when he said he'd tell Max what happened if I tried to put him off employing Harry at the magazine.' She sounded tired. 'In the end I still told Max what I thought: that it was dangerous to let Harry loose on such a wide audience. But Max wouldn't be persuaded. He said Harry had what it took to sell magazines.' She looked at Eve, unblinking. 'That was all that mattered.'

'Did Harry ever tell him about your kiss?'

Samantha shook her head. 'Max might have withdrawn his offer if he knew. Maybe I should have told him, but I... I couldn't bring myself to.'

Harry and her husband had marred her life. Eve cursed them both inwardly as the couple's teenage children clomped down the stairs. Before they got near, Samantha added: 'I'll leave Max once the boys have finished school. I'm just treading water now.'

It was hard to watch Samantha's face as her children gushed about how 'cool' Harry had been. They were flushed with their memories and Eve was glad when they retreated upstairs again.

'Back to their computer games,' Max said, with a chuckle. 'So, are we done?'

Eve leaned forward. 'I'd love to ask a last question or two about Harry's relationship with his readers.'

Keller looked wary.

'Were any of those who wrote in surprised to find out Pippa was Harry?' She wondered if the *Real Story* had had complaints.

'One or two. Even some of the sample letters we published, in fact.' Eve wasn't surprised to find they'd been quoted selectively.

'But they were full of gratitude too,' he went on. 'That outweighed everything else.'

Hmm. 'That's interesting. Only, in my experience, people don't like being fooled. It makes them feel small. What made you decide to hide his real identity?'

The editor shook his head. 'We'd always had a woman up until then, and I didn't want to upset the apple cart. So long as the results were good, it seemed unimportant to me.'

'The results *were* good, then? Only, some of his advice seemed a little… controversial. He suggested the father of a troubled-sounding teenager should leave her home alone for a long weekend to teach her a lesson.' She wondered whether to mention Melody Bentley too, but revealing she'd got proof of Harry's failings might cause him to end the interview immediately.

Keller waved a hand. 'Harry sometimes believed in giving people a short, sharp shock. You have to understand, Eve, that his correspondents were often at their wits' end. That father would have already tried the more obvious solutions to his problems.'

'Not just his problems. His daughter's. And Harry couldn't possibly know that. He gave a deliberately provocative, blanket reply without suggesting the man investigate the cause of the upset.'

Keller shook his head. 'He provided a clear solution that was easy to enact. If it didn't work, the correspondent could look at other options.'

'Did that particular advice engage your wider readers?'

'I'm sorry?'

'I just wondered how many people clicked through on the "Pippa says abandon your daughter" headline. I should imagine shock tactics like that work wonders for your stats. It must go down well with advertisers.'

'I resent what you're insinuating.'

'The thought never crossed your mind?' Eve's heart was racing. She couldn't remember when she'd last felt so furious in an interview.

Keller stood up. 'I think it's time you left, Ms Mallow.'

Eve couldn't wait.

'I will forward you copies of correspondence we've had since Harry's death,' his editor went on, 'praising his work. Many people found it life-changing.'

Too many, Eve guessed. It certainly had been for Melody Bentley.

CHAPTER THIRTY-TWO

Eve was glad of the walk through the biting cold to find the Blue Lion, where she was due to meet Harry's old schoolfriend, Rollo Mortiville. The fresh air helped bring her heart rate down and ease the fury that had blown up inside her.

The pavements were clear of snow, but the buildings were still edged with white, and there were tiny flakes in the air, drifting slowly down. The sky told her there was more to come.

As she moved swiftly, knotting the belt of her coat more tightly round her, she thought of Samantha Keller's revelation. Harry's manipulative approach showed what a dangerous man he'd been. He and his editor had formed an unprincipled alliance. Keller had been driven by money, clearly, but it must have been more complicated for Harry, who'd already inherited his father's fortune.

She glanced to her right and realised she'd arrived at the Blue Lion. Mortiville had explained you reached it via a path running under the upper floors of the pub and the adjacent building. She walked down the arched passageway and found a door with a midnight-blue lion painted on it, against a gold and royal blue background.

Once inside, she went up a narrow staircase and found the interior was reminiscent of a medieval banqueting hall. She surveyed its wooden beams, large brick fireplace and wall-mounted sconces, holding plain white candles. Up above, circles of wrought iron hung from the ceiling, each holding multiple tealights. They must need a full-time member of staff to keep them lit and replenished.

She recognised Rollo Mortiville instantly from the photograph she'd found online: broad and ruddy-faced. He rose from an ancient-looking dark wooden table to greet her. He must have looked her up too.

'Eve?' He was wearing a rugby shirt and pristine jeans. An expensive-looking wool overcoat was slung behind him on a chair and a half-drunk pint sat on the table he'd chosen.

'Rollo. Thanks so much for seeing me. Can I line you up another?' She indicated the drink.

He laughed. 'Wouldn't say no. Thanks. It's the Frontier.'

Eve ordered it for him, and a low-alcohol craft beer for herself.

'So, you were at boarding school with Harry?' She put the drinks down at their table, took a seat and reached for her notebook and pen.

He nodded. 'His dad travelled for work, just like mine, so we were both packed off, as we were motherless as well.' He grinned. 'Mine died; his remarried and hightailed it to New York. Harry had a stepmother, of course, but she hadn't a maternal bone in her body. Just as well for him, or he might have been kept at home. As it was, we had lots of fun.' He rubbed his hands together.

'It sounds like Harry's home life was pretty tough. I guess school might have felt like an escape.'

Rollo took a great swig of his pint. 'I don't think he was too bothered. He was always saying how glad he was to be free of them.'

Always saying? 'He talked about them a lot?'

Rollo's eyes widened and he put down his beer. 'Only to tell me how awful they were. He wasn't wet.'

'Wet?'

'You know, weak.'

Eve tried to keep her face neutral. If Rollo had been Harry's only friend, ready to sneer if he showed his feelings, he'd likely spent his time trying to bury them. She remembered Tristan saying Harry hadn't spoken for a week after his mother ran off to New York.

He'd minded. Who wouldn't? And she bet Rollo had been upset when his mom died too.

'The other boys tried to tease us for being motherless, but it was water off a duck's back,' Rollo went on, grinning again.

'It sounds stressful, being got at all the time. Was the antagonism ongoing?'

He'd moved onto his second pint now, picking it up in his chunky hands. 'No. Harry turned the tables on the poor saps who tried to make us feel small. Got them talking about *their* home lives. Started to point out their parents' inadequacies, and what they should do to improve their lots.'

Identifying troubles the other boys hadn't known they'd had? To make himself feel better and them worse? Maybe that was when he'd learned to manipulate people.

'He was a good listener?' He must have been adept at eliciting confidences at least. Eve had experienced that herself, and it had been the same with the Keller boys, by the sound of it. And then ultimately their mother had discussed her most personal problems with him too.

Rollo smiled and licked the beer from his lips. 'I'd never thought of it in those terms. He enjoyed it.'

Eve turned a page in her notebook, pen poised. 'It was satisfying?'

Rollo nodded. 'A game of stealth. He'd manage to extract one little detail after another, until he knew a lot. And it turned out they had plenty of woes. And then he'd give them advice. By the time he finished they were leaning on him. Hilarious!' He took another draught of his beer.

There'd been an element of control, and it sounded like he'd worked carefully to get it. For a second, Eve's mind ran to her ex, Ian, who still liked to keep tabs on her life and attempt to steer it. Harry had been on a different level, by the sound of it, but there were similarities.

'Did the other boys always do what he suggested?'

Rollo sipped his beer. 'No. He was compelling, and a lot of them hung on his words, but not all.'

'Did he mind? When they rejected his advice, I mean?' She was wondering how much the control had meant to him.

Harry's old school friend gave her a long look. 'Of course he did. No one likes being ignored, do they?'

But most people didn't expect everything to go their way. 'It hurt his feelings, that they didn't trust him?'

'Oh no.' Rollo waved a hand. 'As I say, he wasn't wet.' He snorted. 'He used to get quite angry, as a matter of fact. He often had the last laugh, though. He'd brief against them in the dorm, or drop them in it with a tutor. Whatever. He had spirit.'

He'd fought bullying by becoming a bully. Learned from his opponents' tactics and taken them further, using his skill and intelligence.

'And did you ever meet during the vacations? I understand Harry often stayed with his uncle.'

Rollo put his head back and she saw his smile broaden. 'Oh, yes! Dear old Uncle Tristan and that girlfriend of his. I can't even remember her name. Vi? Di? Something. Harry gave her advice too.'

Eve thought of Samantha Keller and wondered what was coming.

'Pointed out – in a multitude of subtle ways – the many instances where Tristan's behaviour annoyed her, and where their approaches to life didn't match. Until finally she left. Harry said he'd known they weren't built to last. Her actions proved him right of course. Classic!'

Eve was finding it hard not to lose patience with Rollo. Harry had turned it into a self-fulfilling prophecy: Vi or Di might never have left if it hadn't been for his input. How Tristan must have hated him…

She took a deep breath. 'So, I guess all the advice sessions at your school meant you weren't surprised when Harry got work as an agony columnist. Did he tell you right away?'

'Oh, yes. I knew from the start.' He chuckled. 'We'd talk about his work over a beer. And no, I wasn't surprised.'

She was quite sure Rollo would have badgered Harry for details – and not been sensitive in his responses either.

'Do you think he had a lifelong desire to help people?' She made the question over-the-top to see if she got a reaction.

Rollo gave a large shrug. 'Which of us is truly driven by altruism? And does his motivation matter? He got results and he loved his work.'

'Which elements of it?'

Rollo paused for the first time. 'People acting on his advice. We all love being taken seriously, don't we?'

Maybe his job had made Harry feel in control – something he'd probably never experienced at home. He'd first tasted it at boarding school, she guessed, when turning the tables on the other boys. The shift in the balance of power had probably been intoxicating, but nothing could excuse the way he'd behaved.

Eve had five minutes to walk round the corner to the cosy pub where she was due to meet the twins. Inside the Black Bear (all these bears and lions...), she found them gradually unwinding layers of scarf and pulling off their coats.

'Mama!' they said at once, and within a moment they were in a three-way hug-tangle.

'It's so good to see you!' She turned from Nick to Ellen. Their faces were flushed from the cold and the rush across town. 'What news?'

'All well in the highbrow land of culture,' Nick said, laughing. He worked at an arts centre. 'We're sorting out logistics for a one-woman show about life on a nuclear submarine.' He gave a deadpan look. 'It's darkly comic.'

'I can just imagine,' Ellen said. 'And the practicalities sound like a nightmare. All those crashmats for when people fall off their chairs laughing…'

'Thanks for the moral support!' Nick gave her a mock-hurt look. 'Dealt with any amusing patents lately?' Ellen worked at a law firm.

His sister kept a straight face. 'We deal with some world-changing inventions, I'll have you know!'

'Like the potato peeler hand massager, you mean?' Nick grinned as she stuck out her tongue. 'Drink, anyone?'

Two minutes later they were sitting round a small table next to a huge old-fashioned radiator, nursing glasses of wine.

'So what's new with you, Mama?' Nick said.

Eve explained about Harry's obituary. And then – reluctantly – about Camilla Sullivan's murder too.

'Wow,' Ellen said. 'I saw the first death in the paper, but I didn't register it was arson. So you're investigating again?'

'It feels like part of my job now.' She saw anxiety flicker in her children's eyes. 'But I'm taking care, as usual. And the villagers all look out for each other.'

'Except one of them's probably a murderer,' Ellen said, drily.

'Are you working with that ex-cop again?' Nick asked. 'The gardener who keeps his past a secret?'

Eve saw him and Ellen exchange a meaningful look. 'What?'

'Nothing!' Nick gave an innocent smile. 'Just wondered if you were still in touch.'

'Yes, well, I've been keeping him updated.'

'Bet you have!' Ellen said, and Nick laughed.

'Mostly by email.'

'Mostly,' Nick repeated.

Eve joke-rose from her chair. 'If you two are going to spend the whole time teasing—'

'No, no,' they both said at once. 'We'll stop. Promise.'

'How was Christmas with Ian and Sonia?' Eve asked. It wasn't her favourite topic but a subject change would be good.

Her twins glanced at each other, with a look in their eyes that she couldn't read. 'What is it?'

Nick took a deep breath. 'He hasn't been in touch?'

'Well, he announced he's coming to see me in a few days, but he didn't pass on any news.' Eve suddenly felt nervous.

'He and Sonia are splitting up,' Ellen said. 'They mentioned it quite casually just after Christmas lunch. Dad's planning to move out in the New Year.'

Suddenly, Ian's visit took on a whole new significance. Why did he feel the need to travel to Suffolk to tell her in person? Surely he wouldn't suggest they give their marriage another go? For a second she imagined him moving into Elizabeth's Cottage. Her haven. It was unthinkable.

She looked from Nick to Ellen. Were they anticipating the same thing? Would they love it if she and Ian got back together?

'We've been telling him for months now how happy you are with your new life,' Nick said.

Ellen reached over and gave her arm a squeeze. 'That's right. He must know.'

She breathed a sigh of relief. They understood.

CHAPTER THIRTY-THREE

Snippets of information swirled in Eve's head as she lay in bed that night, like the snow now flurrying down into Haunted Lane. Daisy Irvine's failed relationship with Harry vied for attention with Tristan Tennant's resentment towards his super-successful nephew. The fact that Harry had actively driven a wedge between him and his girlfriend made Eve deeply uneasy. And in the background Kerry Clifton hovered, with a pair of candlesticks that might once have been Harry's.

Eve came to in the early hours, with thoughts of Kerry uppermost.

She'd come up with a fresh objection to the possible theft of the candlesticks. Not only would Harry have likely noticed their absence immediately, it would have been hard for her to carry them off the premises undetected, unless he'd been out. But Kerry had talked about him following her round that last day; it didn't sound like he'd left the mill. And the police had concluded he'd stayed home too, according to Robin.

So, smuggling the candlesticks out would have been an issue. They'd be too large to fit in Kerry's handbag, while bringing a more spacious carrier would have looked suspicious… And she'd have to have packed them up carefully too – to protect them and stop them clanking together as she walked out. Would she really have risked all that when Harry was home?

Eve turned over in bed again, away from the window. Her nose was cold. The heating had gone off for the night and it had been forecast to drop below freezing by morning.

Maybe she was missing something. She needed to review Kerry's actions in context. What had been happening, just before Harry died?

She'd have been getting the mill spick and span for his party, Eve guessed. It would have been the first time most of the villagers had been inside since Harry moved in. She might have done extra things that she wouldn't normally…

Eve sat up in bed. *Extra things.* Like having the candlesticks cleaned, maybe? She frowned. Her parents had a pair of silver candlesticks they brought out on special occasions. She'd been allowed to polish them as a child. It had been part of the ritual of preparing for Thanksgiving and Christmas. The thought brought back the tingle of excitement she'd always felt when her father got out the special wadding, impregnated with cleaner, that they used as polish. She could still remember its smell and the way it smeared over the metal. You had to rub and rub it and then suddenly the precious metal went from smeary to bright and sparkling.

Surely that's what you did with silver? You didn't have to take it anywhere. Kerry could have done that at the mill.

But the more she thought about it, the more Kerry taking them somewhere to have them polished explained the facts. She wouldn't have had to sneak them out. Maybe Harry had been particular about his belongings.

Kerry might have looked at the candlesticks, sitting in her house, waiting to be taken to the local antiques firm, say, and decided she'd had enough of Harry's bad treatment. Maybe her murderous thoughts had come from his behaviour, and the candlesticks had been a bonus. Or perhaps someone else had killed Harry and she'd decided to hang onto them, hoping no one would be any the wiser. She might have popped them on the mantelpiece in her front room, little thinking that Camilla would come calling and press her nose against the window.

Not that I have any room to talk.

There was only one antiques firm Eve knew of in the vicinity: a place out on the Blythburgh road. It had changed hands the previous spring, when an offshoot of a long-established company had taken over.

She'd call on them in the morning, and see what she could discover. Turning over one last time, she finally managed to sleep.

The following day, Eve stood in the muffled hush of a snowy world, looking at the sober frontage of Barnes and Sons Antiques. There was no way of knowing if the candlesticks in Kerry's house had really been Harry's, let alone whether he'd asked this firm to clean them. But over breakfast a plan had formed in her head. She thought she could just about get away with her enquiries.

It was interesting to see the store now it was under new owner-ship. Before, it had been dark and full of oddities. Now it was classic in style, with cream walls that offset the beautifully polished and upholstered items of furniture on display. The price tags were eye-watering; the place had definitely gone upmarket. Eve loved old furniture, but she actively preferred items that bore the marks of time. Each dent told a story – harking back to its past. That mattered.

All the same, the objects in the store were impressive: rich, dark wood, sparkling crystal, and gold that gleamed.

Beyond, behind the counter, was a man Eve guessed to be in his mid-sixties. He stood ramrod straight, and was dressed formally in a dark suit, crisp white shirt and tie. As he wished her good morning, he looked like he was suppressing a salute.

Eve walked up to the counter and introduced herself. 'I'm writing Harry Tennant's obituary. You probably read about his death – the horrific fire up at the mill?' She proffered her card, and an email from *Icon*, confirming the commission.

'Of course.' The white-haired man stepped forward. 'Such a tragedy.'

Eve mentally crossed her fingers behind her back. 'I was wondering if you knew much about his passion for antiques? Hobbies always provide a fascinating extra angle on a subject. I was given this photograph of some candlesticks' – she passed him a printout of the one she'd taken the day before – 'I understand they were part of his collection, so I was curious to know more.'

The man peered at the picture, which Eve had edited. She hoped she'd managed to lose the reflections in Kerry's window...

He nodded gravely. 'Oh yes, the Paul de Lamerie pair. George II. 1740s. I can see why you'd assume he was a collector having seen that. It's a passion of yours, too?'

Eve swallowed. Her mouth always went dry when she lied. 'I find antiques fascinating, but I'm very inexpert. All the same, I was convinced these looked special.' She hesitated. 'Someone mentioned you'd cleaned them, so I thought Mr Tennant might have talked to you about his love of antiques more generally.'

'Ah,' the man sighed heavily. 'I wish I'd had the pleasure, but no. A lady who worked for him booked them in to be cleaned, but she wasn't able to bring them, due to the fire. She rang to cancel. Silver has a high melting point, but they'll need timely attention of course. Perhaps their new owner will allow us to look after them, once they've been recovered from the mill.'

Eve's breath caught. Kerry had her tracks covered. If that never happened, she doubted Barnes and Sons would question it.

'So it's not clear if Mr Tennant was a collector more generally?' Eve thought she'd better stick with her fake enquiry.

'I'm afraid not.'

She paused. 'I'm sorry – this is going to sound very ignorant, and it's nothing to do with the obituary. I was just curious about the cleaning process.' She explained how she'd polished her parents' candlesticks as a child. 'I'd assumed people did their own.'

She'd completely lost his respect now, she could see. His eyes widened, making his eyebrows shoot up and his brow crease into multiple furrows.

'Only a qualified expert should even consider taking care of a pair of Paul de Lamerie candlesticks!'

It was as though she'd suggested people ought to perform their own open-heart surgery.

'They're very valuable, I suppose?' Eve said. He'd already written her off as a philistine. She might as well show the extent of her ignorance.

The man made a sound like an anxious horse. 'My dear lady, they are worth upwards of three hundred and fifty thousand pounds.'

CHAPTER THIRTY-FOUR

Over lunch, Eve couldn't get the value of Harry Tennant's candlesticks out of her head. Kerry Clifton had had them in her possession legitimately – temporarily at least – ready to have them cleaned, and probably only Harry knew that. After the fire, she'd rung the antiques firm to cancel, letting them think they'd been buried in the ruins of the mill. Had she known how much they were worth? Maybe she'd investigated. Eve assumed Harry must have given her their details so she could book them in to be cleaned.

Back at home, Eve googled and found a similar pair that had sold at auction for £375,000. What if Kerry had sat in her cottage, looking at them, with Harry's latest criticisms ringing in her ears? The perfect way to steal from him had landed in her lap, so long as she was prepared to stoop to murder.

Tristan Tennant was Harry's heir, down to inherit the candlesticks, but that was only a problem for Kerry if he knew about them. Eve had already guessed they'd been on display in Harry's bedroom. It would explain why Kerry said Camilla's 'level of knowledge' was interesting, and then instantly decided she must have been one of Harry's lovers.

But even if the candlesticks were family heirlooms, and Tristan knew they existed, he probably had no idea whether Harry still owned them. It was likely he'd never question their absence, especially if he didn't know their value. And by that stage Kerry could have quietly sold them on.

Even the killing of Camilla made sense. She was probably the only person who'd discovered Kerry's secret. The timing was bad –

the row at the teashop made Kerry an obvious suspect – but she'd had no choice. She was faced with giving herself up, or eliminating the threat urgently. She hadn't acted the night of the argument, but that could still fit. Murderers were human: she'd have needed space to digest the latest development and nerve herself up to kill a second time. She could have talked her way in, pretended she was penitent and asked for advice on going to the police, perhaps. She was lucky Camilla hadn't already reported her, but she was likely waiting until Palmer was back in on Monday. She'd been the sort who'd prefer to talk to the top brass, and even if she'd thought Kerry was a thief, Eve guessed she hadn't suspected her of murder. If she had, it would have been obvious during their argument at Monty's. Eve bet Camilla had thought of Kerry as small fry.

She shook her head. She needed to work out how to proceed. The urgency left her feeling twitchy.

When she arrived at Monty's to work her session that afternoon, Eve found Viv looking shifty.

'What's up?' she said, walking through the kitchen to hang her coat up in the office.

'New craft market offering.'

Monty's craft section opened off the rear of the teashop. When Eve had first seen it, it had offered an eclectic mix of wares: from the exquisitely beautiful (such as Daphne's crackle-glaze vases) to the downright suspect (a rather odd collection of knitwear, some dark-brown coasters, and something unidentifiable covered with feathers).

When Viv took her on, Eve had put herself in charge of vetting the artists they displayed. She had all the mealy-mouthed tact needed to turn them away if necessary. Viv didn't have the skills; she said yes to everything, then tried to hide the iffy stuff at the back of the displays. Neither of them opted for brutal, hurtful honesty, so they had that in common.

Eve's approach meant the craft market was now full of tasteful wares, and Viv's creativity ensured they were displayed to best advantage, but there were still moments of danger when Eve was absent.

She walked swiftly back through to the kitchen. 'You didn't make any promises, I presume?' It might go either way. It all depended on the confidence and pushiness of the individual.

'I don't *think* I did.' Viv was avoiding her eyes. 'I was tactfully enthusiastic.'

Eve felt her shoulder muscles knot. 'Did they leave a sample? Or photographs?'

'I took one sample. To try to sell. But I definitely didn't promise to take any more.'

Deep breaths. In, two three, out, two three. 'Where is it?'

'I hate it when you use that quiet, dangerous voice.' Viv pulled her best forlorn face. 'And now you're doing that thing with your mouth. Like a snake just before it swallows its prey…'

Eve shot her a look. 'You're being melodramatic. There's no way I could eat you whole. Let's see, then…'

Viv bent down to reach a bag that sat on the kitchen floor. She pulled out a pearlescent cardboard box from inside and lifted the lid.

There was a moment of silence.

'I thought mermaids were supposed to be beautiful,' Eve said at last. 'It looks like Gollum.'

'Aha!' Viv smiled brightly. 'You could tell what it was. Not like when Moira's sister brought in those weird misshapen bits of wood.'

'Can you imagine this alongside Daphne's ceramics? It'll put the customers off their food. And it'll do that for months and months, because it won't sell.'

'You're so harsh!'

'But also correct.'

Viv sighed. 'Yes… I do see that. But the artist – Faye, her name was – was so keen and eager and I, well…'

Eve put her shoulders back. 'Give me her details and I'll sort it out.'

'How?'

'That will require some thought. You owe me one! But I have a plan for the future. I'm going to get business cards printed with my name and Monty's branding. That way you can hand one over next time someone comes and tries to take advantage of your good nature. We can put "Crafts Buyer, Monty's" on them. Suit you?'

Viv nodded and screwed up her eyes as though she was expecting further criticism. Eve decided to let her stew.

Thirty seconds later she opened one eye. 'So what's new?' She followed suit with the second. 'You saw Angie's back? With her and Tammy serving, you'll have time to tell me your news while you make up some marmalade spice cakes. I'm going to sort out more of the red velvet sponges. Then we'll go through and help with the masses.'

Eve had made the spice cakes before. She began to assemble the ingredients. 'For your ears only, right?'

'Of course.'

She told her about the candlesticks in Kerry Clifton's house.

Viv's eyes were like saucers. 'Blimey!'

'I know.'

'Have you told the police?'

Eve shook her head. 'Not yet; I only guessed why she had them and found out their value this morning.' *And you wouldn't have got there without trespassing. What will Palmer make of that?* 'I want to talk to her first – get her side of the story.' Viv was looking anxious. 'Don't worry. I'll pick somewhere safe, out in the open. Or enlist backup.' She sighed. 'Even if I hadn't gathered my evidence by stealth, I couldn't just feed her to Palmer. I've heard he already suspects her, after her row with Camilla. He'd decide it was case closed if he knew about the candlesticks.'

'True. But you have to admit, she looks guilty as hell.'

Eve shrugged. 'On the face of it. But then so does Daisy Irvine.'

Eve scanned the marmalade cake recipe and moved to weigh the butter and caster sugar.

'Are you tempted to tell the police about Daisy?' Viv asked.

'Just a minute.' Eve was still weighing. Viv gave an impatient huff. She already had her ingredients in her mixing bowl and was busy with a whisk.

Eve cut off a chunk of butter and glanced at the scale. Spot on! She tried not to look too smug. Viv wouldn't get it.

'I'm not sure it's right to tip Palmer off about her yet either. Her affair is definitely significant, but if I go to the authorities I'll be putting her marriage and career in jeopardy, even if she turns out to be innocent.' She began to cream the butter and sugar together. 'And it's not fair to be careless with information about her or Kerry. Harry controlled people – meddled with their lives. It'll be unbearable if someone who's innocent suffers even worse after his death because of how I handle things.'

'I'd never thought how morally complex this sleuthing business is.'

Eve gave her a wry look. 'Neither had I.'

'So, what's your plan?'

'I need to find out more about Daisy, and her husband as well. Like you said, his motive for killing Harry was as strong as hers, but I still can't see how he'd have identified Camilla as a threat. All the same, he's as mean as heck. I might take my car along to Andy's Autos and see if I can get him talking. If I work my career into conversation, I can drop Harry's name in. Watching his reaction might tell me whether he knew about his wife's affair. If he had no idea, then he's off the list.' It wouldn't get her any further with

Daisy, though. She needed to find a way to move that part of the investigation forward.

Viv was adding in her eggs with barely a glance at her hands. 'Don't chat if you're alone together at the garage. How would I cope if I lost you? I'd be at the mercy of every kitsch crafter in the county.'

'Thanks so much for your concern!'

'So you're digging for more on Kerry, and Daisy and Dan Irvine.'

Eve nodded. 'And Tristan Tennant.' She filled her in on her trip to London, including the news that Harry deliberately frightened his uncle's girlfriend away. 'He's right up there with Daisy and Kerry as a suspect – though I've heard the police are giving him a load of attention, so I guess it's reasonable to focus my efforts elsewhere. I feel I've got more chance of making headway with Kerry than they have, so I'll keep going.'

The marmalade spice and red velvet cakes were safely cooling, and Eve was near the end of her shift, when she spotted Kerry Clifton through Monty's window, trudging across the village green, a bag of groceries over her arm. She must have been to Moira's.

If Eve wanted to catch her alone for a quick word, the situation was perfect. She'd been feeling uneasy about her secret knowledge all afternoon. What if her decision to keep the police in the dark had unforeseen consequences?

'You look like a dog that wants to be let out,' Viv said, following her gaze.

'Hmm. Thanks. You know I said you owe me, after the Gollum mermaid debacle…?'

A look of glee came into Viv's eyes. 'You're seriously planning to run out on a session you promised to work? You never do that! I love it. It makes you so much more relatable.'

Eve gave her a tired look.

Viv glanced around the teashop. Tammy and Angie had left for the day, but there were only two tables still occupied. 'Go on! She'll be gone otherwise. I think I'll cope.'

CHAPTER THIRTY-FIVE

Kerry Clifton was crossing from the village green to reach the top of Dark Lane by the time Eve caught her. Harry Tennant's former cleaner must have sensed something from Eve's expression. She no longer looked like a friendly Mrs Tiggy-Winkle; there was an irritable set to her jaw.

'What do you want?' She carried on walking and Eve matched her pace.

She hadn't anticipated such an early opportunity to tackle the woman, but ideas for how to do it had marshalled themselves as she neared her quarry.

'It's just an odd thing that's come up while I've been researching Harry's obituary. One of his contacts told me he was a keen collector of antiques.' She might as well reuse the story she'd invented that morning. 'It's always interesting to mention a subject's hobbies in an obituary, so I decided to stop by at Barnes and Sons. As the nearest dealers, I guessed they might have talked with him about his passion.'

Side on, Kerry Clifton's poker face was pretty good. It was unfortunate for her that the cheek nearest Eve was twitching…

'We ended up talking about a pair of Paul de Lamerie candle-sticks Harry owned.' Well, that was true, as far as it went. 'I gather you'd booked them in to be cleaned.'

They were part way down Dark Lane, just yards from Kerry's house. Eve needed to make her point before the woman disappeared inside.

She took the plunge. 'That's what you and Camilla Sullivan argued about, at the teashop, isn't it? She'd seen them through your window, I guess. She knew Harry would never have given them to you as a present. Even if he'd been a kind and generous boss, a gift worth three hundred and fifty thousand pounds would be quite something. But he wasn't kind and generous, was he? Tristan told me about the cruel way he treated you.' She'd leave Moira out of this. 'Yet you wanted me to believe otherwise. You hoped everyone would accept he'd given you the silver as a token of his gratitude. It might have worked if I hadn't found out their value.'

Kerry Clifton's lips had gone white. 'You've fathomed a lot out.'

'It fitted with everything Camilla said.'

The woman took a deep breath. 'Every single thing I do blows up in my face!' Her tone was exasperated, upset – injured even. It wasn't what Eve had expected.

'Taking the job with Harry in the first place was a disaster. When he was being friendly and chatty, pestering me for the neighbourhood gossip, he was good value. But his temper could turn in an instant. He hated anyone questioning his judgement and he liked everything just so. Might as well have worked for a perishing dictator! And then, when I finally decided to get some advice about what to do, I wrote to Pippa Longford! And Pippa was Harry!'

She tugged distractedly at her hair with a gloved hand.

'What was his reaction?'

She'd gone still, her eyes on the middle distance, face pale. 'He laughed. But not out of amusement. I think it was more' – she paused a moment – 'anticipation. He was thinking ahead. He was perfectly calm on that occasion – as though he'd got what he wanted. He said to me: "Ah, dear Kerry. What a foolish thing to have done. But don't worry, there'll be no recriminations. At least, not today." Then he smiled in a way that put the fear of

God into me. It was like he was promising to get his own back when I least expected it. I knew I'd be looking over my shoulder until that happened.' She shook her head suddenly and put her shoulders back. 'I should have walked out then and there, told him to keep his precious job. But I needed the income. It was a bit of luck that the vacancy at Seagrave Hall came up. I planned to walk out on Harry dramatically, in order to take it, but I didn't get the pleasure.'

It explained how she'd landed the new job so quickly. It would be easy enough to check she was telling the truth about the timing.

'But when I heard Harry had been killed,' Kerry went on, 'I realised I still had the candlesticks. He'd been careless with them. Didn't even know how much they were worth until I emailed Barnes and Sons a photo to get a quote for the cleaning job. And he let me take charge of them, for all his horror when I smashed one of his damned glasses. He was too lazy to drop them off himself. And there they were, sitting on my mantelpiece...'

'So you cancelled the job, knowing everyone would assume they were somewhere in the rubble at the mill?'

She held her head up high and nodded. 'I didn't think Harry's Uncle Tristan would miss them. He'll be loaded now he has his nephew's fortune: all the money that was handed down by Harry's father. That travel business must have been worth a bomb. I thought the candlesticks would be fair compensation for the rotten way Harry treated me. But no. Camilla nosy-beak Sullivan had to spot them through my window. And they weren't clearly visible, let me tell you! She must have craned her neck to see them!'

Eve thought of her own spying at Kerry's place and hoped her blush wasn't obvious.

Kerry's shoulders slumped. 'I think I knew even before her visit that it wouldn't do. Camilla's outburst just popped the lovely bubble I'd been blowing.'

What did she mean? Eve waited as Kerry tugged open her bag and pulled out her phone. She dragged off her right glove, fiddled with the screen then showed it to Eve. A text message, sent on Saturday evening, after her row with Camilla, and before her murder on Sunday night.

Dear Mr Tennant – so sorry for your loss. I wanted to let you know I have some candlesticks of Harry's that I will need to pass on to you. They were due to be cleaned so escaped the fire. Apologies for the delay in getting in touch. It took me a while to get hold of your number. Yours, Kerry Clifton.

She scrolled down so Eve could see the reply.

Dear Kerry, thank you for your sympathy and for letting me know about the candlesticks. Please may I pick them up when I'm in Saxford next Friday? Perhaps you could let me have your address? Kind regards, Tristan.

Eve recognised his mobile number. It was the one he'd given her for any follow-up queries, and was distinctive, with three consecutive fours in it.

'I don't reckon he knows how much they're worth either,' Kerry said, bitterly. 'Otherwise he'd have probably driven straight over to fetch them. I'm hoping he won't take them to Barnes and Sons for a valuation. There'd be questions asked after what I told them.'

Eve shook her head. 'I'm sure they'd just put that down to a breakdown in communication. It's candlesticks disappearing that would ring alarm bells, not them materialising unexpectedly.'

Kerry huffed and nodded. 'Hopefully. That would mean something going right for once. A small compensation for a series of kicks in the teeth.' She dipped her head, then looked Eve in the eye. 'I'm sorry if you think ill of me, but I can't claim I'm sad that Harry's dead, or that I would have felt guilty about keeping the candlesticks. I just guessed Camilla would tell the police. This way I could pretend I'd always intended to give them back.'

Eve nodded. 'Can I ask you one more thing?'

The woman arched her eyebrows. 'I'm sure you're going to, anyway.'

'I remember you telling me you smelled the perfume of two different women in Harry's bedroom – suggesting he was having an affair with them both.'

Kerry's expression was sour. 'It's not my job to protect his reputation. Camilla was one, I reckon, or at least she wore the same perfume, and went beetroot when I mentioned it.'

'I wondered about the timing. Do you think Harry strung both women along for a while?'

Her expression cleared for a moment. 'Not that long. A week or so maybe? Camilla won out. I carried on smelling her perfume right up until he died. The other one wore something more cloying. I remember thinking, maybe Ms Cloying found out about Ms Classic and walked out.'

It all fitted with Tori Abbott's account of Harry and Daisy's row in the early autumn. She'd guessed they'd broken up. Eve could tick her cross-check off her list.

Kerry gave her a quick look. 'I've heard about you, you know. Moira told me you've done some investigative stuff before.'

'It's hard not to piece things together when you have information in front of you.'

'I can imagine.'

Viv was standing in Monty's, peering out of one of the bay windows. Eve hoped the remaining customers hadn't wanted her attention, given it was trained on the village green. She moved towards the door as Eve crossed the snow-covered grass.

'Well?' she said, as Eve whisked inside, shutting out the bitter cold.

Eve did a quick check of the tables. The last two groups were draining their pots of tea. 'Innocent explanation,' she replied in an undertone.

Viv raised her eyebrows. 'Really?'

'Well, semi-innocent.'

Viv moved behind Monty's counter, further from the occupied tables, and Eve followed. 'Explain.'

She updated her quietly. 'Kerry was certainly tempted to do the wrong thing. And of course, she could have spun me a line, if she'd killed Harry to get her hands on the candlesticks, then regretted it and wanted to make herself look innocent. But' – she closed her eyes for a second and pictured the woman – 'the way she talked was wrong for that. She wasn't at all nervous – defiant, more like. And mad as heck at fate. She thinks the candlesticks would make a lot more difference to her life than to Tristan's.'

'She's probably right on that score, given he'll get Harry's cash anyway.'

Eve nodded. 'And ironically enough, Tristan might be the killer, which she probably realises. But she'd have found it difficult to sell them on, I guess, even if Camilla never reported her to the police. People would have asked questions; they're just too valuable.'

When the last customer left the teashop, Eve went through to the office.

'What are you doing?' Viv followed her.

'I'm going to email the Gollum mermaid artist.'

'What on earth will you say?'

'I've just remembered there's a fantasy crafts store a little way up the coast. I'll tell her our clientele aren't right for her and point her in their direction.'

'Nice. I like the idea of palming her off on someone else.'

Eve gave her a quelling look. 'I genuinely think her work will fit right in there. The only trouble is' – she opened her email – 'the mermaid might end up next to an actual Gollum figurine. There'll be no hiding the likeness then.'

Back at Elizabeth's Cottage, Eve gave Gus his supper and settled down to prepare hers.

'So, I think Kerry Clifton's off the suspect list,' she said to his wagging tail, as he tore through his food and she fetched onions from the fridge. 'I don't think she'd have hung onto Harry's candlesticks, even if Camilla hadn't challenged her – she was just sorely tempted.'

She picked out a sharp knife from the kitchen drawer and began to chop the onion. 'But Daisy Irvine and Tristan Tennant are still top of the leader board. The trip to Andy's Autos tomorrow might tell me where to place Daisy's husband, Dan. And I still need to do more work on Tori Abbott. Maybe Moira's story about a young lover is true. And she *could* have sneaked out of the friends' house where she and Hector were staying to set fire to the mill.'

She sat down a short while later to a light pasta supper with white wine and mushroom sauce, her laptop open on the table in front of her. How could she follow up on Tori? Idly, she put the woman's name into Google. Some articles about opposition to a local planning application came up. Tori had been on the steering committee protesting against the building work: a new housing development on the outskirts of Saxford. In the end, the protesters had won the day.

Looking further down the Google results she found references to the woman showing her horse in county competitions. She clicked through to look at the photos, but of course, Tori would never allow herself to be caught on camera with a lover. Eve took another mouthful of mushroom and pasta. She'd descended into the realms of nosiness and was enjoying it.

A moment later, she switched from looking at general search results for 'Tori Abbott' to images only, skimming past photographs of other Toris and homing in each time she recognised the subject.

She'd almost finished her pasta when she found one that made her pause. She hadn't really expected to find anything useful, but there was just a chance she'd been wrong. Needing a larger version of the image, she clicked through to the website it came from, which belonged to a county magazine.

Gus was sitting at her feet, under the kitchen table, and she bent down to fuss him. 'Don't look now, but I think I might have found Mrs Abbott's fancy man.'

A moment later, she'd printed out a copy of the image. First thing tomorrow, she'd check it with Moira.

CHAPTER THIRTY-SIX

Eve's first mission on Thursday was to show Moira the photo she'd found online the night before. After that, she was going to take her Mini Clubman to Andy's Autos, the garage where Daisy Irvine's horrible husband Dan worked.

The thought had made her stomach screw up over breakfast and she had indigestion. But he and Daisy were key suspects and the visit made sense as a next step.

Dropping in on Moira felt very relaxed by comparison. She secured Gus's leash to the hooks outside the store. 'Won't be long!'

Her dachshund gave her a doubtful look.

'Well, okay, it does depend on how chatty Moira is.' Mildly chatty, five minutes. Intense, dial that up to ten.

She ruffled Gus's fur, then stood up straight and pushed the door open, setting the bell jangling.

'Oh, Eve!' Moira said. 'How are you getting on? I was just this minute talking about you to Deidre Lennox. I said I was bound to have an update for her soon!' Moira needed her gossip supply topped up regularly. 'Have you reached any conclusions about poor dear Harry and Camilla's deaths?'

'Not yet.' She wasn't going to confide. She might as well stand on the roof of St Peter's with a megaphone. 'I do have something to check with you, though.' She took the printout she'd prepared the night before from her bag and put it on the counter.

'Ooh!' Moira put a hand over her mouth, showing off her plum nail polish. 'Where on earth did you get this, Eve?' She was quite breathless. 'That's him! The young man I told you about who ducked out of sight when I went to deliver the Abbotts' shopping!'

She was practically licking her lips.

Eve kept her expression neutral, though it wasn't easy. 'According to the magazine who took the photo, that's Tori's son.' Eve guessed she'd identified the right man, as soon as she saw the pointed beard and earring. He'd clearly rebelled against his parents' conventional habits. It instantly felt more believable than Tori falling for someone like that. If Eve had been brought up by the Abbotts, she'd have rebelled too.

Moira looked thunderstruck, a blush creeping up her neck. 'Really? Oh, but I thought… But then, why did he duck out of sight? That's ever such odd behaviour. And there was the laughter too. I feel quite embarrassed now. But I really did think…'

'Well,' Eve smiled guilelessly, 'you always said you were convinced there was an innocent explanation.'

Moira blinked. 'Ah, well, yes, of course. It's just… But no, you're right. Him being her son – well, that makes *much* more sense.'

Eve had rarely seen her look so disappointed. Her brow was furrowed; it was clear she was still wrestling with the facts.

'Maybe he was in his pyjamas or something,' Eve said. 'That could be why he ducked out of sight. And why he laughed. People do giggle when they're embarrassed.'

Moira smiled herself at that point. 'Well, of course, that's true. And it was a morning delivery – late morning. So maybe he hadn't yet dressed and was feeling ashamed about it.'

Privately, Eve wondered if Tori had warned her son about Moira: how long he might have to spend on the doorstep, answering her questions, if he showed his face. He'd probably been laughing like a child playing hide-and-seek, when he realised he'd almost been caught.

Moira fanned her face with her hand. 'Anyway, that's that.'

Eve managed not to laugh until she got outside the store and halfway across the village green with Gus. *Not bad.* But her mirth evaporated at the thought of her next errand. There was nothing funny about Dan Irvine.

Things got off to a promising start at Andy's Autos. The drive over had forced Eve to focus on the snowy lanes, but in the back of her mind, the details of her planned approach had settled in her head.

By the time she entered the garage front office she felt in control, which was just as she liked it. The place was quiet too. No other clients currently, and two men on the desk, wearing air-force-blue overalls. One was leaning over an open newspaper, the other doing something on his phone. Eve recognised the one with the phone as Dan Irvine, from the 'Our Team' page of the outfit's website. It was the other who glanced up first, which wasn't ideal, but when Dan raised his eyes from his screen a moment later he stirred himself more quickly than she'd imagined. She turned to him, hoping the second man would return to his reading, and the tactic worked.

'What can we do for you?' Irvine said, his eyes on hers. It was slightly disconcerting, the way he looked at her so intently.

She sighed. 'I'm not sure. My "check engine" warning light's coming on intermittently.' She turned to indicate her Mini Clubman, which was visible through the glass front of the reception area. 'It's showing yellow, not red, but I was worried about driving further until I'd had it looked at.'

Had she rattled off her explanation too fast? Made it sound rehearsed? She'd found it harder than usual to pull off; it was the way he looked at her.

His gaze was still steady. 'What's the power like? Any stuttering as you put your foot down?'

She had to swallow before she answered; couldn't help herself. 'No, nothing like that.' She wanted the chance for a quick chat while he performed some simple inexpensive checks, not to shell out loads for a proper once-over.

His expression was meditative. 'All right. I'll have a look.' He turned to his colleague, who was still behind the desk. 'You might as well go off for your break, Jim.'

The man picked up his newspaper. 'Cheers.' A second later he disappeared through a door to a back office. Eve found herself hoping he'd stay on site. She shouldn't have a reason to fear Dan Irvine. He didn't know her from any other local. Yet the very air around them seemed laced with tension.

He held the reception door open for her. Ahead, she could see his reflection in her Mini's windows, towering behind her. His neck looked almost as wide as one of its hub caps. She was reminded of a bull and felt anxious for Daisy Irvine. She wouldn't feel safe, living with a man like Dan.

He came round to her left side as she reached the car. 'It's unlocked?'

'Yes.'

He pulled the door open. 'I'll need to plug in a scan tool, just under the steering wheel.' He crouched down, but his eyes were still on her. 'Haven't seen you here before.'

It was the sort of opening Eve was looking for. 'No, I moved to Suffolk quite recently. I wanted to get out of London, and as I'm freelance, I could be flexible.' She was one step closer to being able to mention her profession and her current subject. She'd make sure she was watching Irvine's eyes when she did.

But the mechanic had paused, tool in hand. 'Here less than a year?'

The question was oddly specific. She answered as smoothly as she could. 'Around sixteen months.'

'Where'd you get your MOT done?'

'Martin's.' She didn't like the look in his eye.

'So what made you choose us today?'

Thank goodness she'd hashed through the questions he might throw at her. 'Martin's were busy. Driving in the snow makes me nervous at the best of times. I didn't want to risk carrying on if the car has a fault.'

He never once broke eye contact. 'I see.'

Why did she get the feeling he didn't believe her? It was a reasonable explanation. She fought the urge to lick her dry lips.

At last, Irvine turned and plugged in the tool, but of course, she knew what it would tell him. The code would say a problem with the fuel cap. He'd find the cap was loose, because she'd loosened it, but not cracked, because she knew that it wasn't. He'd tighten the cap, charge her for his time, then send her on her way.

By this point, she'd intended to be having a cosy chat about his life at the garage, and hers as an obituary writer, and what an intriguing proposition Harry Tennant was.

'What's it like working here?' she said. She could at least try to get her project back on track.

He glanced at the screen on his scanner, then up at her. 'Fuel cap.'

It looked like he wasn't going to answer her question. He went straight to the cap, peered at it, then screwed it on, forcefully. '*Someone* hadn't tightened it.'

'Must have been like that since I last filled up,' Eve said. 'Now I think about it, that was when the light started—'

'Why were you hiding outside my house on Monday evening?'

She caught her breath. 'Excuse me?'

'I saw your car parked down the lane when I went upstairs. My wife and I heard something in the bushes, and the cat yowling. At the time I thought I'd seen a shift in the shadows next to the moggy. But when she appeared I brushed it aside. It was only when I went up to the bathroom and saw your Clubman from the window that I wondered. You drove off a moment later, but now, here you are again.' He took a step closer. 'What's your game?'

She mustered her best I'm-outraged-at-the-tone-you're-taking voice. 'That was your house? How was I supposed to know? Frankly, I've no need to tell you what I was doing there. I wasn't on your property.' She folded her arms for good measure and fixed him with her stare.

Dan Irvine gave her a long look. 'You'd better go, now your fuel cap's sorted. Forget the bill – just get lost.'

Eve got into her car with as much dignity as she could muster. She felt hot and prickly all over, and her legs were shaky. And she'd learned nothing – except that Dan Irvine might now be a danger to her, and that she was frightened of him.

As she turned her key in the ignition and pulled slowly out of the garage, another car drove in. A VW Polo. Eve caught her breath. Through the window she saw Daisy Irvine. Maybe she was filling up her car on the way to work. Eve had noticed the wedding boutique didn't open until ten.

Daisy's eyes caught hers through the window. For a moment she frowned and Eve thought she might not place her, but then a look of recognition flooded her face.

Recognition – and fear.

Eve still felt shaky when she let herself into Elizabeth's Cottage. Gus dashed up to her, his tail thumping.

'I'm every bit as pleased to see you, buddy,' she said, crouching down to greet him. He was now combining frantic scampering with excited paws on her lap. The snippet of normality made her smile for a moment. She gave him a hug, appreciating his warmth and the smell of his fur.

'I messed up,' she told him, as she stood again. 'Dan Irvine makes me more uneasy than anyone has in a long time.' But had he got anything to do with the murders? Daisy had clearer motives and opportunities for killing both Camilla and Harry, but Dan seemed meaner.

Eve still hadn't stopped shivering. She sighed. She ought to do some work on Harry's obituary. Standing there fretting wouldn't help. 'Let's go through to the dining room and light a fire.' It might stop her shaking.

As usual, she'd laid out the kindling and logs the night before, so all she had to do was strike a match to the rolls of newspaper underneath.

She sat down to plot the structure of her article, but it was hard to concentrate with all the adrenaline coursing round her body. She managed to focus for an hour or so before giving up again. Gus was snoring gently as she went to the kitchen to fix herself a hot chocolate.

She was just trying to restart her work when her mobile rang. Robin.

'*Nice work on Kerry Clifton.*'

Eve had emailed him an update the night before. She'd been vague about how she'd set eyes on the candlesticks, not specifying it had involved looking through a *rear* window…

'I've got more news. I must send you a full round-up – or I can give you the basics now?' What would he think about her visit to Andy's Autos?

'*Thanks – it'd be good to get my fix.*' She could hear the smile in his voice. '*But if you've got a lot to tell me, why don't we meet?*'

'Sure.' That might help, actually. She could explain better face to face. 'Where would suit you? And what time?' She imagined using one of the usual clandestine rendezvous points: the burned oak in Blind Eye Wood or the old mooring block, by the estuary.

'*Given the weather, I wonder if we should try a new venue,*' Robin said. His tone was light. '*How about a bar in town?*'

'A bar?' It was unexpected. He was asking her for a drink?

'*I don't suppose anyone will spot us in Blyworth. Most of the Saxfordites never venture beyond the Cross Keys.*'

He had a point. Meeting there shouldn't trigger a flurry of awkward questions about their relationship, and an assumption that Eve must know about his past life. 'Okay. Sounds good.'

'*Can you be on the far side of the Old Toll Road bridge at eight? I'll pick you up.*'

'Thanks.' This was starting to sound semi-social. Eve felt a flurry of nerves tickle her stomach.

'*We could visit Tristan Tennant's place – what was it?*'

'The Hideaway.' Of course, this was work. The case. Robin missed life as a detective and wanted to see some of the relevant locations, that was all. She took a deep breath. It was okay; there was no need to be anxious. 'Sounds like a plan. Maybe I can do some more digging while we're there. I'm worried I've been neglecting Tristan.'

'*Excellent. See you at eight, then.*'

'Great. I'll be there.'

She'd just gone back to her laptop to revisit her obituary plan when there was a knock at the door.

Gus looked like he'd been dreaming of rabbits, his back legs and nose twitching. Now he sprang up, his eyes suddenly wide, and barked for all he was worth.

'You'll frighten them away, you know.' No one would guess he was small from the noise he made.

She was so preoccupied with the thought of a drink with Robin that she hadn't considered who might be calling.

Out on the doorstep was Daisy Irvine.

CHAPTER THIRTY-SEVEN

The sight of the wedding boutique owner gave Eve a jolt, but of course, she'd given her a business card. She should have anticipated this. The look on the woman's face made her insides twist.

'What did you say to my husband? How did you find him?'

She was wearing the black velvet coat Eve had seen her in before; it showed off her waist-length blonde hair. A black beanie protected her from the cold, but Eve guessed she was beyond noticing it. Her face was pinched, with tinges of deep red on her cheekbones and her neck.

She took a step forward, but Eve had no intention of letting her in. 'I was about to take my dog for a walk,' she said, indicating Gus, who was poised by her feet. 'If you want to talk, you can come with us.' As she spoke she slung on her coat and bent to put Gus's on too.

'It's not for you to dictate terms.' Daisy's voice was barely controlled.

'Gus needs his exercise.' She pulled on her boots, grabbed her bag and stepped outside. She'd make for the village green and keep to well-populated areas. 'Besides, I thought you didn't want to speak with me.' Diplomacy had gone out the window; the sight of Daisy brought back the adrenaline rush from earlier in the day.

'That was when I thought you'd be decent enough to leave me alone. Now I know you're just like any other journalist: out to dig dirt and make trouble.' She dashed after Eve, up Haunted Lane, the rooks cawing in the trees. 'I'll ask you again, what did you say to Dan?'

Eve turned. She shouldn't have let fright get the better of her; it was important not to escalate the situation. 'I'm sorry. Let's start again. I didn't say anything untoward. I asked for advice about a warning light on my dashboard. Nothing more than that.'

It was the literal truth.

'He asked if I knew you.' Daisy caught her breath. It was bitterly cold, the air almost uncomfortable to breathe, but Eve could tell it was more than that. Daisy was seriously afraid. But of Dan, or of being found out? Or both? 'I told him I'd seen you in the shop.'

Heck. Eve could have done without him knowing that.

Daisy seemed to catch her expression. 'I had to. He always knows when I'm lying. He doesn't believe the problem with your car today was genuine. He thinks you're after information.'

Eve wasn't surprised about that, especially now he knew she'd been loitering round Daisy's boutique as well as at their house and his garage.

'Does he know about you and Harry Tennant?'

Daisy took another sharp intake of breath – a sob almost. 'What do you want?'

'Not to cause trouble. Truly. But I'm interviewing Harry's friends and contacts so I can write his obituary. It's likely I'll end up talking to the person who killed him and Camilla Sullivan. In the interests of self-preservation, I'm keen to find out who they are, sooner rather than later.'

Daisy was looking sideways at her as they crossed Love Lane and began to skirt the village green. She glanced quickly over her shoulder, then spoke in an undertone. 'You think I'm guilty?'

'You had a motive for both murders.'

Daisy's shoulders went down. 'You know about Camilla and Harry too.'

'She admitted they were close.' Eve could see the pain in Daisy's eyes.

'Oh yes, they were "close" all right.' Her tone was bitter. 'Look, if you want to talk as we walk then I need more privacy. The sea's that way, isn't it?' She pointed down Heath Lane. 'Harry and I walked there once, by moonlight. Dan was away overnight on a stag do.'

Eve hesitated. It would probably be deserted down on the beach, and they'd be well out of earshot of the nearest house; the heath lay between the sea and the village. But if Daisy had a weapon on her it must be small. Her bag was tiny. If the woman was going to chase her up the shoreline with a paring knife she'd probably come through it alive.

'All right.'

Gradually, the quiet of the snow-covered village gave way to the noise of the coast: the sound of the herring gulls' cries as they scavenged for food and the North Sea, pounding relentlessly on the shingle.

The cottages on Heath Lane were squat and covered with thick, snow-topped thatch; they looked like they were hunkered down against the cruel weather. Once they were past them, Eve turned again to Daisy.

'How did you find out Camilla and Harry were lovers?'

But the walk seemed to have given the woman time to think better of confiding. She stared ahead at the turbulent sea as Gus strained to be let off his leash.

Eve tried again. 'It sounds like you're in trouble and it might help to talk.'

'I don't see how.' Eve could barely hear her words above the sound of the sea. She shook her head. 'I wish to goodness I'd never written to the *Real Story*'s advice column. I buy the magazine for the celebrity news. The reports on weddings, that kind of thing. Clients expect me to be up with the latest gossip: who just got married and what they wore.' She turned to Eve. 'Things… well, things weren't great with Dan, and I needed support. Because I already bought that paper it was Pippa Longford I wrote to. I've got friends who've written to similar columns and felt so much better after getting an outside view. I thought it would be the same for me – Pippa always came up with radical solutions, and I imagined that's what I needed. A completely fresh take. But in the end, writing that letter turned my life upside down.'

Eve released Gus. He tore down to the sea's edge as the water drew back, then dashed up the shingle-strewn sand again as the waves crashed onto the shore. It would turn into an endless game of chase.

'What happened?'

The woman gave a deep sigh. 'I didn't worry about hiding my email address. Not that I used my professional one, of course, but my private one mentions my full name and the year I was born.' She hung her head. 'So stupid, but I didn't expect Pippa to be an unscrupulous man who lived round the corner. My Twitter handle uses the same format, and that account has my photo. And of course I gave my home county, like the instructions tell you. Anyway, long story short, he identified me and decided to reply direct, rather than through the newspaper column. He managed to make me feel we were almost acquainted already, because we were both local. He said he'd seen my name and picture in a county magazine, advertising A Bicycle Made for Two.'

She shoved her hands into her coat pockets and began to walk up the coast, staring ahead. 'He made me feel so special. He said my letter had worried him.' She wiped her eyes with the back of a gloved hand. 'He made a big deal of apologising for approaching me in person, and knowing it was unethical, but he said he wanted to help. And I believed him, God help me.' She still hadn't looked at Eve since she'd started her story.

'It was a shock to find out "Pippa" was male, and local, but he seemed so kind, and I'd hit a low point. Dan's been making my life hell for the last couple of years.' She blinked away tears. 'Before long, Harry and I weren't just talking. Not that he rushed me into bed. He was too clever for that, controlled enough to play a waiting game.'

Now, at last, she turned towards Eve. 'That's what it was to him. A game. I was a conquest. He spent weeks telling me I should leave Dan. I thought he meant…' Her eyes were as bleak as the sky.

'When he finished with me, he said he'd had "fun" and that of course I should leave Dan, but not because of him. Just because he was clearly no good as a husband.' She paused and looked out to the horizon. 'I'd got suspicious. Guessed he was seeing someone else. I smelled her perfume on him. And when I confronted him, he said: "Well, you're still with your husband, aren't you? It's not as though we're exclusive. And anyway, I'm not the sort to settle down. You must have guessed that by now."' The bitterness in her voice had intensified. 'He made me feel such a fool, and suddenly, he and Dan seemed similar, not different.'

Eve could hardly believe what she was hearing. Harry Tennant had abused his position so cruelly, with a total lack of conscience. He'd treated her like his old enemies at school: manoeuvred until he was in a position of power. In the back of her mind, Eve wondered how she'd have coped with Harry's games, if he'd lived. Would she have rued the day they met? 'He had a duty of care to all his correspondents. You were totally in the right.'

But the facts made Daisy's guilt seem all the more plausible.

'How did you know it was Camilla that Harry moved on to?' Eve asked, when Daisy said nothing.

'I knew her.' Daisy's tone was wretched. 'I always recommended her flowers to people who came to buy wedding dresses, and she'd put in a good word for my business in return. When I smelled Chanel No. 5 on Harry's shirt, I remembered seeing them exchange glances when they crossed paths in the shop. I challenged him on it, and he admitted it was true. It was almost as though he was curious to see my reaction – like a scientist watching a lab rat. He told me' – she took a great gulp of air – 'he told me he needed to be with a proper grown-up for a change. Someone sophisticated – his equal. She was several years older than him. A lot older than me. I was beside myself.' Her voice was so quiet now. 'I don't know how long I stood outside the mill for, crying. He'd invited me over for a stolen afternoon on early closing day, but it didn't pan out the way I'd imagined.' She bit her lip. 'So yes, I had an excellent motive for murdering them both, and I know you suspected me before I told you all this. But look at me. You know I'm telling the truth. I didn't do it.'

Eve hesitated. Daisy must have read the sympathy in her eyes, but Eve couldn't rely on gut instinct for something so serious.

When she didn't speak, Daisy took a step towards her. 'Why would I wait all these months before killing them? You know that makes no sense. I discovered this last October.'

But Eve remembered Daisy's bitter tone intensifying as she'd quoted Harry, saying he wasn't the sort to settle down. 'Because Camilla let slip she and Harry planned to marry.'

Daisy took a sharp intake of breath. After a moment she tried to cover her tracks. 'I didn't know that.'

But Eve was sure she was acting; she'd heard the rumours. 'For what it's worth, I think that was Camilla's fantasy. I have the impression Harry was honest with you; he'd never have made their relationship permanent.'

She watched Daisy's eyes carefully. Relief. She was glad. If she'd killed Harry for that reason, wouldn't Eve have seen anguish instead?

'It's none of my business,' Eve said, 'but I think Harry might have been right about leaving Dan. He frightened me when I spoke with him this morning.'

Daisy looked down at the sand and shingle. 'He's scared me lately.'

'Do you think he might have killed Harry out of jealousy? And then maybe Camilla if she somehow found him out? Has he ever met her?'

Daisy shook her head. 'Not as far as I know, but if she suspected him, I suppose she could have made enquiries that put him on his guard.'

It was possible. 'So, Dan knew about you and Harry, then?' She'd never answered, the first time Eve asked.

Daisy closed her eyes a moment and nodded. 'Seems he found out quite early on. And carried on spying on us, collecting information, working out how to turn the thumbscrews most effectively. He only told me what he knew after Harry had dumped me; he heard me crying and guessed what had happened. And one day, he and Harry came face to face. Dan got a request to tow a car out of a ditch, and when he turned up, Harry was waiting with it.'

It was as Eve had speculated. Hector's car trouble had brought them briefly into contact.

'When Dan came home he was really out of sorts. Once he'd pulled the car out, he tried the engine and made some excuse to look under the bonnet. He'd thought the car was Harry's, and tampered with something in the hope he'd have an accident. He's a terrible husband but a knowledgeable mechanic.

'It was only after he'd finished that Harry told him the car belonged to some surgeon, who'd had to get to work urgently.' Daisy shook her head. 'Dan couldn't adjust the engine again without Harry seeing, and he couldn't drive the car to the medic's house either, in case it was he who had an accident, so he had to tow it. And then the surgeon's wife was home, so he had to make an excuse to go poking around in the engine in their driveway. He was livid; he blamed me for the whole thing.'

'Daisy, that's attempted murder, right there. You have to go to the police!'

'I can't,' she said. 'He'd explain it away; it would be my word against his. And my motive for the double killing is just as strong as his. Stronger, probably.'

Eve didn't know what to say. 'What about leaving him, for your own safety?'

Daisy shook her head. 'Even though he tampered with Harry's car, I still wonder about the killing. Doing something stupid on the spur of the moment is one thing – I could see that. He's hot-headed and cruel. But underneath it all, he's a coward. I couldn't imagine him risking his freedom once he'd taken a step back and thought about it.'

Daisy must have seen the doubt in her eyes.

'If I leave Dan, he'll ruin my business. He's been subbing me for the last year, when sales fell, but it's more than that. I don't just sell wedding dresses, I sell fairy tales and dreams. Dan would make sure everyone knew my life was a lie. He'd drown out the truth – how unhappy he made me – and focus on my affair with a murdered man. He'd portray himself as the hard-working wronged husband. I'd love to leave him, believe me, but my business is everything to me. One day I'll work out what to do.'

'If you ever decide you need help, do you know who to call?'

She nodded.

'And you can ring me anytime too, for what it's worth.'

She gave a wry smile. 'Thanks, but if I do need help I'll probably pick someone who's never suspected me of murder.'

Fair reaction, really.

Daisy stalked off up the beach and Eve called Gus. 'How are you doing, buddy?' she said, crouching down to pet him. 'Me? I have to say, I've felt better.'

CHAPTER THIRTY-EIGHT

Eve was sensible. She didn't usually spend hours deciding what to wear. She assessed the occasion, knew instantly what was required and went with it. And yet before her date with— No, before her *meeting* with Robin to catch up on the case, she'd changed her clothes four times. The fact sat there like a small uncomfortable stone in her shoe as she climbed awkwardly into the passenger seat of Robin's battered van.

Viv had been the problem, even though she had no idea what was going on. Her voice had worked its way into Eve's mind as she stood in her bedroom, surveying the contents of her wardrobe: *You really think that's suitable? Might as well wear a bin bag...*

Eve's subconscious had fought back: *We're having a catch-up. This is practical. And no one dresses up these days, unless they're twenty and going clubbing. At the age of fifty...*

Viv's voice had been straight back in there: *Yes, fifty. Not a hundred and fifty. Don't you ever find being uber-practical gets a bit boring?*

'Sorry about the transport,' Robin said, breaking into her thoughts. There were no streetlights but she could see the contours of his (rugged) face in the moonlight.

'Not at all; it's great.' She hadn't expected the van to be immaculate, what with his gardening business.

'I hope you don't end up covered in bits of mud.' He glanced across at her.

'It'll blend in with my coat.' She was wearing the chocolate-brown one. Quite smart. Did he think it was over the top? 'It was a good idea of yours to do a proper review. And the venue's perfect; I still need to find out more about Tristan Tennant.'

She caught his shadowy half-smile. 'The case wasn't the only reason I suggested getting together.'

Eve's stomach fluttered. Back to square one. She was fifty now, yes, but still, most definitely, part teenager. Time to shift focus...

'I had a run-in with Daisy Irvine's husband today.'

He whistled, his eyes on the dark road ahead now. The snow-covered verges glittered in the van's headlights, but heating puffed from the vehicle's vents, keeping the interior warm. 'Really? How did that come about?'

He'd think she'd walked into trouble. Primarily because she had. 'I took my car to Andy's Autos to report a fault.' She saw him open his mouth and rushed on. 'I have to admit, things didn't work out as planned.'

She told him how Dan had sent the other mechanic off on his break, then proceeded to reveal that he'd seen her car the evening she'd listened in on his and Daisy's conversation. Robin already knew about that adventure, though she'd played down how risky it felt at the time, making a joke of the cat's appearance.

He'd still emailed back to suggest she might like to be more careful in future...

They'd entered Blyworth now. They must only be a minute from Tristan Tennant's wine bar. The drink ahead loomed large. Robin seemed entirely at ease, which made Eve feel less so. She was used to being the grounded, level-headed one.

But this was crazy. It wasn't as though she and Robin could ever be an item. Going public would mean half the village pummelling her for details of his mysterious past. Telling them she didn't know would make Robin seem even more suspicious (and make her look like a gullible jackass). But admitting the truth was also out; it might put him in danger from his corrupt former colleagues and their criminal contacts. Ergo, a relationship was off-limits. The thought left her feeling calmer again.

Robin parked in a side street round the corner from the Hideaway. As Eve let herself out of the van, Viv's voice materialised in her head again. *You'd have to be secret lovers. But hey, who would want* that *kind of excitement?*

Eve focused on the icy pavement and let the cold evening air do its work. At least their conversation shouldn't dry up, even if she felt nervous. The day's news would keep them going past closing time, despite using up Andy's Autos on the way.

There was only one other couple in the bar and just one member of staff: a woman with sleek mahogany-brown hair and bright red lipstick, her white blouse and black waistcoat visible above the counter. She matched the classy aesthetic of the place, but it looked as though Tristan's presentation wasn't enough to attract the locals. Still, it was a Thursday night; perhaps it did better at weekends.

The woman smiled and leaned towards them with all the eagerness of a person bored with their evening so far. 'Would you like to see the wine list?'

Robin raised an eyebrow at Eve.

'Actually, I'd love a gin and tonic.' The spirits still looked untouched. They'd go off if she didn't lend a hand.

'And a bottle of the low-alcohol Ghost Ship, please.'

'Thanks for driving.' The aftermath of the day and her nerves for the evening left Eve feeling quite ready for the gin.

'You've only recently opened?' she said to the barmaid, partly to make conversation and partly to see what she'd say. She remembered the answer: the bar had launched six months earlier.

The woman smiled rather tightly. 'That's right. Early days.' Her tone was artificially bright.

'I love the classic décor.'

'I hope everyone else agrees with you.' The woman glanced away quickly as she put their drinks on the counter.

'Thanks.' They paid, then moved to a table well away from the bar so they could talk freely.

'I suppose Dan might ask Daisy if she's aware of you, now you've crossed his radar twice,' Robin said, pulling out a chair to sit down.

She took a deep breath as she dropped into a seat opposite him. 'I'm afraid he already has.'

'Ah. Care to elaborate?'

She told him about Daisy's visit, pausing midway for a swig of her gin. At last, she'd passed on the whole story. 'I found myself believing her. Pouring out what happened seemed like a cry for help, though I can't deny she had every reason to kill Harry and Camilla. And there's Dan to consider, too. If Daisy's to be believed, he's already had a go at taking Harry out, though I still don't buy him as Camilla's murderer.' She put her head in her hands for a moment. 'I don't know what to do. I guess I should be relaying all this to Palmer. But if I tell the police what Daisy said about Dan then I'll be putting her in danger too. And they might arrest her on the back of what I say.' She glanced up at him. 'All suggestions gratefully received.'

His look was sympathetic. 'Sometimes you have to tell what you know and rely on someone else to take the next step. Admittedly, I wouldn't trust Palmer to make a cup of tea, but Greg's on the case too, and he's different.'

She sighed. 'I know, but the damage to Daisy would be the same. I realise I can't just leave it, but maybe I can tackle it from another angle.'

Robin nodded. 'I thought you might suggest that. Via Tori Abbott?'

They were on the same wavelength. *Ugh.* She was feeling a connection. This wasn't helping her think straight. 'That's right. I can check Daisy's story about Dan hanging around at their house to "fine-tune" Hector's car – see if she thinks he behaved suspiciously. If Tori backs Daisy's story, I can decide what to tell the police.'

Robin's blue-grey eyes were on hers.

'I know. The delay's not ideal, but Tori probably told Palmer about Harry's "Venus" already; hopefully they're not totally in the dark.'

'Perhaps. But even if she has, do you think he'll have managed to identify her? My guess is you're several steps ahead of him.'

Eve felt uncomfortable; that was where her excuses for not intervening sooner fell flat. 'You might be right. Daisy didn't mention being interviewed.'

Robin sipped his beer. 'What if I talk to Greg and make sure the police know about Harry's second lover? If they're still trying to identify an unknown blonde, I can tell him Camilla met Harry at A Bicycle Made for Two, and the woman who works there has golden waist-length hair. Greg's subtle; he won't go in all guns blazing.'

Some of the tension eased from Eve's shoulders. 'That would be great. Thanks.'

Without warning, he put out a hand and rubbed one of her recently de-tensed shoulders. It tensed again. Thank goodness she hadn't just taken a mouthful of gin; she'd probably have choked.

She hadn't worked out how to respond before he removed his hand again and her panic-induced paralysis released her.

He was smiling, a hint of laughter in his eyes. 'You had quite a day of it, then?'

She nodded.

At last, he looked more businesslike. 'So, where are we at? Daisy, Dan and' – he lowered his voice still further – 'Tristan are all possible perpetrators for Harry and Camilla's murders, with Daisy having a direct motive for both killings. And the others maybe killing Camilla if she'd found them out.'

Eve nodded. 'And Judd and Melody Bentley are outside possibilities, as you pointed out.' She whispered too now: 'As Tristan's still a strong candidate, I guess I shouldn't waste this opportunity. Another drink?'

He grinned. 'Same again, thanks.'

She went to the bar and placed a repeat order. 'I wonder,' she said, as the barmaid prepared the drinks, 'did you ever meet Harry Tennant? I'm writing his obituary; I came here to interview Tristan about him on Sunday.'

The woman rolled her eyes. 'Oh yes, I met Harry.'

'Not a fan?'

She smiled. 'He was very charming, but full of himself. Sorry. I shouldn't speak ill of the dead.'

Eve smiled. 'No problem. It's important to make my article truthful; I want to hear people's genuine impressions.'

The woman looked down. 'He irritated me. He sort of implied I'd made a mistake, taking this job.' She shrugged and turned to ring her and Robin's drinks up on the till. Eve handed over a ten-pound note and she thanked her.

'I'm the bar manager,' the woman went on, handing back the change, 'and it's my first senior role. He – well, he implied I could do better. He said if Tristan had followed his advice, he'd have put a whole load of money behind the business, but they couldn't agree.' She took a deep breath and spoke very quietly. 'The worst of it was, Harry could see we were struggling. It was like he was showing off that he could have helped but wasn't going to.'

At that moment, a door behind the bar opened and Tristan himself walked in.

'Excuse me.' The bar manager blushed scarlet and bent to rearrange some glasses on a shelf behind the counter.

Eve met Harry's uncle's eyes. His gaze was slightly unfocused. The clientele might not be wading into the Hideaway's spirits, but maybe Tristan had been. Whether he'd killed Harry and Camilla or not, he must be under a lot of strain.

'Back again?' he said to her.

'Yes, but only for a drink this time.'

He looked beyond her, to where Robin was sitting, and his shoulders relaxed a little. 'Oh, I see. I'm glad you chose the Hideaway.'

'I loved the atmosphere when I came to interview you. The bar makes me feel special, as though I'm in first class on a classic cruise liner, or at some swanky New York hotel.' His emotional look in response tugged at Eve's heartstrings. 'How have you been? It must be such a difficult time.'

He heaved a sigh. 'I'm taking things slowly. There's a lot to sort out.'

If the bar was struggling, he'd need Harry's money as quickly as possible. Probate would take ages, but Kerry stealing the candlesticks was a lucky break for him. If he took possession of them unofficially, maybe he could sell them without waiting for the formalities and boost his capital.

'What about you?' Tristan said. 'How's the obituary coming along?'

It was the opening she needed. 'It's been *interesting*.' She tried to inject a lot of meaning into her final word.

Tristan raised an eyebrow and leaned forward on the counter. 'What do you mean?'

Eve glanced left. The bar manager was serving two new customers who'd just come through the door. 'I'm sorry – it feels wrong to say this to a relative – but it sounds as though Harry made life difficult for several people. I guess family members don't always see what goes on.' She waited with bated breath to see if her strategy worked.

'Don't worry,' Tristan said at last. 'I saw that side of him. Whatever you write in *Icon*, it won't be a shock to me.'

Eve sighed. 'He hurt you too?' She was still standing over the drinks the bar manager had poured for her and Robin. She took a sip of her gin and tonic and Tristan reached to pour himself one as well. Another small dent in the spirits.

He nodded, then suddenly closed his eyes.

Eve saw a tear appear on his cheek and watched him wipe it away hastily with a handkerchief.

'I'm sorry,' she said. 'I understand his challenging behaviour started way back when he was in school: manipulating the other boys, finding out their secrets, taking control. And of course he was living with you during the holidays. If he took the same approach at home, it can't have been easy.'

The man looked at her with bloodshot eyes. 'It wasn't. The truth is, we had a difficult relationship, and I'm finding it hard to mourn him.' His voice was low. 'I feel so damned guilty. He was my responsibility as a child. I ought to be bereft.'

'He treated you badly. It's not your fault.'

She saw his chest rise and fall through the thin white shirt he wore. 'He needed me. I'm sure that's why he moved here. He might have spent his time taunting me, but I think I was still a prop. One of the few constants in his life. He had a difficult childhood.' He stood up straight. 'I can imagine how this looks, and the police already think I'm guilty, but their theories make no sense. He drove me up the wall, but he was my brother's child and his behaviour's been going on for decades. Why would I act now, just after having dinner with him, when I'd look like a prime suspect? And I had no idea he'd made no will, and that I'd inherit.'

At last, Eve was ready to carry her and Robin's drinks back to their table.

'That looked like an interesting conversation,' he said quietly, after he'd thanked her. 'An update for the journey home, perhaps?'

On the way back to Saxford, in the privacy of Robin's van, Eve relayed what Tristan had said.

'Interesting.' His eyes were on the road. 'What do you think?'

Eve sighed. 'I feel sorry for him, but I'm still not sure he's innocent. The "why would I act now" argument doesn't hold water. Who knows what they talked about over dinner, the night Harry died? Harry told the bar manager he'd offered to back the Hideaway financially but pulled out when he and Tristan couldn't agree on an approach. Maybe that argument resurfaced. Money worries at the bar might have come to a head.'

Robin nodded. 'More than possible, I'd say.'

Tristan was still on the list.

Robin dropped Eve off on the Old Toll Road Bridge on his way back into Saxford. His cautious attitude to being seen meant there was no awkward doorstep moment.

She thanked him for the lift and was just opening the passenger door to climb down from the van when he spoke.

'Eve.'

She turned.

'Yes?'

'I hate the fact that there's been a double murder in the village, that goes without saying, but I'm enjoying the teamworking. Sorry about the cloak-and-dagger stuff.'

Viv's voice filled Eve's head. *Secret lover.* Shut up!

'No problem.' She climbed out. 'And I'm enjoying it too.'

She saw his smile in shadowy profile as he drove off into the night.

CHAPTER THIRTY-NINE

Eve spent the following morning working at Monty's, but her mind was on her plans for the afternoon: a trip to the Abbotts. What would they tell her about Dan Irvine's visit, the day Hector had car trouble?

It was just after lunch when she set off with Gus to their house; they took the village route for a change. The snow had started to fall *again*. It was still beautiful, but Eve was beginning to wonder when the conditions would change. It made getting about difficult, especially now there was snow on top of ice. Gus looked similarly doubtful as he glanced up at the sky.

By the time they reached Old Yard Lane, fresh flakes had covered the previous layer and the bare trees went from being edged with white to weighed down by it again, blending into the snow-filled sky beyond. The birds had gone quiet and Eve's footsteps made no sound; everything was muted.

She was part way along the lane, at the far reaches of the village, when she saw a truck, parked in the gateway to a field.

Andy's Autos. The cab was empty.

Eve swallowed and scanned the road ahead. Gus pressed his tartan-coated body against her ankles and she looked down at him. 'Dan Irvine isn't the only person who works at that garage.' All the same, the sight left her uneasy. And if Irvine was mixed up in Harry Tennant's death, revisiting Saxford might be related.

Nerves built in her stomach as they walked on. It felt like a game of grandmother's footsteps. No one would hear them coming in the snow, so they'd take whoever they found by surprise. And if that happened to be Dan Irvine, Eve didn't like to think of his reaction.

It was only a second later that she saw him. He came round the corner from the direction of the Abbotts' house. Black woollen beanie and donkey jacket, dark jeans and heavy boots, he was a bulky presence, tramping through the whirling snowflakes.

There was no avoiding his line of sight. He walked towards her with a heavy tread, his eyes on her all the way.

'What the hell are you doing here?' he said, when he got close. He didn't raise his voice: his tone was low and threatening, with a hint of derision. 'First you go to my wife's shop. Then you stray onto the land next to our house and visit the garage, and now, here you are again.' His venomous look went from her to Gus, who growled and moved in front of Eve.

'I described you to Daisy after you visited the garage – asked if she'd met you. She admitted you'd been in the shop but I knew there was something extra she was keeping back. I took a look at her mobile, then went through her bag.

'You weren't just some casual shopper. She had a business card amongst all her rubbish. Eve Mallow. I googled the name and your photo came up. I've found out all about you.'

Eve digested the information. He'd know she specialised in celebrity obituaries. And the only celebrity death round here lately had been Harry Tennant's. And if he'd googled, he'd probably found articles about her input into previous murder investigations, too. He'd likely guessed she suspected him. There was no point in lying now.

He was very close to her, leaning forward. Gus mirrored his stance with bared teeth, head raised as high as it would go.

'What's your game?' Irvine's chest rose and fell. 'Are you following me?'

'I had no idea you were here. I'm on my way to visit the Abbotts.'

His eyes narrowed and left hers for a moment. Had he been with them too? Was it something to do with him tampering with their car, when he'd thought it was Harry's? They were in a position to give him away, if they'd noticed his strange behaviour the day their car came off the road. Perhaps he'd wanted to creep in to double check nothing he'd done was detectable. That could be why he'd left his truck down the lane. Maybe he'd managed to access the Abbotts' garage secretly. Or perhaps he'd been on a fact-finding mission: wanting to know who the couple might have told about his extended visit to fine-tune their car's engine.

'What do you want with them?' His tone was sharp.

'They knew Harry Tennant and, as I'm sure you've discovered, I'm writing about him.'

Suddenly Irvine stepped back and put his shoulders down. It looked like it had been an effort.

'I know how I must have sounded, the day you listened in to mine and Daisy's conversation.' The smile he gave didn't reach his eyes. It made Eve's skin crawl. 'Jealous. Vindictive. Bitter. And you weren't mistaken. I'm all of those things. When I found out she'd had an affair with Tennant I punched a hole through the wing of a rust bucket we had in at the garage. That's how angry I was. But that's me. I'm hot-headed. And who wouldn't see red, under the circumstances?'

He grinned again. Did he really think he could build bridges with her? He'd just admitted to searching his wife's bag and phone. And she'd heard him treat her like dirt in a casual way, born, she was sure, of long-term habit.

'You can't tell me it's unnatural,' Irvine went on. 'I'm still livid with Daisy. But' – his eyes left hers again – 'I love her. And as for killing Harry Tennant – that's crazy. It's true I felt like flattening him when I heard, but setting the mill on fire? If I'd taken my revenge on Tennant I'd have wanted to see the whites of his eyes – have him acknowledge the wrong he did me.'

He'd put on a good act. She didn't sympathise with him on any level, but a tiny part of her believed his very last sentence.

'Didn't you feel tempted?' Eve said. 'To tackle him face to face, I mean?' She wished she could ask about tampering with the car, but it was impossible. It would be clear Daisy had told her.

Irvine gave her a long look. 'Very. But I've got a good job, and I'd be out on my ear if I started beating up our customer base.'

'So Harry used Andy's Autos? Beyond when he waited for you to deal with Hector Abbott's car?'

The mechanic's eyes flickered. He hadn't known she was aware of that. Eve cursed herself; her words might be enough to make him wonder what Daisy had said.

'The Abbotts mentioned it,' she added, evenly. 'They were explaining how Harry had been a good neighbour.'

Irvine snorted. 'There was nothing good about him. But no, I meant generally. Bosses tend to object when you beat people up, whoever they are. And everyone's a potential customer.' He sighed disgustedly. 'It's written on our office noticeboard.'

He turned away abruptly and stamped towards his truck, smacking his hand on its frame angrily before he got into the cab.

Eve walked on up the lane and tried to steady her breathing. As Irvine started his engine, she bent to ruffle Gus's fur. 'Heck, I'm glad he's gone.'

She rounded the corner and walked up the Abbotts' snow-covered drive.

Tori was in the kitchen, and met her eyes through the window. A moment later she was at the door. 'You have more questions? Would you like to come in?'

Eve shook her head and indicated Gus. 'I won't – thank you. But I did have an additional query. It's a bit of an odd one. I'm here about Dan Irvine, from Andy's Autos.'

Tori double-took. 'What's he got to do with all this?'

'He just came to see you?'

She nodded. 'All part of the firm's service, apparently. A courtesy call to check Hector's car's been working well since they dealt with it.'

It was pretty odd to come in person; he could have asked that over the phone. 'And has it?'

Tori frowned and Eve wondered how much to say.

'To be honest, Mr Irvine's come up in my research into Harry's obituary, and I don't know what to make of him.'

'Ah!' Her expression cleared. She stepped towards Eve and folded her arms, a conspiratorial look in her eye. 'I see. It was good of him to come and check on the car, of course, but I feel the same way. And…' She frowned. 'Oh, I might as well say it! He took a call while he was here, from the woman I saw in Harry's window. Her face came up on his phone screen when it rang. I don't know what it was all about, but it wasn't professional to have it in front of a client.'

Eve raised an eyebrow.

'He said some horrible things to her. Though I could hear her too and she sounded furious. It was hard to know who was most angry.'

'Did he threaten her?'

'No. She sounded as aggressive as he did.'

Daisy had seemed resigned and depressed when she'd visited Eve, but maybe things had escalated since then.

'Tori, I wanted to check one last detail about Dan Irvine, if I may,' Eve said. 'After he returned Hector's car here, I gather he had to hang around to do something extra to the engine. I wondered if you were home and remember him looking under the bonnet?'

Tori frowned. 'Who told you that?'

Eve hesitated. 'His wife mentioned it.'

The furrows in her brow intensified. 'How odd. No. I'd been away overnight, but I was back by mid-morning. He returned Hector's car after I got home, but he headed straight off. I didn't see him again until today, and the car's been fine.'

Could he have reversed the tampering without the Abbotts seeing him – come back later, say? It wasn't what he'd told Daisy. 'If he'd come back without telling you, could he have done something extra to the car without you spotting him?'

Tori frowned, as well she might. 'No. Once he returned it, I locked it in the garage. It's my Fiat that stays out on the drive.'

Eve walked slowly home with Gus. There was something odd going on. Could Daisy Irvine have lied about Dan tampering with Hector's car? Or had Dan's mysterious visit to the Abbotts that day been to threaten Tori not to admit that he'd worked on it?

It would explain the home visit.

That evening, as Eve reheated the second half of her mushroom pasta sauce for supper, her mind was still on the Irvines. Who was lying? Daisy, to try to frame Dan? Or Tori, because she was scared to tell the truth? Eve tried to imagine Dan threatening her, to keep her quiet. Tori wouldn't frighten easily, Eve was sure, but she was no fool. If he'd told her not to talk, she might have decided to obey for the time being while she worked out what to do. She'd had no time to think; Eve had arrived immediately after the mechanic's visit. And if Tori did speak out, she'd want to confide in the police, not Eve.

But as she put on spaghetti to cook, she forced herself to accept it could have been Daisy who'd lied. Trying to frame Dan might seem like her only way out if she thought her guilt was about to be revealed. If her plan worked, she'd still have to deal with the fallout: the publicity might put people off shopping at her store, and the financial support from her jailed husband would be over. But it would be better than being found guilty herself.

Everything inside her rejected the idea that Daisy was guilty. She'd seemed so raw and honest when she'd visited Saxford. Dan was a far more likely villain on the face of it. But Daisy had been hurt. She'd probably put up with horrendous treatment from Dan over the years. Maybe after that, Harry's betrayal was just too much. And each time Eve tried to make Dan fit as the killer (Why would he have visited the Abbotts at home if he wasn't threatening Tori?), her logical side ruined it. (Maybe rich customers get platinum treatment; they're probably worth it in the long run.) The arguments against him combined with her gut feeling that Camilla would never have let him into her house.

She clung to Tristan as another possible killer, but in her heart of hearts, Eve felt Daisy was pulling ahead of him. Camilla would probably have welcomed her in with open arms and a glass of sherry.

But Eve didn't want it to be her.

CHAPTER FORTY

Eve tried to work on Harry Tennant's obituary in the dining room the following morning, but concentrating proved hard again. Ian's arrival in the village and their planned dinner at the Cross Keys that evening loomed large. Why had she agreed to see him? And what if he was going to suggest they give their marriage another go? She'd never be able to relax enough to eat Jo's—

Her mobile rang, making her jump. Gus, who'd been lounging on her feet, shot her a look of mild annoyance. 'Well, if you will use me as a pillow…' She pulled the phone from her pocket.

Robin. Nerves tickled her stomach. He must have news.

'*Eve.*'

'Is everything okay?'

'*Dan Irvine's been found dead. He was working late at Andy's Autos. Alone. Except someone arrived to keep him company, then clobbered him over the head.*'

'Same weapon as for Camilla?'

'*The police think so. They've arrested Daisy Irvine.*'

Eve knew she was a prime suspect for Harry and Camilla's murders; the facts pointed strongly to her guilt. But still she found herself baulking at the way things were panning out. 'What's their case?'

'*What you'd imagine. They know she had an affair with Tennant, and that he passed her over for Camilla. Daisy knew Dan was working late at the garage and she didn't raise the alarm when he failed to come home. And as you discovered, the Abbotts heard her having an acrimonious call with him when he dropped in on them yesterday.'*

Eve had emailed Robin an update before she went to bed and, of course, he'd have spoken to Greg, as they'd agreed at the Hideaway. The arrest was probably down to her as much as anyone. She felt so guilty.

'*On top of all that,*' Robin added, '*Daisy told you Dan had tampered with Hector's car, thinking it was Harry's, but the Abbotts say he never hung around to reverse what he'd done like she claims.*'

'They still say the same now Dan's dead? I was wondering if he'd threatened them into keeping quiet.'

'*I'm afraid it doesn't look that way. The police think she hoped to pin everything on Dan, but lost it with him at the last minute.*'

It sounded so open-and-shut, but nagging doubts filled Eve's head. 'That all makes sense, but my gut tells me something's not right.'

'*You might want to marshal your thoughts. The police know you were asking the Abbotts about Dan Irvine yesterday. And Greg's aware you and Daisy spoke too, after I asked him to look into her quietly. He's had to give Palmer that information because of what's happened. Sorry.*'

It was inevitable. 'I understand.'

'*I'll keep you posted if anything fresh comes to light.*'

'Same.'

'*Speak soon, Eve. And take care…*'

His words broke through the sinking feeling in her chest. 'I will.'

She got up and walked towards the kitchen to get a glass of water, glancing over her shoulder at Gus. 'I need to be dispassionate and think this through again.' She took a deep breath. 'If Daisy got away with Dan's murder, she'd likely have inherited his money and become sole owner of the house. Her customers might associate her business with violence and scandal, but she could have afforded to move away and start again, with some capital behind her.' She shook her head as she crossed the kitchen. 'But I can't believe she killed Dan with that plan in mind. After all, what chance did she have of escaping prison? She knew she was a prime suspect for the murders, even before his death. And he was a big guy. If she's guilty, she'd have to have taken him completely by surprise, and delivered a knockout blow before he could retaliate.'

She filled her glass and looked down at Gus, who'd followed her through. 'I just don't see her thinking it would work.'

But the fact was, Daisy could still have been overtaken by anger. Not everyone planned life to the nth degree and kept themselves under control. Daisy had been devastated by Harry's betrayal and probably tested to the limit by Dan's behaviour. Maybe she'd gone to Andy's Autos to have it out with him, taking the weapon she'd used on Camilla for protection, then snapped, seizing her moment when his attention was elsewhere. Or perhaps he had proof she was guilty, and all other considerations went out the window. With an attack driven by such passion or desperation, she could have dealt a lethal blow.

Eve strode through to the living room and put on her coat. 'Let's go for a walk, Gus. I need some air.'

A moment later, she and her dachshund were outside, he in his tartan, she in her chocolate-brown wool. They turned left up Haunted Lane, past the snow-laden oak tree and up Love Lane towards the Old Toll Road bridge.

Eve crossed to the far side of the river this time, before following the bank that led towards the mill. Maybe seeing the spot where it had all started would trigger something useful.

As they trudged through the snow, Eve's mind turned to Tristan Tennant and Judd and Melody Bentley. If Daisy was innocent and her husband dead, someone else was guilty. And what possible reason could any of them have for killing Dan Irvine? Whereas Daisy had plenty; it would be no surprise if she'd finally snapped.

The mill was up ahead now: a blackened shell against a backdrop of white and grey, surrounded by its protective wire panels to keep out trespassers. The day was gloomy and quiet.

Her phone ringing in the hush made her start. She didn't recognise the number.

'*Eve? It's Daisy. Daisy Irvine.*'

'Daisy. Are you okay?' The question was instinctive. Whatever she'd done, in that moment Eve felt she was dealing with a person who needed help.

'*You don't believe I did it.*' It was a statement. She must have gathered as much from Eve's voice.

But Eve was rational. She didn't have enough evidence to accept her own gut feeling. 'I don't know what to think.'

'*You said last time we met to contact you if I needed help. I'm calling you rather than anyone else right now. Don't let me down.*'

'Daisy, I know you lied. The Abbotts say Dan never hung around at their house to check on their car's engine, the day he towed it out of the ditch. He dropped it off then left immediately. So he can't have tampered with it like you said.'

'*What?*' There was a moment's pause. '*No, Eve, you have to believe me, that's the story Dan told. If it's not true, then it was him who lied.*'

She sounded panicked. And completely genuine.

'The Abbotts say they heard you being aggressive towards Dan when you called him yesterday.'

'*I was upset. He raised his voice and so did I. But I wasn't aggressive. I was in tears.*'

'And the police wonder why you didn't try to contact them or Dan when he didn't come home last night.'

She gave a despairing sigh. '*I was relieved not to see him. He told me when I rang that he was working late. I assumed he'd gone out drinking afterwards and slept on someone's sofa. It wasn't unusual.'* Suddenly, she dissolved. *'I loved having the house to myself.'* She spoke through sobs. *'He was a bully, always putting me down. It was so much better when he wasn't there.'*

Palmer wouldn't question her guilt when she broke down and said things like that.

'Please believe me, Eve. I didn't do this – any of it. Someone else is guilty and happy to see me suffer.'

Eve promised to keep digging for information, however hopeless it seemed. After she'd rung off, she walked up close to the wire-panelled barrier round the mill.

'Honestly, Gus, I just don't think she did it. She's too raw. If she's lying she's the best actress I've met.' But why would Dan lie about tampering with Hector's engine?

She stood, staring at the mill, imagining the killer doing the same thing. Waiting for the flames to take hold. An act of hatred, but a controlled one.

Or possibly a coldly clinical way of erasing a threat. It could be either.

Most evidence had been burned to a cinder. That, and the remoteness of the mill and the time of the attack provided the perfect cover, with the Abbotts absent…

At that moment, Eve heard a noise. The squeal of brakes from across the river. It looked like the Abbotts had a visitor. Some speed freak screeching to an uncontrolled stop in the drive.

Eve could just see the car in question, between the Abbotts' garage and their leylandii hedge. She moved slightly beyond the mill to get a better look.

A moment later, she realised Tori Abbott was staring back at her. She'd just emerged from the passenger seat.

Beyond her, a figure stumbled out of the driver's door.

Hector. Not visitors after all, then.

Eve gave them a wave and Tori waved back, a sort of mini salute.

Eve didn't think much of Hector's driving. If that was how he parked a car she'd want to make sure she never landed in his operating theatre.

It was at that moment, still facing Harry's old neighbours, that fresh connections started to form in Eve's mind.

CHAPTER FORTY-ONE

The link between Dan Irvine, Harry Tennant and Hector Abbott. Tori denying Dan had done extra work on Hector's car. Suspicion thrown on Daisy. But it didn't have to be she *or* Dan who'd lied.

It could have been Tori.

Possibilities filled Eve's head. *What if?*

Hector had looked unsteady as he emerged from his vehicle. And the way he'd slewed the car across the drive… She remembered the surgeon standing by the fire at Elizabeth's Cottage on midwinter's evening. He'd found her spirits.

When the Abbotts left for the night, Eve recalled Tori leaning on her husband, saying she'd overdone it, but as they'd moved towards the door, she'd felt they were supporting each other. Maybe Tori hadn't been drunk at all. Perhaps she was covering for Hector, who'd been laying into the alcohol. She wouldn't have wanted the neighbours talking.

Eve bent down to attach Gus's leash. 'Buddy, I'm not sure what this means, but something tells me we should head home, right now.'

Thank goodness the Abbotts were on the other side of the river. She started to walk at speed. There was no need to urge Gus on; he'd picked up on her urgency.

Hector's car was the link. Why hadn't she seen that before?

She focused, trying to remember everything she knew about the accident.

Or had it been an accident? Suddenly she felt muddled.

Snippets of conversation came back to her. Hadn't Tori referred to the car breaking down? 'Conked out', she'd said. But what had Daisy told her? Eve frowned. She was sure she'd referred to Harry waiting with the car of 'some surgeon' until Dan pulled it out of a ditch.

Tori massaging the truth, to protect her husband's reputation, after he'd driven off the road?

'Heck, Gus.' Eve quickened her pace further. 'Hector was on his way to work that day. Maybe he landed in a ditch because he was drunk, then went straight into the operating theatre…'

And Harry would have seen the state he was in. His words at the open house came back to her. He'd said his party would be 'a chance to see if everyone's keeping their New Year's resolutions'. A veiled message to Hector? Hector who'd put it out that he was considering retirement, but who'd changed his mind once Harry was dead.

And then another scene from the midwinter party flashed in her head, when she'd shown Tori, Hector and Harry the place where the boy, Isaac, had hidden under her house. Tori had said how horrible it must have been for Isaac to know his life would be over if he was caught. *No chance of a future. And all for one small, forgivable misdemeanour.*

Forgivable in Isaac's case, most certainly, but not in Hector's, where his transgressions could cost lives. And Harry had replied: *Thank goodness we live in modern times, where punishments fit crimes.*

A chill washed over her. All that evening behind the polite, light way they'd spoken, secret messages and hidden threats had been issued. She was sure of it. Tori had done a good job, telling everyone how keen she was for her husband to retire – giving Harry the impression he was going to get his way.

'I think Harry gave Hector an ultimatum,' Eve said to Gus. They were slip-sliding along the bank now. Real speed was difficult because of the conditions. 'Resign or be outed as unfit to work. But Hector thought of a third option…'

And somehow, Eve guessed, Dan Irvine had cottoned on to the fact that Hector had been driving drunk too, and become a target. Maybe the accident had looked odd; it would have been before the icy weather. Dan would have felt deeply antagonistic towards Harry. Perhaps he'd asked how he'd managed to land in the ditch – accused him even. At which point he'd have discovered the car didn't belong to Harry at all. Eve imagined the conversation: Harry holding up his hands. *Nothing to do with me, I assure you. Let's say it's just as well the owner took a taxi for the rest of the journey…*

Dan delivered the car back to the Abbotts' home, so he'd known where to find them. Maybe he'd eventually realised Hector had a reason to keep Harry quiet.

What had he been doing at their house the previous day? Sounding them out? Making an inept attempt at blackmail? Revealing, while he was there, that he'd be working late at his garage.

It all fitted.

As for Camilla, the gossip about her and Harry's affair was rife after her row with Kerry. Maybe Hector believed Harry had told her about his drink problem. Or perhaps even the fear of that possibility had been enough to seal her fate.

Daisy had probably only escaped because Harry stopped seeing her a while back, before he knew Hector's secret. Instead, it looked as though she'd become the Abbotts' scapegoat – the more they'd found out about her, the better she'd fitted.

Eve tugged her phone from her pocket, ready to call Robin, but it rang in her hands before she could key in his number.

CHAPTER FORTY-TWO

The voice on the phone sounded bored. '*Eve Mallow? It's Blyworth police here. We'd like to send a constable over to interview you about your recent contact with Daniel and Daisy Irvine. When will you be in?*'

The cold air caught in Eve's throat as she struggled to keep her nerves in check. 'I…' Instinct told her it was urgent to get her message across. What if the Abbotts were planning to intercept her? Eve pictured Tori's face as she'd stood, staring across the river.

She had a horrible feeling she'd guessed something was about to click. Hector Abbott's driving was enough to make anyone pause for thought.

'I need to speak to you urgently about Dan Irvine's death.' She tried to put as much authority into her voice as possible.

'*Which is why I'm calling,*' the woman said. '*What time would be convenient?*'

Palmer had likely told the whole team she was a pain who enjoyed muscling in. The woman on the line probably had instructions to keep her at arm's length.

'It's too urgent for that. I need to tell you now. Or rather, is Detective Sergeant Boles there?' Eve felt a spark of hope rise in her chest.

'*No, I'm afraid not. We're all very busy.*'

She took a deep breath, hastening along as she spoke. 'Could you please listen? This is important. I think I know who killed Harry Tennant, Camilla Sullivan and Dan Irvine.'

'*It's all about the evidence now, Ms Mallow.*'

'I believe Hector Abbott, who lives opposite the mill, is an alcoholic who was continuing his job as a surgeon when he was unfit to work. Harry Tennant looked after his car when he'd driven it—'

'*I'm sure our constable will be very interested to hear your theory,*' the woman cut across her. '*Can you be at your house in twenty minutes?*'

'If the Abbotts don't get to me first. I'm walking back along the River Sax from the Old Mill now.'

'*Lovely.*' She didn't think the woman was listening. '*DC Dawkins will be with you.*'

As Eve hung up, almost sobbing with frustration, she caught movement. It was down the bank, behind the reeds that bordered the marshland.

The breath went out of her.

Tori Abbott had appeared, her face contorted. It was just as Eve had feared. She must have read her look of realisation from across the river – and then acted on it immediately, racing round to the Old Toll Road in her car, ready to join the path along the Sax. All the while, Eve had been closing the distance between them. And now, she'd have heard every word of Eve's phone conversation.

Instinctively, Eve turned to run in the opposite direction and cried out in fright as she came face to face with Hector. He'd been immediately behind her, his eyes narrow. He was breathing heavily. He must have run to catch her up after parking his own vehicle further up the bank, only she hadn't heard him. That blasted phone call.

He was holding something. Eve blinked, unable to process what she was seeing. It looked like a sword.

She spun round again. Tori was up the bank now, holding a kitchen knife. Something from her perfectly appointed home…

Gus barked and the woman's furious eyes fixed on him.

'Go!' Eve shouted, dropping his leash. 'Go, Gus – get to safety!' She clapped her hands behind him and pointed towards the village. *Don't be brave. Not now.*

But her dachshund stood firm. He was still making a lot of noise.

Tori leaped towards him, knife in hand, as Eve looked on in horror. On autopilot, she dived left.

Tori changed course in an instant, to focus on her true prey, but her lunge towards Gus had spooked him at last, and he took off along the bank.

Eve was caught between the Abbotts. One armed with a knife, and one... she swallowed as she looked at Hector's weapon again. It really was a sword. In his other hand he held what looked like an ordinary walking stick.

Suddenly, she put the two together. Hector Abbott owned a swordstick. Some relic of a monied ancestor: a gentleman about town in the eighteenth or nineteenth century.

She took an automatic step back, but Tori was right behind her. 'I'll take your phone, thank you.'

It was still in Eve's hand. Could she outrun them? But even if she risked it, they were blocking her exit routes along the bank. She'd have to wade through the marshes or attempt to cross the river. In each instance it would be two against one and they were armed. Hector's sword had a long reach and knives could be thrown.

She handed over the mobile.

'I don't think the police will believe your fairy tales,' Tori Abbott said. 'DI Palmer mentioned you when he interviewed us. He doesn't think much of you, does he? I'm inclined to agree. Hector may like a drink or two, but he's never lost a patient because of it. By killing you and the other three, he can carry on working. He'll save many more lives that way. And the more I find out about Harry, the more I feel he was a waste of space. That's certainly true of Irvine too, though I liked Camilla.' She shrugged. 'There will always be collateral damage. Turn around and be quick about it. We're going back to the mill.'

Eve felt winded, her strength gone. Her legs trembled as she turned towards Hector. He edged along as she did, keeping the sword up, pointed at her stomach.

He'd probably attended the sort of school where you learned fencing. If he was drunk when he drove into the Abbotts' drive he must still be inebriated now, but he looked in control. Of the sword at least, perhaps not of his actions. His eyes were frightening. She could see how angry he was. He believed it was his right to carry on as before.

Her mouth was so dry she could hardly speak. She swallowed to try to ease her throat. 'What's your plan?' It came out as a croak. 'If you stab me, you're bound to leave an extra trail of evidence. You can't carry on like this. And when I'm found the police will remember what I said on the call. Daisy's in custody. They can't blame her this time.'

Tori was right by her shoulder, ready to tackle her if she tried to run. Hector was just ahead, still walking sideways.

'Oh, the police won't find a murdered woman,' Tori said. 'They'll find one who died by accident. An overly curious obituary writer who couldn't accept the police's version of events. One who revisited the scene of the original crime to look for clues; who ought to have known better than to enter the mill when it was crumbling. Palmer will conclude you were overconfident and arrogant. It's what he thinks anyway.'

What? They were going to make her go inside the mill? Stage an accident?

'It's been standing ever since the fire. There's no reason it should fall now.' Eve's teeth were chattering. 'And there's a barrier round it.'

'Held together with cable ties. We've brought some wire cutters for the purpose, to leave near your body. As for the mill, I saw the CSIs use a cherry picker to investigate the upper floor. No one dared put their full weight on the boards, but you'll be able to clamber up there on the rubble that's accumulated. And when you fall, if you're not badly injured initially, you will be by the end. I suspect the pathologist will find it hard to work out whether the rubble fell on you naturally or had a helping hand. One brick to knock you out, and then we can arrange the rest quite artfully.'

They were already at the barrier. Hector manoeuvred behind Eve and forced her forward as Tori half turned to tackle the cable ties. She used the wire cutters she'd mentioned, drawn from her pocket, the kitchen knife still in her other hand. A moment later she was dragging the barriers apart.

Horrible images reared in Eve's head: thoughts of the suffocating rubble burying her.

Tori joined her husband behind Eve, and they pressed in close, forcing her through the gap, towards the mill's doorway. There was nowhere to run.

'Go on.' Hector's voice was barely controlled. Eve thought he'd use the sword if Tori wasn't there. His wife's cold eyes were on him.

'Better my way,' she said, as though placating a toddler about to have a tantrum.

Eve stepped slowly over the threshold. Bricks had fallen through part of the upper floor where it had collapsed, and more rubble had collected where the wooden lintels over the windows had burned through.

'Step onto the debris and make your way up,' Tori said. 'Keep climbing. Move the bricks as you need so you can get higher. It's what you would do if you'd come here to investigate.'

The worst of it was, Tori was right. This was just the sort of thing Palmer would imagine she might do. He was wrong. She'd never take such a risk. But it was what he thought that counted. Robin and Viv would protest – say it didn't ring true. But what sway would they have?

Even if the woman from the police station remembered what she'd said about the Abbotts she'd probably assume Eve was delusional. And if the story reached Palmer he'd never believe it. Who could be more respectable in his eyes than a surgeon and his horse-riding county wife?

'Go on. Higher.' Tori's voice was clear and controlled.

Eve glanced over her shoulder, out of one of the collapsed windows. She could see no one. She was starting to realise how clever the Abbotts' plan was. If she crossed the first floor and it collapsed it would be a miracle if she didn't at least break something. And as the boards gave way, everything precariously balanced on top would come crashing down with her. It wouldn't take much to ensure she took their secrets to the grave.

Her eyes were above the level of the first floor now. It was a miracle it was still holding up. The joists under it were thinned and blackened, the floorboards almost burned through, uneven, sloping. Her gaze fell upon a pile of broken pieces of mirror – the one she assumed Harry Tennant had had on his ceiling. The police must have moved them aside as they recovered his body. As well as the rubble below, she'd have a hundred shards falling around her. The thought made her feel sick.

A hundred shards…

Eve was still wearing her overcoat, with its large patch pockets. Tori and Hector were way below her now, poised to step forward if she tried to retreat, but primed to leap away when the floor came down.

'You're wasting time!' Tori said. 'Hector will come after you if you don't get up there. He can stand safely on the rubble and reach you with his sword.'

Eve took another step towards the first floor to placate her, but as she moved, she reached surreptitiously for bits of the broken mirror. Her thick gloves were a godsend, protecting her from getting cut.

She crammed her pockets with shards, picking the ones of medium size. They'd be heavy enough to throw straight.

'Go on, Hector,' Eve heard Tori say. 'She needs some encouragement.'

And then she heard the sound of his sword scrape on something down below.

She needed no other spur. She grabbed more shards from the upper floor and began to fling them at Hector, aiming low. Even in that moment, she couldn't bring herself to target his head. What must it take to stand over someone and beat them to death?

Hector stumbled backwards, over the mill's threshold, confusion flooding his face.

After a second, he tried to re-enter the ruin, but Eve threw another shard, and another, staying within reach of the supply. He moved back again, raising his arm to shield his head as she threw a little higher.

Tori was growing impatient, but when she pushed past Hector, Eve redoubled her efforts, flinging the wickedly sharp glass at the woman's shins.

She moved back too, stumbling over her husband. Eve kept going until she could no longer reach the couple from where she stood, on top of the rubble.

What should she do? Follow them, her pockets full of shards, and get them to retreat further? But that was unsustainable. She'd run out before long.

The alternative was to stay put and keep attacking each time they came back. Maybe, just maybe, DC Dawkins would raise the alarm when she didn't show for their appointment. Or someone might pass by.

Eve's spirits plummeted again. The chances were horribly thin. It was bitterly cold. Most villagers would be huddled indoors by their fires.

At that moment, Hector appeared in the mill doorway again.

And this time he was holding a sheet of corrugated iron. Eve remembered seeing it, sheltering Harry's recycling. Hector had it held high as a shield. Eve tried to aim a shard of mirror at his feet, below the metal.

It went wide, and Hector kept on coming.

CHAPTER FORTY-THREE

Eve knew she was fighting for her life. She took a brick from the heap she was climbing on and hurled it with all her strength at the corrugated iron Hector was carrying. This time she didn't trouble about where she aimed.

The brick hit home at the top of the sheet, forcing it back. She heard a howl of pain and in the same moment, she caught movement through the window, away along the bank, towards the village.

She lobbed another brick as hard as she could. Then another as Hector stumbled backwards.

Tori had been right behind him, but now she turned abruptly. Eve could hear shouting. And barking? Gus?

Eve flung another brick, then craned to see what was going on. The distant shapes were coalescing into people. And, straining on his leash, her beloved dachshund. Thank goodness someone had him safe. If he'd been allowed to run free he'd likely be there by now, ready to attack the Abbotts, but hunting dog though he was, he couldn't win against a sword.

Hector had dropped the iron sheet now. He and Tori stood like rabbits in headlights.

And then they ran.

Up the river, away from the group of people.

And into the path of a couple of police officers approaching from the opposite direction. Hector brandished his sword, but Tori shook her head at him.

It was too late.

A moment later, a small group of familiar faces were shouting instructions to her above those of DC Olivia Dawkins and a young uniformed sergeant. Viv was holding Gus, who was straining to get into the mill. Angie bent to soothe him, and almost immediately he rolled over to have his tummy tickled.

Hmm. Not *that* upset then…

Viv was giving Eve a look like a mother who'd found one of their children doing something inadvisable.

Behind her were all three Falconers. Jo strode forward to join in the bellowing.

And behind *them*, was Robin. His eyes were anxious, but when Eve's gaze met his he grinned and wiped his hand across his brow.

CHAPTER FORTY-FOUR

The next day, Eve was sitting opposite Viv, at a corner table in Monty's, a plate of sloe gin and spice cakes between them. They were well down a pot of Darjeeling and being waited on hand and foot by Angie, Sam and Kirsty.

'I'll take you for an actual sloe gin in the pub later,' Viv said.

'That'd be good. Though I can't tonight.'

Her friend's face took on a look of appalled sympathy. 'Oh, of course. Ian. I can't believe he gave you a hard time for missing your dinner date yesterday.'

The only thing keeping Eve going was the prospect of a catch-up with Robin after the pub. 'Please don't call it a dinner date. Or any kind of date. I'm only meeting him for a drink now. I told him I wasn't up to a meal.'

He'd been put out about that, too. After extending his stay by one night, thanks to her 'crazy exploits', he'd clearly expected her full attention all evening.

'Quite right. I do wish you'd let me come along. I'd love to see him, and I'd sit quietly in a corner somewhere…'

'No! I feel awkward enough as it is.' The thought of her impending doom was awful. 'Still, it'll give me the chance to thank the Falconers.'

'You already did. Around a thousand times. They know you're grateful.'

Gus had run all the way from the river to the Cross Keys, where Toby immediately guessed something was up. He, Jo and Matt had left their bar staff in charge and followed Gus, in the hope he'd lead them to Eve. ('Just like Lassie,' Viv had said, giving her dachshund a cuddle.)

Meanwhile, Sylvia and Daphne had spotted DC Dawkins, knocking vainly at the door of Elizabeth's Cottage. When the woman told them she and Eve had an appointment, they'd instantly decided something was wrong too. ('We know you're not cavalier about that sort of thing,' Daphne had said.)

It was at that moment that Robin had arrived, apparently. 'He'd been trying to call you to rearrange a gardening appointment,' Sylvia said, but her knowing look told Eve she hadn't entirely bought that story. 'Something made him anxious when he couldn't reach you. Then DC Dawkins mentioned you had an alternative theory about who was guilty. She'd only got a garbled message. Something about monks, she thought. It was Robin who worked it out. The Abbotts. Who would have thought it?'

Dawkins had called her colleague, who'd said vaguely that Eve might be by the river – which was also where Gus was dragging the Falconers. Meanwhile, Viv and Angie saw the crowds rushing up Love Lane and dashed out, leaving Sam and Kirsty in charge at Monty's.

DC Dawkins called backup, and a couple of colleagues approached the mill from the south, while she and a sergeant rushed along from the north, just about managing to overtake Eve's friends.

'Once we knew you were in danger there was no stopping us,' Viv said.

Eve felt mushy inside. 'That's so touching.'

'You know we all love you. And you're really useful about the teashop too.'

'Yeah, thanks.'

'Don't look at me like that. By the way, have you seen today's *Real Story*?'

Eve shook her head, and took another sloe gin cake.

'They've published Harry's last advice column posthumously. And there's a letter in it I think will interest you. It's from MS, Suffolk.'

'What?' From Moira? Could it be?

Viv called the column up on her phone and handed it to Eve.

Dear Pippa,

I really feel quite embarrassed writing this, but a friend recommended you to me, and your words are always ever so reassuring.

My husband and I have been together for many years now, and though he's not the most talkative of men…

That certainly sounded like Paul.

… we have a good, solid marriage, really probably better than most people could hope for. But in the bedroom department, shall we say, the excitement has been lacking for a number of years now. We're both on our feet all day and tired during the evenings. I wonder if I could…

Eve scrolled down.

'Eager for the smut, I see,' Viv said.

Eve waved a hand. 'I'm just trying to assimilate the details as quickly as possible.'

'Yeah, right.'

Eve took a sip of her tea.

There's no need to be embarrassed. This is a common problem and I'm glad you got in touch.

Eve skimmed Harry's advice, from the role-playing to the mention of leather, oil and blindfolds. 'Take it away.' She handed the phone back to Viv. 'I'm getting images I'll never unsee. Poor Moira. No wonder she was embarrassed when she realised she'd poured her heart out to a male neighbour and not some anonymous, motherly expert down in London. It figures that Harry would go for the kinkiest advice. He was all about click-bait.'

'It fits with Camilla recommending his services to the locals for entertainment purposes too.'

'Absolutely.' But it had gone way beyond idle amusement for Harry, Eve guessed. He'd liked to manoeuvre his acquaintances like so many chess pieces on a board.

Eve arrived early for her Cross Keys ordeal and had to walk round the village green to avoid any extra time with Ian. She could see him, sitting in one of the pub's windows. She wished he hadn't chosen a table in full public view, lit up by the cosy lights inside. She'd be the latest news in the village store tomorrow, and not just because she'd escaped a pair of murderers.

He rose from the table as she walked through the door, and leaned in immediately to kiss her on both cheeks.

Eve felt herself go crimson as they approached the bar. Toby served them, and she thanked him again for his help the day before, earning a raised eyebrow from Ian, who knew none of the details. A moment later they returned to their table with their drinks.

'Why did you ask for an extra large glass of wine?' Ian said, as he sat down with his pint of Adnams.

'Because that's what I wanted.' She'd said it as a joke, to relieve the tension after the drama of the weekend, and Toby had laughed.

'Extra large isn't the correct terminology.'

'It was obvious what I meant.'

'So you make a habit of it, I assume?' Ian had that look in his eye she knew so well. Chiding and patronising, amused but censorious.

It was actually rare, but she had no intention of justifying herself. 'I do whatever I feel like.' She did. It was great. Suddenly she thought of the twins' words. 'Ian, Nick and Ellen said you're breaking up with Sonia. I'm sorry. It was nice of you to hold it together for them over Christmas.'

He waved her comment away. 'It was just the adult thing to do.'

Eve always acted like an adult too, so why was his response so maddening?

'Eve.'

Her stomach tensed. She was glad she hadn't agreed to dinner; she'd never have digested it. 'Yes?'

'I wanted to come to you. You know, before I put myself back out there.'

'I'm sorry?'

'Before I get back into the dating game. I wanted to come to you first.' He was looking a little irked at her obtuseness. 'To give you first refusal.'

Like he was a house on the market. 'Oh, I see. Gee, Ian, that's so generous of you!'

He smiled graciously at her.

Totally oblivious. 'But I'm really happy being single. Thanks all the same.'

His nostrils flared and she smiled to herself. If she'd made him sad, she might have felt guilty, but she hadn't. He was shocked by her levity. He didn't want her, not really, she'd just be less effort than finding someone new. And he wanted her to want him.

What a jerk.

*

Robin opened the door of his cottage. It led straight into his kitchen and Eve dashed inside so he could shut out the cold. He had a fire lit, and going into the small room was like walking straight into a warm hug. Her relief at leaving Ian at the pub was profound.

She slipped off her coat and hung it next to Robin's on some hooks by the door. 'Thanks again for coming to look for me yesterday.'

He laughed. 'Just one of the Saxford posse.' There was a moment's awkward silence. 'Are you all right to stay?' He shot her an apologetic look. 'Moira mentioned your ex is lodging at the pub. If you want to spend your evening with—'

She cut across him. 'I really don't. Thank you.'

'Ah.' He gave her a quizzical look and pulled out a chair for her.

A moment later she was sitting opposite him, explaining the chat she and Ian had had at the Cross Keys. 'If he'd wanted me back because he genuinely missed me—'

'I can see that would have been different.' He cut across her this time.

She shook her head. 'No, I was going to say the result would have been the same, only I'd feel sadder. As it is, there's no need to give the matter another thought.'

His smile was as warm as the room. 'I see. In that case can I get you a glass of wine? I've got some red warming.'

'I just had an "extra-large" Shiraz at the pub.' What would she be like after more? She was in grave danger of giving herself away.

He grinned as he rose from the table. 'Understood. No pressure. Though if you want a drink, I could get some cashews as well?'

She took a deep breath. 'All right. That sounds good, thanks.'

In the end he put out cashews, olives, a plate of Italian meats and cheeses and some French bread. 'You need to build up your strength after yesterday. And this evening, by the sound of it.'

They sat and ate and talked over the case. 'Do the police know why Dan Irvine went to visit the Abbotts?' Eve asked.

Robin nodded. 'Tori and Hector aren't talking yet, but the techs found a sent email on Dan's laptop, making veiled references to the circumstances surrounding Hector's accident. He suggested they "have a little chat", to "protect both their interests". Hector emailed back to arrange a time. Their story about him going round as a courtesy call was rubbish. It's pretty clear Dan planned to blackmail them. He wasn't very subtle.'

'And of course Hector and Tori knew he'd be working late at the garage. They overheard him telling Daisy not to wait up, from what she said.'

Robin nodded. 'That call was a bit of luck from their point of view. They could suddenly see their way clear to framing Daisy. Harry's "Venus" literally popped up before their eyes, and she had reason to kill all three victims.'

'Poor Daisy.' Dan's death was a horrific thing to deal with, even if he'd been abusive. And her clients always would associate her with the murders, but at least she was in the clear now. 'I guess the germ of that idea was already forming when Tori put me onto her. She knew Daisy and Harry had quarrelled and parted. I'll bet the Abbotts kept a close eye on the comings and goings at the mill once they realised they might want to get rid of Harry. It would have reassured them that Daisy hadn't made a comeback. As it was, she was perfect, out of the picture, with a motive for the killing.'

Robin nodded grimly. 'Tori must have been ecstatic when she realised Harry's "Venus" was also Dan Irvine's wife.'

'I know. I keep imagining their minds working as soon as they saw her image flash up on Dan's phone. Their plan to frame her fits with Tori lying to me and the police about Dan Irvine, too.

I admitted it was Daisy who told me he'd hung around to tweak Hector's car's engine, the day it was towed home. And they were already setting her up to take the rap for all three murders. It was in Tori's interests to make Daisy look dishonest.' She'd thought quickly and been so calculating.

Eve's mind ran through the full chain of events now. 'What about the other deaths? Tori and Hector sneaked out of the house where they were staying, I presume, to kill Harry. Maybe Tori drove, given they arrived in one piece.'

'They never seemed like serious suspects before, but the police have checked the traffic cameras now. They've got them.' He gave her a wry look. 'You're right. Tori did drive. They took her car.'

'She said the whole village knew they'd be away that night.' Eve thought back to the woman's words. 'As far as the Saxfordites were concerned, they were in the clear.' It had been sickeningly clever. 'And they talked Camilla into letting them in?'

'As a near neighbour, they knew her – went to each other's houses for sherry, apparently. So it probably seemed natural to Camilla that they'd go round to offer sympathy, once the details of her and Harry's relationship got out. Greg's assuming they went to test the water: to see if there was any sign she suspected them.'

'I guessed they might have worried about pillow talk.'

Robin nodded. 'Greg imagines something went wrong while they were with her. As you know, Camilla was prone to hint she knew Harry's secrets; that could have prompted them to act. Or Hector might have made Camilla suspicious when he talked about Harry. He has a short fuse, and what with that and the drink…'

It was an awful thought. 'Either way, Camilla couldn't have suspected them before that night, or she'd never have let them in. So she'd have been unguarded in what she said.'

'That sounds right. And they know now that the weapon was Hector's cane…'

She visualised the solid silver knob on top of the swordstick. 'He walked right in there with everything he needed to kill her. The cane looks like such an innocent item but it's two weapons in one.'

She shivered and Robin put another log on the fire. His eyes met hers. 'Let's do this again sometime soon, after all the police interviews are over.' He smiled. 'If you'd like to, that is?'

Eve's heart felt like it was skipping round her chest. People would be bound to notice if they made a habit of it. They'd ask her about him. *Secret lovers.* Shut up.

'That sounds nice. Thanks.'

Harry Tennant – agony columnist

Harry Tennant, known to many as the agony aunt Pippa Longford, was killed on 2 January in Suffolk, aged forty-eight. A man and woman have been arrested for his murder.

Tennant's advice column in the *Real Story* garnered a huge following and many readers wrote to the paper after his death to praise him. But none of his correspondents knew his real identity; he kept his true self private. This was echoed in his face-to-face dealings with friends, acquaintances and lovers, too. Some of them gleaned part of the truth about the man, few – maybe none – the whole.

Behind Tennant's successful adult façade lay an unsettled childhood. He was just seven years old when his mother left the family home in Surrey for a new life in New York, and his father, Darius, was seldom present. His work as the founder of the adventure travel company Way Out There meant he played little part in Harry's upbringing. Darius Tennant's death in a helicopter crash must have been another emotional blow for the teenage boy, but it had less effect in practical terms.

Harry was already used to being shuttled between boarding school and the home of his uncle, Tristan, where he spent his vacations. Though Tristan never tried to send him elsewhere, it seems the situation was uneasy. Harry had already discovered his passion for diagnosing people's problems and steering them in what he regarded as a better direction. He believed he was able to anticipate troubles that had yet to arise; some might argue his interventions made them a reality.

His approach risked playing with the emotions of friends and relatives, but maybe it was his way of seizing some autonomy in a life where he'd had almost none.

He took these childhood traits with him to the *Real Story*. Although some found his help invaluable, his advice fell short in more complex situations. Having gained some control, it seems he found it impossible to let go, and that included failing to admit when experts were better placed to help than he was. He was prone to making eye-catching and controversial recommendations. It endeared him to his editor and casual readers, but had serious consequences for a correspondent on at least one occasion.

That said, some readers found his domineering style compelling. He leaves behind many fans who say he changed their lives for the better.

Eve sighed. People were so complex; it was hard to get the introductions to her articles just right. Harry had caused a whole lot of hurt. He'd been deeply malicious, but damaged too. She could see how he'd become the man he was. Anger built inside her, against Petronella and Darius Tennant, and Rollo Mortiville too, though they were also products of their own upbringings.

She clung to the good news she'd had since wrapping up the case. She'd managed to contact Lottie Briggs, Melody Bentley's former colleague at the estate agents. The bully, Patsy, was still at work, but Lottie was helping her latest victim. She'd managed to witness the bullying and was now supporting an official complaint against Patsy. Apparently several of Melody's ex-colleagues had found their voices, now they realised the tide was turning. Lottie had contacted Judd's sister about coming back into the office with a legal representative to discuss her treatment. Things were on the up, so Judd ought to be a lot happier too.

Matters were more complicated for Tristan and Daisy, but they each had plans. When Tristan contacted Eve after her run-in with the Abbotts, to check she was okay, he said he was going to rethink his approach to the Hideaway. It sounded like his bar manager had come up trumps. She had new ideas that would work with the atmosphere he was aiming for and build on it: an exclusive range of cocktails, superior finger food, and some private booths for people entertaining business guests. It sounded promising.

As for Daisy, she'd contacted Eve on her release to thank her for working out who'd killed Harry and living long enough to tell the police. It was as Eve had imagined – she couldn't face carrying on in Blyworth. But the money she'd been left meant she could start again elsewhere once the legal formalities were complete. It was too early to make firm decisions, but she was already looking at locations for a new home and wedding boutique. A friend who helped run the Blyworth store planned to relocate with her as part of her ongoing team. They'd been scouring maps together and googling the competition. Daisy was down, but most certainly not out.

Meanwhile, Kerry seemed to be enjoying her new role at Seagrave Hall, and Moira had been alarmingly buoyant at the village store that morning. Maybe she'd benefited from Harry's advice.

Gus joined Eve by the dining table. 'Let's not think any more about it,' she said. 'I'm bound to bump into her and Paul together at some stage and if I've pictured them… Well, anyway. How about a walk?'

Gus dashed towards the front door.

A LETTER FROM CLARE

Thank you so much for reading *Mystery at the Old Mill*. I do hope you had as much fun working on the case as I did! If you'd like to keep up to date with all of my latest releases, you can sign up at the following link. Your email address will never be shared, and you can unsubscribe at any time.

www.bookouture.com/clare-chase

I got the idea for *Mystery at the Old Mill* while reading one of the agony columns in a Saturday paper. The reader had entrusted the columnist with some deeply personal information and in response she got a caring and perceptive take on a difficult topic, which I'm sure must have helped. But it got me thinking about what it might cost someone to pass on such sensitive details if the paper was less upstanding, and the columnist downright immoral.

If you have time, I'd love it if you were able to write a review of *Mystery at the Old Mill*. Feedback is really valuable, and it also makes a huge difference in helping new readers discover my books for the first time. Alternatively, if you'd like to contact me personally, you can reach me via my website, Facebook page, Twitter or Instagram. It's always great to hear from readers.

Again, thank you so much for deciding to spend some time reading *Mystery at the Old Mill*. I'm looking forward to sharing my next book with you very soon.

With all best wishes,
Clare x

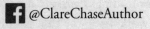 @ClareChaseAuthor

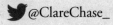 @ClareChase_

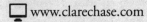 www.clarechase.com

ACKNOWLEDGEMENTS

Much love and thanks as ever to Charlie for the pre-submission input, George for the manuscript check and Ros for the cheerleading and feedback on each end product! Love and thanks also to Mum and Dad, Phil and Jenny, David and Pat, Warty, Andrea, Jen, the Westfield gang, Margaret, Shelly, Mark, my Andrewes relations and a whole bunch of family and friends.

And as always, I'm more grateful than I can say to my fantastic editor Ruth Tross for her inspired input. It makes a huge difference. I'm also indebted to Noelle Holten, for her dynamic promo work. Sending thanks too, to Leo Darlington, Peta Nightingale, Kim Nash, Alexandra Holmes, Fraser, Liz and everyone involved in editing, book production and sales at Bookouture. I feel so lucky to be published and promoted by such a skilled and friendly team.

Thanks to the wonderful Bookouture authors and other writer mates for their friendship. And a massive thank you, too, to the hard-working and generous book bloggers and reviewers who take the time to pass on their thoughts about my work. Their contributions are invaluable.

And finally, but importantly, thanks to you, the reader, for buying or borrowing this book!